Praise for Catherine Bybee

Wife by Wednesday

"A fun and sizzling romance, great characters that trade verbal spars like fist punches, and the dream of your own royal wedding!"

—Sizzling Hot Book Reviews, 5 Stars

"A good holiday, fireside or bedtime story."

—Manic Reviews, 4 1/2 Stars

"A great story that I hope is the start of a new series."

—The Romance Studio, 4 1/2 Hearts

Married by Monday

"If I hadn't already added Ms. Catherine Bybee to my list of favorite authors, after reading this book I would have been compelled to. This is a book *nobody* should miss, because the magic it contains is awesome."

—Booked Up Reviews, 5 Stars

"Ms. Bybee writes authentic situations bad in such an equal way . . . Kee seat . . ."

—Rea , 5 Stars

"*Married by Monday* was a refreshing read and one I couldn't possibly put down . . ."

—The Romance Studio, 4 1/2 Hearts

NO LONGER PROPERTY OF RANGEVIEW LIBRARY DISTRICT

I0956453

Fiancé by Friday

"Bybee knows exactly how to keep readers happy. . . . A thrilling pursuit and enough passion to stuff in your back pocket to last for the next few lifetimes . . . The hero and heroine come to life with each flip of the page and will linger long after readers cross the finish line."

—*RT Book Reviews*, 4 1/2 Stars, Top Pick, Hot

"A tale full of danger and sexual tension . . . the intriguing characters add emotional depth, ensuring readers will race to the perfectly fitting finish."

—*Publishers Weekly*

"Suspense, survival, and chemistry mix in this scintillating read."

—*Booklist*

"Hot romance, a mystery assassin, British royalty, and an alpha Marine . . . this story has it all!"

—Harlequin Junkie

Single by Saturday

"Captures readers' hearts and keeps them glued to the pages until the fascinating finish. . . . romance lovers will feel the sparks fly . . . almost instantaneously."

—*RT Book Reviews*, 4 1/2 Stars, Top Pick

"[A] wonderfully exciting plot, lots of desire, and some sassy attitude thrown in for good measure!"

—Harlequin Junkie

Taken by Tuesday

"[Bybee] knows exactly how to get bookworms sucked into the perfect storyline; then she casts her spell upon them so they don't escape until they reach the 'Holy Cow!' ending."

—*RT Book Reviews*, 4 1/2 Stars, Top Pick

Seduced by Sunday

"You simply can't miss [this novel]. It contains everything a romance reader loves—clever dialogue, three-dimensional characters, and just the right amount of steam to go with that heartwarming love story."

—Brenda Novak, *New York Times* bestselling author

"Bybee hits the mark . . . providing readers with a smart, sophisticated romance between a spirited heroine and a prim hero . . . Passionate and intelligent characters [are] at the heart of this entertaining read."

—*Publishers Weekly*

Treasured by Thursday

"The Weekday Brides never disappoint and this final installment is by far Bybee's best work to date."

—*RT Book Reviews*, 4 1/2 Stars, Top Pick

"An exquisitely written and complex story brimming with pride, passion, and pulse-pounding danger . . . Readers will gladly make time to savor this winning finale to a wonderful series."

—*Publishers Weekly*, Starred Review

"Bybee concludes her popular Weekday Brides series in a gratifying way with a passionate, troubled couple who may find a happy future if they can just survive and then learn to trust each other. A compelling and entertaining mix of sexy, complicated romance and menacing suspense."

—*Kirkus Reviews*

Not Quite Dating

"It's refreshing to read about a man who isn't afraid to fall in love . . . [Jack and Jessie] fit together as a couple and as a family."

—*RT Book Reviews*, 3 stars, Hot

"*Not Quite Dating* offers a sweet and satisfying Cinderella fantasy that will keep you smiling long after you've finished reading . . ."

—Kathy Altman, *USA Today*, "Happy Ever After"

"The perfect rags to riches romance . . . The dialogue is inventive and witty, the characters are well drawn out. The storyline is superb and really shines. . . . I highly recommend this stand out romance! Catherine Bybee is an automatic buy for me."

—Harlequin Junkie, 4 1/2 Hearts

Not Quite Enough

"Bybee's gift for creating unforgettable romances cannot be ignored. The third book in the Not Quite series will sweep readers away to a paradise, and they will be intrigued by the thrilling story that accompanies their literary vacation."

—*RT Book Reviews*, 4 1/2 Stars, Top Pick

Not Quite Forever

"Full of classic Bybee humor, steamy romance, and enough plot twists and turns to keep readers entertained all the way to the very last page."
—Tracy Brogan, bestselling author of the Bell Harbor series

"Magnetic . . . The love scenes are sizzling and the multi-dimensional characters make this a page-turner. Readers will look for earlier installments and eagerly anticipate new ones."
—*Publishers Weekly*

Doing It Over

"The romance between fiercely independent Melanie and charming Wyatt heats up even as outsiders threaten to derail their newfound happiness. This novel will hook readers with its warm, inviting characters and the promise for similar future installments."
—*Publishers Weekly*

"This brand-new trilogy, Most Likely To, based on yearbook superlatives, kicks off with a novel that will encourage you to root for the incredibly likable Melanie. Her friends are hilarious and readers will swoon over Wyatt, who is charming and strong. Even Melanie's daughter, Hope, is a hoot! This romance is jam-packed with animated characters, and Bybee displays her creative writing talent wonderfully."
—*RT Book Reviews*, 4 Stars

"With a dialogue full of energy and depth, and a twisting storyline that captured my attention, I would say that *Doing It Over* was a great way to start off a new series. (And look at that gorgeous book cover!) I can't wait to visit River Bend again and see who else gets to find their HEA."
—Harlequin Junkie, 4 1/2 Stars

Staying *For* Good

Also by Catherine Bybee

Contemporary Romance

Weekday Brides Series

Wife by Wednesday
Married by Monday
Fiancé by Friday
Single by Saturday
Taken by Tuesday
Seduced by Sunday
Treasured by Thursday

Not Quite Series

Not Quite Dating
Not Quite Mine
Not Quite Enough
Not Quite Forever
Not Quite Perfect

Most Likely To Series

Doing It Over

Paranormal Romance

MacCoinnich Time Travels

Binding Vows
Silent Vows
Redeeming Vows
Highland Shifter
Highland Protector

The Ritter Werewolves Series

Before the Moon Rises
Embracing the Wolf

Novellas

Soul Mate
Possessive

Erotica

Kilt Worthy
Kilt-A-Licious

Staying *For* Good

A
MOST LIKELY TO
Novel

CATHERINE BYBEE

This is a work of fiction. Names, characters, organizations, places, events, and incidents are either products of the author's imagination or are used fictitiously.

Text copyright © 2017 Catherine Bybee
All rights reserved.

No part of this book may be reproduced, or stored in a retrieval system, or transmitted in any form or by any means, electronic, mechanical, photocopying, recording, or otherwise, without express written permission of the publisher.

Published by Montlake Romance, Seattle

www.apub.com

Amazon, the Amazon logo, and Montlake Romance are trademarks of Amazon.com, Inc., or its affiliates.

ISBN-13: 9781503939172
ISBN-10: 1503939170

Cover design by Shasti O'Leary Soudant

Printed in the United States of America

This one is for Brandy
Because sometimes friends are the only
family you have

Prelude

The walls of a double-wide were the dividing factor of separation between a trailer and a house. Technically, it was her home, her house . . . but everyone in River Bend who wanted to dig at Zoe's status made sure they referred to it as a *trailer*. Her BFFs, Mel and Jo, never said *trailer*. Even on nights like this . . . when the calendar said it was early summer but the evenings in River Bend, Oregon, didn't get the memo. Those paper-thin walls that lacked insulation and girth didn't do a good job of keeping away the cold.

The rain had held out for her high school graduation but had started to dump buckets after her friends arrived to celebrate their freedom.

Zoe glanced over at Mel, who was fast asleep on her half of the pullout sofa bed that did a shitty enough job as a sofa and had no business being a bed. It was, however, off the floor, and if Zoe thought the walls were thin, the floor was worse. Jo curled up on herself in a recliner that should have been taken to the curb a decade before . . . but that was probably when her mom had swiped it off the sidewalk.

Between the three of them, they'd managed to down half a bottle of tequila and polish off an entire pizza. The night swam with emotions. First the reality of finishing high school, then Mel's bombshell that her parents were getting divorced and she would likely leave River Bend for good.

High school Zoe could say good-bye to, not a problem . . . but not Mel. It was always assumed one-third of the River Bend trio was going off to college. Mel was the smart one, great grades, strong family. When she waved her acceptance letter to USC in front of Jo's and Zoe's faces, both of them joined their friend in her excitement. Neither of them thought for a minute Mel's parents would announce their divorce and move from River Bend when Mel reached for her high school diploma. The divorce was anyone's guess . . . but the fact Mel's parents were moving away essentially cut off Mel's ticket to return to River Bend on holidays and summers.

And that sucked!

Zoe lay there with Jose Cuervo swimming in her head, and the conversation that had stuck with the three of them until they'd passed out.

Their fellow high school seniors had voted their predictions on what the graduating class was going to do with their lives.

Mel managed top honors with *most likely to succeed*. A USC education would propel her to the top of whatever chain Melanie Bartlett decided to climb.

Jo found herself at the bottom of the honor roll with *most likely to end up in jail*. Considering JoAnne Ward was always the one to score the liquor and did a bang-up job of pissing off her father, Sheriff Ward . . . and doing just about every delinquent thing a teen could do and not end up in jail . . . yeah, it was only a matter of time. Seemed Jo was always trying to prove she was more than a cop's daughter. Because Sheriff Ward had the ultimate respect of the citizens of River Bend, everyone looked the other way at Jo's shenanigans. *Eventually* always managed to catch up, and one day Sheriff Ward wouldn't be able to help his little girl.

Then there was Zoe . . . her *most likely to* was the most disturbing of all.

Zoe Brown: Most likely to never leave River Bend.

Zoe had felt physically ill when she'd read the yearbook with that spelled out in print.

The thin walls of her mother's home felt thinner, the air thicker, the temperature colder. This was not what Zoe wanted for her life.

She wanted to see the world. Wanted the ability to wear clothes that matched. She wanted furniture that wasn't cast off from someone else. And a car. She wanted a car. Working for all those things in a town as small as River Bend would mean nothing but long, hard hours at two or three jobs, and then maybe by the time her ten-year class reunion came around, she would have a couple of them. Or maybe she wouldn't. What happened if her father managed parole? That asshole was doing fifteen to life for armed robbery, and her mother had yet to divorce him. Her younger brother and sister were just entering junior high. Zane had been angry since birth, or so it seemed, and Zanya was syrupy sweet to the point of falling for the wrong guy as soon as she noticed boys existed.

If Zoe didn't leave River Bend to find a life outside of her family, she would probably be raising her own kids under a roof that made rain sound like hail and with chairs that stank of cigarettes even when no one in the house smoked.

Zoe shook her thoughts from her head and closed her eyes.

That's where she saw Luke.

Her knight . . . her savior. The only reason she managed to keep her chin high through the halls of River Bend High. Well, Jo and Mel helped with that, but being Luke's girlfriend for the better part of two years had kept her sane. Outside of her BFFs, she shared everything with Luke. Well, almost everything. Her fear of never leaving River

Bend was something she shielded from him. His father owned the auto repair shop in town, and Luke was super talented with everything that required oil and gasoline to run. His family reminded Zoe of what a family should be. His mom taught Zoe the basics of cooking and baking, things she loved to do. Luke's father's even temper and kind spirit gave her faith that not all men beat their families.

Luke was a big reason River Bend thought Zoe would never leave town.

High school sweethearts marry young in small towns.

Zoe admitted, if only to herself, that marriage to Luke would grant her so many things her life wouldn't have without him. A family. Some stability . . . maybe even a house with real walls and thick carpet.

But what happened if Luke fell off his bike, crashed a car? What would happen if five years from now, with two point five kids, and all the bills that came with that life, something happened to the man she married? Her entire life could blow up in the span of one day, one bad accident . . . one bad anything! How would she survive?

Double-wide and smelly sofas . . . that's how.

Zoe shot up in bed with enough of a gasp that her friends opened their eyes.

"What the hell, Zoe?" Jo squished the tiny pillow she was slobbering all over and shoved her head back into it.

Mel reached over, started to pat Zoe's arm, then squeezed. "You're stone cold. What's wrong?"

Zoe felt the rise and fall of her chest moving too quickly.

"I have to break up with Luke."

Her declaration woke both her friends up.

"What?" Jo and Mel both asked at once.

Chapter One

Eleven Years Later

"Cut!"

"It's a soufflé, Felix. You can't say *cut*." Zoe felt the heat of the open oven flow up her face as the lights from the studio shone down. She held herself in suspended animation while the camera crew scrambled with enough noise for her to know they weren't filming.

"Zoe, don't move." Felix held his hands in the air as if he had a supernatural power that would keep her from shuffling her feet. Truth was, he kinda did. While the five-foot-six, two-hundred-pound balding man might be able to keep her from moving, the chocolate soufflé in her oven-mitted hands was not going to comply.

She couldn't shove the thing back into the oven to keep it puffed up, and removing it completely would make it deflate quicker. Hence the reason the low heat of the oven was cooking her stage makeup to a glowing 120 degrees. Huddled close to the oven, Zoe felt her brow growing damp.

"Felix!"

"Camera two, zoom in on the soufflé. Someone dust Zoe's face!" And when that someone didn't move fast enough, Felix yelled, "Now!"

Zoe's didn't let the tractor beam of her eyes leave her creation. The crown of her soufflé was perfect . . . just the right amount of brown on the edges, the perfect smell of mouthwatering calories no one needed but everyone wanted. The countdown for the damn thing falling was ticking like a clock on a bomb, and she was holding still as if said bomb were strapped to her waist and one move would set if off.

Someone shoved a fat-bristled makeup brush on her face, dusting away the glistening moisture so she didn't shine on camera.

The middle of her dessert started to breathe, and Zoe's heart rate shot up. "Hurry!"

Felix clapped his hands several times. "Quiet . . . everyone quiet on the set!"

Zoe painted on her smile and awaited her cue.

Yet her baked masterpiece was the one that followed her director's instructions.

The second Felix yelled *action*, Zoe opened her lips to deliver her lines about the proper care of a soufflé when removing it from the oven, and poof! The middle collapsed and at least three people on set said *damn* at the same time.

"Cut!"

Zoe straightened her back and hit the oven door with her knee to slam the thing shut.

"Damn it, Felix." Cussing out the director might prove detrimental to a celebrity chef with lesser clout, but Zoe had earned her stripes and often called the shots. Besides, Felix loved her.

No longer caring if the food looked awful, Zoe all but tossed the dish on top of the counter and moved out of the hot lights of the staged kitchen.

No less than a dozen sets of hands scrambled around the cameras and the microphones hanging from long booms hovering above.

Felix stood in front of camera two, quietly scolding the man behind the lens.

It was Zoe's second soufflé of the day, and she wasn't sure there was another one in her.

She waited patiently while Felix finished his direction before turning her way. "Darling, I'm sorry." He had to reach up to pat her face.

"*Cut* is not a word we use when removing this from the oven. I told you that."

"The angle was all wrong. The finished dish is what makes everyone think they can do it . . . makes your audience think you're a goddess of the kitchen." It was hard to stay mad at a man who had a slight lisp and made grand gestures with his hands as he spoke. He called himself the Vanna White of the director's chair. The only things those two had in common were their taste in men and their expansive shoe collections.

Zoe removed the tiny apron that was mostly for show and handed it to him. "I told you soufflés were a bad idea."

"The harder the dish, the better the ratings, darling. Now stop complaining and start mixing." He gently nudged her apron back into her hands.

She handed it back.

"I need to eat."

Felix swiveled to the counter and picked up the crock with the soufflé. He dropped it back on the counter almost as soon as his fingers touched the thing. He blew on his fingertips like a three-year-old. "Eat that."

"If I ate everything I cooked, I'd be as big as you."

He shrugged without argument and patted her slim hip. "We can't have that." He turned to the crew. "Everyone, we're back in thirty. Princess Zoe has to eat."

Zoe grinned, kissed Felix's cheek. "One more shot at this today. Get it right."

He was already turning away. "We will, darling. Rupert!" he yelled in the opposite direction.

She walked past the cameras, out from around the fake walls of the set, and down the narrow hall to her dressing room, which sounded more glamorous than it was. A lighted mirror and a rack to hang her clothes on sat in one corner, while two chairs that once sat in a nearby office building surrounded a tiny table. A locker suitable for the gym at her old high school was used to lock up her purse. As much as she'd love to think her belongings were safe, there were too many nameless people running around who might be more than willing to lift her wallet.

A knock on the door caught her attention.

"Hey, Zoe . . . Felix said you needed to eat."

September was a twenty-two-year-old production assistant whose name and bubbly personality had landed her the job.

"Anything other than chocolate."

"Salad . . . sandwich?"

"Yes, and sure."

September smiled and left the doorway.

Zoe kicked off her high heels, which she'd never cook in when in her own kitchen, and removed her purse from the tiny locker. She fished her cell phone from the bottom and checked her messages. Her real estate agent was supposed to have called, or at the very least texted that morning with a new list of potential properties in the Dallas area.

It was time for Zoe to put down some roots. She'd traveled most of the past eight years after taking second place on the first season of *Warring Chef*. Her spot, even if one slot away from number one, had launched her career and turned her into a celebrity. She took regular guest spots on Chef Monroe's weekly syndication, which had her flying to New York several times a year. She also hosted holiday specials, like the one she was filming now, for a popular food network, which wouldn't air until Christmas, some eight months away. Her day job, if she could call it that, was taking the head chef position in the posh section of West Dallas, called Trinity Groves, two weekends a month. Everything else she did to earn money cooking was on location, at a charity event . . . or some kind of red carpet ordeal where she was just as big a draw as the Hollywood elite sitting at the dining tables.

Zoe glared at her blank screen: no messages and no missed calls.

It had been a big decision to consider buying property, and she was anxious to jump on it and move out of her two-bedroom apartment.

It was the right thing to do. "Darn it!"

Zoe flopped on the small chair and rested her head against the wall. The hairdresser would simply have to deal with it.

Her eyes fluttered closed right as her phone, sitting beside her, rang.

The screen lit up with the image of her mother. It wasn't often Sheryl called, which gave Zoe's heart a jump in her chest.

"Hey, Mom."

"Hi, honey . . . I hope I'm not interrupting anything." Her mom always sounded as if she were on the edge of a breakthrough announcement. Considering their family dynamics, she often was.

"I'm on a break. Is everything okay?"

There it was, Sheryl's anxious sigh followed by a telltale groan. "It's Zanya."

Zoe's baby sister was now a mother with a three-month-old. Without hearing the details, Zoe could tell by her mother's tone that this wasn't a call about disaster striking. "I assume Blaze is okay."

"Your nephew is fine . . . it's Zanya. I think she's pregnant again."

Zoe was sure her jaw dropped enough to invite a flock of birds to nest inside. Of all the things her mother could have said, Zanya being knocked up before her vagina had healed from pushing nine pounds of Blaze out wasn't expected.

"What?"

"I found a pregnancy test in the bathroom."

Zoe sat forward, head in her hand. That lack-of-food headache was quickly shifting into something that would need more than protein to fix. "Was it used?"

"No. She can't do this a second time. I knew when she started seeing that ass again things would go downhill."

That ass was Blaze's father, Mylo Barkov. "You can't expect him to sit out on his son's life."

"Fine. He doesn't have to sit out, but he doesn't have to stick it in her again!" Zoe found a smile on her lips at her mother's crass and pointed statement, despite the severity of the situation. "Can you talk to her? She won't listen to me."

"You might be jumping to the wrong conclusions."

"Pregnancy tests don't just land in your cart at the market, Zoe."

Zoe rubbed the bridge of her nose. "No, they don't." And thank God she'd never had a scare like the one her sister was going through. Zanya was barely able to drink legally in a bar and was a single mother who'd dropped out of school and had no real employable skills outside of retail and service work. Which in a small town the size of River Bend meant she'd be living in her mom's mobile home for years to come. Seemed her sister was living the life Zoe feared and ran from. Too bad she hadn't been able to take her baby sister with her when she'd left all those years ago.

"I have to be back on set in twenty minutes. Is she there? Or should I call back tonight?"

"She's gone. But please call as soon as you can. If she isn't knocked up again, she needs to have someone slap her into closing her legs."

"Mom!"

"I mean it, Zoe. I love you kids, but I don't need to raise another lot. I'm willing to help, but Blaze is a full-time job by himself. I can't have another one around here. I'm getting too old for this crap."

Late forties wasn't old. Many hard years of life, however, gave Sheryl the appearance of a woman ten years older.

September slipped into the room with a bag in her hand.

Zoe raised her index finger in the air and finished the conversation.

"I'll call her, Mom. Try not to stress about this. It's probably a false alarm."

"Damn well better be."

"I've gotta go."

"Call her," was her mom's final demand.

Zoe ended the call and tossed her phone on the sofa with a moan.

"That bad?" September asked from the door.

"Why can't family call just to say hi? Why is it always drama?"

September started to laugh. "Friends call to say hi. Family call when they need something."

~

"I feel guilty," Zoe moaned.

"Because you're living your life?" Mel asked after getting the scoop on the Zanya situation.

"Because I'm not there keeping my baby sister from making more mistakes."

"You're talented, Zoe, but stopping your sister from having sex isn't a skill you have."

Zoe rested her head in her hands as she spoke on the phone. "I haven't been there for her. My mom isn't exactly the perfect role model, and we both know Zane can hardly take care of himself, let alone be a big brother for more than ten minutes at a time."

"You're her sister, not her mother. You can open the communication door, but she needs to walk through it to make it happen."

Zoe knew her friend was right. "Still feel guilty."

"I'll talk to her. Make sure she knows I'm here to listen. Being a single mom is hard. It's easy to fall into the trap of sticking with the wrong man to make it easier."

If anyone knew that, it was Mel. Her eight-year-old daughter was born before Mel turned twenty. The baby daddy was a piece of shit, rest in peace.

As the words rolled around in Zoe's head, she pictured Hope's father the last time she'd seen him alive. Nathan had tried to gain custody of Hope for all the wrong reasons. Went so far as to hire thugs to make Mel look like a bad mom. Everything backfired on the man, and one of the thugs he'd hired did a hell of a lot more than set Mel up for an unwinnable court battle.

"You didn't stick with Nathan for long."

"No, but it wasn't easy on my own. I can't say I wouldn't have caved if he'd lost his selfish gene and stepped up early on."

"It would never have been good with that man."

"Don't I know it. If I knew men like Wyatt were out there, I wouldn't have ever slept with Nathan to begin with."

"Yeah, but then you wouldn't have Hope. And you wouldn't have made it back to River Bend and met the love of your life."

"Who knew you were such the romantic?" Mel teased.

"I'm not."

"Speaking of Wyatt . . . has he called you?"

Zoe felt a smile on her lips. He hadn't, but she knew why Mel was asking.

"Nope, why?"

"Oh, I don't know . . . ask you my ring size, maybe."

Zoe giggled. "I don't know your ring size."

"Six. We've talked about this."

"I must have forgotten." Wyatt was working up the right time to pop the question. The question everyone already knew the answer to.

"You're just as frustrating as Jo. Maybe I should put my ring size on the box of condoms."

"I'd hope you're on the pill by now," she teased.

"I am, but I've forgotten to take the damn things twice now. We need backup."

"How is it you've forgotten something as important as a pill?" Mel was the smart one, or so Zoe always thought.

"I kept them on the bathroom counter. Someone moved them, and I forgot to take it. I remembered the next day."

"Where did you find them?"

"In my makeup bag. I never put them in there."

"How did that happen? I can't imagine Wyatt doing it." Mel worked alongside Miss Gina at her bed-and-breakfast. She had the caretaker's room and a private bath that wasn't cleaned by the staff brought in on busy weekends. For the most part, the large Victorian home held only Miss Gina, Mel, and Hope. Plus the occasional overnight guest otherwise known as Wyatt. Though Wyatt had his own place just outside of town.

"You're probably just being blonde."

"Ha-ha! Very funny." Melanie was as blonde as Zoe was dark haired. "So when are you coming to visit us again?"

Considering Zoe had spent more time in River Bend in the past six months than she had in ten years, the question should have felt out of place. It didn't. Still, returning home always tore a piece out of her heart. Well, returning didn't so much as leaving again.

"I'm actually in the process of buying my own place."

"Really? You're buying a house?"

Zoe had a hard time stretching the truth. "I haven't found what I want yet. So my weekends off are busy with open houses and such."

Mel paused. "Oh . . . is that right?"

"It is. Production this week hasn't gone well. I'll be on set most of the month."

"Huh." Mel didn't sound convinced.

"You should come visit me."

Laughter met Zoe's suggestion. "And pull Hope out of school? Not to mention I'm barely on my feet again. I've just about saved enough to buy a beater."

"Do you even need to buy a car?"

"I can't keep asking Miss Gina for hers."

Zoe nodded even though her friend couldn't see her. "I get it. Now's not a good time for me to fly in."

"I get it. But you have to promise me something."

Mel's voice dropped as if what she was going to say meant business.

"Sure, what?"

"You have to promise me you won't avoid coming back because of Luke."

Zoe hesitated . . . took a deep breath.

"Of course not."

"Zoe?" Mel used her Mom voice.

"I told you and Jo I wasn't going to disappear. I won't." She would just find a way for her friends to visit her once in a while and then slide home and hope she didn't see him.

Just thinking about him made her heart hurt.

She'd done really well for ten years. Ten years of avoiding Oregon. Ten years of pretending Luke was just a high school romance. Ten years of getting on with her life. She'd even managed a few lovers in that time. They never lasted, and she never tried to push any relationship past the physical.

Even those encounters were far apart.

Then, when she'd returned for her ten-year reunion . . . those encounters stopped altogether.

Maybe the lack of any quality naked time was the reason she'd been thinking more and more about her high school flame.

"I'm holding you to that."

"I'm sure you will."

"Glad we're on the same page . . . now, about Wyatt . . ."

For the next ten minutes, Zoe listened to all the ways Mel was planning to drop hints on styles and sizes of rings.

Like a good friend, Zoe listened and offered advice.

When she hung up, she realized that once Wyatt did pop the question, what would follow would put Zoe in River Bend more often than not. Between bridal showers, dress rehearsals, and the actual wedding, she'd need a permanent room at Miss Gina's B and B.

And avoiding Luke would be impossible.

Chapter Two

Luke skirted out from under Jo's Jeep and wiped his dirty hands on the rag sitting on the ground by a workbench. Led Zeppelin music pounded inside the garage, giving his brain the opportunity to work without thought. Music had always been white noise while his hands dipped inside an engine.

He rummaged around until he found the part he needed and headed back under the car.

"Luke? You under there?"

A familiar voice cut through the music. "Yeah. Just a sec."

He tightened the hose with a clamp and left the underside of the Jeep again.

Wyatt stood to the side of the SUV, his eyes on the space Luke should be working in. Luke knew his friend's question before he even asked.

"When will this lift be fixed?"

"Our guy in Eugene can't get here until next week."

"That sucks."

"Tell me about it. This is the third time this thing has broken down in the past year."

"Maybe it knows how much you love crawling under cars on your back."

Luke rubbed the ache in his tailbone with the reminder. "At least most of the cars around here are lifted a few more inches than what the kids are driving these days."

"Hey," Wyatt said with a laugh. "I'm still a kid."

"You drive a truck."

"Still a kid."

Neither one of them were kids any longer. But twenty-eight and twenty-nine weren't exactly old.

"What brings you by?"

"Can't I just drop in to say hi?"

Luke gave a single nod. "Yeah, but that happens later with beer. Middle of the day drop-ins mean you need something." Which was an absolute sign that they weren't kids and both of them had jobs.

Wyatt pointed two fingers in Luke's direction. "Right. Two things. First, I need a starter for the track meet on Thursday."

Stopping a workday to fire blanks into the air and watch kids run around a track was a nice diversion in his week. "Two o'clock?"

"Yep."

"And the second thing?"

"I wondered if you could drive into Eugene with me on Saturday."

"What for?"

"I found a couple of used cars I wanna check out for Melanie."

Luke found himself staring. "You're buying Mel a car?"

Wyatt shrugged his shoulders. "She needs one."

"She'd rather have a ring."

Wyatt smiled with a shake of his head. "Which is why I'm looking at used cars and not new ones. I think she'd flip a gasket if I told her we need to wait on a ring because of a new car."

"What are you waiting for anyway?" It was obvious that Wyatt and Mel were headed toward marital bliss.

For a minute, it wasn't apparent if Wyatt was going to answer. Then he sucked in a long breath. "My house is almost done."

Luke thought as much. Wyatt had lived in his home for six years now and had existed in a constant state of construction. Only after he met Mel and it was obvious they were crazy about each other did Wyatt fast-track his own project. Considering Wyatt was the one you called for any and all general contracting needs in River Bend, it was a continuous joke that his own home sat half-finished.

"I knew there was a reason for the fire in your step. How much longer will it take?"

"I'm pushing for a month. Any more and I think Mel will be writing the number six on every street sign and notepad in town."

Luke narrowed his eyes. "Six?"

"Her ring size. 'How about a six-pack, Wyatt?' 'Are six tacos enough?' 'Did you know that most women wear a size six ring?' There isn't a day that goes by that I don't hear the number. I've even started betting Miss Gina how many hints I'll get in a day."

The thought of Miss Gina shelling out betting money to Wyatt brought a grin to Luke's face.

"Poor Mel."

"Not sure what she's worried about. I told her the day was coming."

"You have me there. I haven't gotten to the ring stage of a relationship." Not since high school . . . and at that time, he was young and dumb, as they say. "You might wanna give her a ring before she tattoos your arm in your sleep."

"I doubt it will get to that . . . branding with a fire iron, on the other hand . . ." They both laughed at the image that swam between them like a cloud. "So, Saturday?"

"Yeah . . . of course." Luke ran a hand through his slightly long hair. "I could get out of town."

Wyatt let a sly smile pass his lips. "Maybe we should make it a guys' weekend. See if we can't get you laid."

Luke would have taken offense if his buddy wasn't on to the basic needs of a man in a small town. "Won't Mel worry?"

Wyatt shook his head. "If she thinks that's who I am, then rings wouldn't be on the table of discussion."

Luke knew his friend was right. Mel took some time to trust, but when she did, she did with her whole heart. Besides, Wyatt wasn't that kind of guy.

"So we drive up Saturday, drive back Sunday?"

"If you find yourself busy Sunday, I'll bring the new car back without you," Wyatt said.

Sounded like a plan.

Luke slid back under the Jeep with a tiny lift in his chest after Wyatt left. Something to look forward to other than the underside of a car and the same dozen streets of the town he'd called home since he was born. He hadn't had a serious relationship in town since Zoe . . . and that had been eleven years ago. He had the occasional hookup, but most of the time he left town for that. Nikka had scratched his itch in Eugene for a few years . . . nothing serious. It helped that she was a little older and didn't look at him as anything but a bed warmer. The arrangement worked for both of them.

But it got old and Nikka had eventually moved on.

An out of town anything was way past due. Maybe he should convince Wyatt to take a weekend in Vegas for a bachelor party.

Yeah . . . that sounded good.

Vegas weekend.

Lots of women in Vegas.

When he pictured the women, he thought of long legs, thick dark hair . . . full, lush lips.

He squeezed his eyes shut and pushed Zoe from his head.

Luke took his frustration out on a stubborn cap holding Jo's oil inside the engine. Only testosterone had a strange ability of giving strength that wasn't there a few seconds before.

The taste of motor oil never was something he'd learned to like.

He pushed away and managed to grab a nearby bucket to capture what his face hadn't. His father took that moment to kneel down and peer under the Jeep.

"Don't say it," Luke warned.

His father simply started laughing until the deep rumble walked out of the garage and into the office.

"I need to get laid," Luke whispered to himself.

~

"I need your help."

"Need me to arrest someone for you?"

Zoe once again cradled the phone to her ear. This time she was outside a coffee shop, her tablet open as she searched the Internet.

"Nothing like that. You told me last winter you were in need of a vacation."

Jo chuckled before she spoke. "What's a vacation?"

"That thing you do every once in a while to take a break from that thing you do to earn a living."

"What does me leaving my post have to do with helping you out?"

"I'm buying a house."

"Yeah, Mel said something about that. That's exciting."

"And I can't decide. Is it too big, is it too small? Wrong neighborhood? I don't want to mess this up. It's a big step. I'd feel a lot better if someone I know and trust was here helping me narrow down my search."

"You want me to come to Texas to help you house search?"

"Yeah. I know it's short notice . . . but there are several great options that are having open houses over the weekend."

"This weekend?"

"Don't sound shocked. If I'd asked you to plan a week away a month from now, you'd come up with an excuse." Zoe paused and waited for Jo to deny her claim.

She didn't.

"I could use a weekend away. Just make sure we have time to . . . play."

Zoe smiled into the phone. "You mean hook up?"

"God, yes."

Zoe laughed. "I'll plan a long weekend."

"I can cut out early Friday and take the late shift on Monday."

"Like anything happens in that town on a Monday night."

"Hey," Jo almost shouted. "You'd be surprised."

"You're right. I would. So Friday . . . text me your flight plans."

Zoe disconnected the call, opened up the calendar on her tablet, and blocked out the weekend using Jo's name. Because Zoe knew her friend would still have her cell phone in her hand, she sent a final command via text. Leave your gun and badge at home.

Zoe waited for the snarky friend inside the cop to show up. The dot, dot, dot on the screen proved her rebel friend was still in there somewhere.

Fine, but I'm bringing my handcuffs.

Instead of delivering the news to Jo with a phone call, Luke washed up and walked through the town to the station, where he was sure he'd find her.

The town sheriff didn't leave the station midday unless the weather socked in hard, making driving conditions on the outside of town dangerous. There wasn't a need to patrol River Bend all that often. While Jo made some effort to vary her routine, she'd fallen into the same patterns as her old man all those years ago. A drive through town in the morning . . . again around happy hour, if you could call the group of yahoos that went to R&B's after four the happy hour crowd . . . and another stroll after dark. Summers varied a little more due to the teenage population scoring liquor and playing a little too hard. They too knew Sheriff Ward's routine and avoided her wrath. Or maybe Jo looked the other way so long as no one got hurt or attempted to drive.

Luke pushed through the door to the station and greeted the longtime clerk. "Hey, Glynis. She in?" He nodded toward the back office.

"Does she have somewhere else she needs to be?"

He chuckled and moved behind the desk before briefly knocking on Jo's door and letting himself in.

Jo was standing over a filing cabinet, a stack of papers in her hand. "Hey," Luke said, capturing her attention.

"Oh, hi." She seemed surprised to see him. A little nervous even.

"How is your busy crime-fighting day?" He laughed at his own joke and took a seat.

"Don't jinx me. I'm trying to get out of town." Jo actually winced as she said the words.

"You, out of town? As in a vacation?"

She shrugged. "I guess you can call it that."

She didn't elaborate.

In fact . . . she turned back to the cabinet and started searching through her files.

"Where ya going?"

"Uhhh . . . Texas." She pulled some papers and nudged the drawer shut without making eye contact.

Texas. He understood the strange affect of his friend. "How is Zoe?"

"Good. She's good." She took a hasty seat and put on a fake smile. "How is my Jeep?"

Luke rolled with her change in subject. "It needs a new starter. I ordered it, but it won't be here until Saturday."

"That bites. I'm flying out on Friday."

"Why does that bite if you won't need your car?"

"Need to get to the airport. I'm not taking a squad car and leaving it there."

"I can give you a ride."

Jo took a moment to stare at him before saying, "You ride a motorcycle and drive the occasional tow truck."

"I can take my dad's truck."

"It's okay. I don't want to put you out."

No, she didn't want to have him hyperaware that she was visiting Zoe. The whole town seemed to think he was a walking nerve when it came to his high school flame.

"You're not putting me out. In fact, Wyatt and I were planning to drive into Eugene on Saturday. Let me see if we can't make it a day earlier and avoid two trips."

Jo hesitated but then started a slow nod. "Okay. That sounds . . . okay, sure."

Who knew doing a favor for a friend would sound so painful.

"So my starter is fried, huh?" Jo shifted the subject once again.

"Yeah. I should be able to get it in on Monday."

"That would be great." When she glanced at the clock, he took it as a signal to move along.

Luke pushed to his feet and patted the top of her desk. "I'll get back to you on the carpool into Eugene."

"Thanks, Luke."

"No problem."

He made his exit with a nod to Glynis.

The pine-scented air of River Bend filled his lungs as he walked down the block. He waved at the high school principal, who drove by before Luke jaywalked across the street. A breeze caught the wind chimes that hung from the eaves of the crafty gift store.

He shoved his hands in the front pockets of his jeans as he rounded the corner.

Sam's diner drew his attention. He noticed Sheryl's old car and glanced inside the windows. Zoe's mother brought a wave of mixed emotions inside him. He saw Zoe in her mother's eyes, but that was about it. Sheryl's hair was at her shoulders, and instead of the sleek black color of Zoe's, she had a mousy brown that had started to gray. The woman was weathered beyond her actual years. Sheryl had been a big reason Zoe had fled their hometown. And for that, Luke had a hard time liking the woman.

He'd never felt the need to leave River Bend. But lately, he wondered if that was a mistake. The world outside his town was huge, and he'd yet to experience much of it.

Unlike Zoe, who had seen more countries than he had states.

Luke hesitated only a second in front of Sam's diner before walking the rest of the way back to the shop.

He walked into the open garage, past Jo's Jeep, and into the office. A note on the phone said his father had gone home for lunch.

Luke glanced over his shoulder to the open workspace. Where else could a garage be left completely open and unattended without the worry of someone walking in and ripping them off?

He wasn't sure he wanted to be in a place where people had to continually lock the doors. Yet boredom had set in like a growing cancer over the past year.

Ever since Zoe had returned, albeit briefly, for their class reunion.

Her face, along with many others, reminded him of how little he'd done with his life.

Maybe it was time he took a long, hard look in the mirror and determined if he was happy, or if he was simply lazy.

Instead of contemplating his internal drive, he picked up the phone and dialed Wyatt.

Taking an extra day in Eugene sounded like an excellent plan.

Chapter Three

"The town will not fall apart without you there, Jo. Relax."

"You're right . . . you're right." She looked out the back window of Wyatt's twin cab truck before twisting around to focus on the road in front of them.

Luke placed his arm around the back of his seat and watched a play of emotions cross Jo's face. The woman was a mess.

"When was the last time you took time off?" Wyatt asked from the driver's seat.

"Uhm . . ."

Luke glanced at Wyatt and back at Jo. "Unless you sneak out of town when I'm not looking, I'm guessing the answer to that was back before you took the badge."

"I have days off."

"You have overnights off . . . leaving town for something other than work is what the rest of the world calls a vacation."

"I've gone away a couple of times. And look who's talking. When did you leave town last, Luke?"

It was his turn to stutter. "Uhm . . . ah . . ."

"Exactly! Pot to kettle."

"I drive into Eugene quite a bit," he said.

"Which is an extension of our backyard."

She was right. "I should get out more. It's a big world out there."

"I always thought I'd see more of it," Jo said.

"You still can," Wyatt said. "It's not like you're old."

Jo frowned as if in disagreement and continued to stare out the window.

"He's right, you know."

"I didn't see anything of the world when my dad was sheriff, and I don't anticipate the opportunity to now."

"Doesn't mean you can't change that."

Her eyes skirted past his and out the back again.

That's when it hit him.

As much as Luke felt as if all his options in life were spelled out for him, that any big changes had already happened, they weren't. He made enough money to live a simple, comfortable life in a small town, working in a garage with his father. He had a modest home of his own. Yeah, his parents had helped him with the down payment years ago and refused to accept any payment back. The anchor to River Bend was his parents, a job he didn't hate, and a lifestyle that suited him. What was Jo's anchor? Her job . . . which, if he had to guess, she wasn't in love with. Her friends . . . and the legacy of her father. For Luke, staying in the town he'd grown up with had been a choice. A logical one. For Jo it was an obligation, a weight that kept her looking out the back window of Wyatt's truck en route to the airport.

The desire to learn Jo and Zoe's weekend plans wasn't just from his slight obsession with his old flame. He wanted to know that Jo would get her mind off River Bend. She needed to remember how to live a little.

"What kind of crazy plans do you and Zoe have this weekend anyway?" he asked.

"I doubt *crazy* is a word we'll use."

"Neither of you knit."

She smiled. A smile Luke didn't see on his friend's face as often as he once had.

"House hunting."

The image of houses in Texas did a dance in his head. It took a full thirty seconds for what that meant to sink in. "Zoe's buying a house?"

"Sounds like it."

"Wow." He hated the knot in his throat. Hated that he knew her buying anything anywhere meant she wasn't going to move home. He'd waited for years for word of her getting married. Or at least word that she was in some kind of meaningful relationship with one of those Hollywood types she always surrounded herself with. When he'd seen her at their ten-year high school reunion, and then again when Mel's daughter, Hope, had gone missing, he'd felt his heart weeping once again.

Jo nudged his arm off the back of the seat.

His eyes snapped up.

"Do yourself a favor, Luke. Don't ever go to Vegas."

"What?"

"You have no face for poker," she told him.

Hiding his emotions was something he had learned to do in Zoe's presence, but apparently not with Jo and Wyatt. "I'll have to work on it before the bachelor party."

Jo sat forward, all her attention out the back window shifted. "Bachelor party?"

Wyatt slammed his arm across the seat to knock a little wind out of Luke's chest. "Oops."

"Something you wanna share, Wyatt?"

Wyatt glanced in his rearview mirror, then over at Luke. "Someday."

"Someday? As in someday soon?"

Wyatt shrugged.

Jo lifted her eyebrows in question toward Luke.

"Don't look at me. Man code and all. When the day comes, however . . . I think Vegas is in order."

"Mel will not want a Vegas wedding," Jo said.

"Bachelor party in Vegas."

Jo nodded in understanding and placed a hand on Wyatt's shoulder. "Just don't let this one near a poker table, okay?"

"Deal."

"I'm not that bad," Luke defended himself.

At the same time, both Jo and Wyatt said, "Yes you are!"

"Damn it's hot here!"

Leave it to Jo to greet her with a smile and a bitch.

Zoe made a slightly girlish giggle and squeezed her friend hard once she'd passed through the doors outside the secure zone of the airport.

Jo offered a one-arm hug, holding on to her duffel bag.

"It's Texas . . . we're always hot."

She dropped her bag and shrugged out of her jacket.

Zoe reached down. "Anything in baggage claim?"

"It's a long weekend. How much do I need?"

Zoe tested the weight of the bag with a bicep curl. "So long as you left your weapons at home."

Jo glanced around.

"It's Texas. We like guns here."

"Not in an airport."

Zoe slid her Ralph Lauren sunglasses over her eyes and led Jo toward the garage that housed her car.

"I can't believe you didn't bail," Zoe said once they were in the car with the air conditioner cranked on high.

Jo released a long-suffering sigh and rested her head back. "I considered it, but my vagina protested."

Zoe busted out.

They arrived at the booth to pay the parking fee, but were unable to speak to the attendant because of their laughter.

Just when the laughter ebbed, Zoe glanced at Jo and started giggling again.

"How long has it been?" Zoe asked.

"I can't even tell you. It's embarrassing."

"You can and will tell me. I need to know if you're going to jump on the first penis that presents itself or if you're going to make him work for it."

"And here I thought we were going to look at houses."

Zoe turned onto the frontage road that led to the freeway. "We'll do that, too. I have a few houses to look at tomorrow. I scheduled time with the Realtor at one, and again at two on Sunday. So we can live large at night and sleep in the next day."

"I like the way you think, Brown."

Zoe liked how every once in a while Jo would use her last name as if it were a badge. Zoe had always considered it a curse.

"So really . . . how long since you hooked up with something that didn't involve a battery?"

"Almost two years. Wait!" Jo glanced up as if the answer to Zoe's question were written on the underside of the visor. "Nope, two years."

"That sucks."

"Yeah, well . . . hooking up in River Bend is out of the question, and Eugene is too far away for anything with any regularity."

"Not if you met the right person."

Jo twisted in her seat and pointed two fingers to the right side of her chest. "You know what my badge has taught me?"

Zoe thought she knew what her friend was going to say but let her say it anyway. "What's that?"

"That cops aren't meant to have a love life."

"That's stupid. Lots of cops are married."

"And even more of them are divorced."

Zoe slowed for traffic and kept half an eye on Jo as she spoke. "You don't have to get married, or divorced. You can simply date someone once in a while."

"Problem with that is most of the guys I have met, limited though they were, all bailed the second I told them my profession."

"Men like to take care of women. Most don't know what to do with someone as independent as you." Zoe knew that from personal experience.

"I think it has more to do with the kind of guys I'm attracted to."

"You always liked the bad boys in high school," Zoe reminded her.

"That hasn't changed," Jo said with a sigh. "Conflict of interest at this point in the game."

"So the two years is more because you've avoided the whole scene . . . or no one has presented himself?" Zoe eased off the freeway and headed toward her apartment.

"Both. But thinking he will present himself by materializing on my doorstep is probably an unrealistic expectation."

Zoe smiled. "Stellar evaluation."

"I should be a detective."

Zoe parked and turned off the car.

The heat hit them as they pushed open the doors. "I don't think I could ever get used to this," Jo told her.

"This isn't even that bad. Summer is worse."

"A whole lot hotter than home."

Zoe didn't want to think about River Bend being home. "Yeah, well . . . drama creates its own heat."

Jo followed her inside, where the air conditioner was already running.

"Speaking of drama, have you spoken with your sister?" Jo asked.

Zoe tossed her keys in a bowl by the front door and placed her purse on the same table. "She isn't pregnant. Thank God!"

"So I heard."

"But she could have been, hence the pee stick in the bathroom." Zoe walked through her place, inviting Jo to follow. She stopped in her second bedroom and waved a hand at the bed.

Jo took the hint and placed her bag on the chair beside it. "I was a little worried I'd have to cuff your mom to keep her from ripping off Mylo's dick."

"She'd have to stand in line. I'd be more worried about Zane."

Zoe's brother was the unpredictable one. Took after their father with his temper.

"Zane has kept his nose clean since last summer." Jo sat on the bed and did that bounce thing people did when testing the mattress. "He has a legitimate job in Waterville, and Josie says he hasn't been a regular for months."

Josie owned R&B's, the local bar in River Bend.

Zoe had heard the same news from her mom, but hearing it from Jo meant there was truth in the information. Her mom tended to sugarcoat ugly things. Well, not when it came to a possible second grandchild. But when it came to Zane, their mom had always looked the other way, blamed herself for a lack of a father in his life.

Zoe leaned against the bed. "I hope it continues."

"You and me both. Nothing worse than policing my best friend's brother."

The image of her father shot to her head. "What about your best friend's dad?"

Jo lifted an eyebrow.

"He's up for parole in a couple of months."

"He never makes it."

The tension in Zoe's shoulders tightened. "He's not in jail for murder. He'll eventually get out."

"He has a hard time staying out of fights, Zoe. Which adds time to his existing sentence and doesn't make the parole board happy. I don't think he's going anywhere soon."

The two of them never spoke about her dad. To hear Jo speak with such conviction told Zoe that Jo knew more than just the basic facts of how the parole process worked. "You've been keeping up on his case, haven't you?"

Jo simply shrugged. "You'd do the same if you were me."

Zoe leaned down and hugged her friend. "I love you."

She felt Jo's hand rest on her back, and then it offered a little shove. "I'm horny, but you don't have the right parts."

Zoe hugged her harder before letting thoughts of her father drift away.

"You've got that James Dean thing going . . ."

The woman beside Luke at the bar had short dark hair, an easy smile, and slurred words. He'd offered to buy her a drink before realizing how many she'd already had going in.

"What do you know about James Dean?"

She reached forward, pushed hair from Luke's forehead, and nearly fell off the bar stool.

Beside him, Wyatt laughed into his beer.

"It's the hair."

Luke caught her before she ended up in his lap.

A prospect he might not have minded if she were sober.

Her glazed eyes passed over him and on to Wyatt. "Your friend is kinda cute, too."

Wyatt wiggled his fingers in the air in a wave. "Hey, darlin'."

"Oh . . . that's cute."

Seemed like everything was *cute* to this one.

"It's Trish, right?"

Trish slapped a hand on Luke's shoulder and leaned close enough for him to smell the alcohol in her pores. "You remembered."

"Ah-huh . . . right. Did you come with friends tonight?"

Trish twisted a little too fast and wobbled while pointing to the far side of the bar, where two similarly dressed women were playing pool with several men.

Instead of suggesting that Trish meet up with her friends, Luke used the excuse of a need for the bathroom, leaving Wyatt to fend for himself.

He approached one of Trish's friends, who held a pool cue in one hand, a beer in the other. "You came with Trish?" he asked, pointing behind his back toward the bar.

The woman offered a toothy smile. "Is she getting into trouble?"

"She's pretty hammered. Think maybe she should have someone watching out for her before she ends up in a truck bed with a stranger."

Toothy Smile rolled her eyes. "Hey, Jen. We need to rescue Trish."

The woman she called Jen swung her gaze toward the bar and moaned. "Not again."

The two of them handed off their cues and wove through the crowd. Once they had Trish's attention, Luke watched Wyatt pick himself up off the bar stool and make his way across the room.

"You wouldn't believe what she offered to do to both of us." Wyatt was grinning.

"I can imagine." Luke tilted the rest of his beer back and set the empty bottle on a nearby table.

~

"What are you drinking?"

Zoe forced a smile over her shoulder. The man asking her the question had been beside the guy who was now getting his ass beat on a dartboard by Jo. Military short hair, thick shoulders, thick neck . . . and from what she could see by the grin on his face, thick ego.

"Perrier with lime."

His smile wavered.

"I'm driving." Not that she needed to explain, but she did anyway.

"Jack and Coke," he told the bartender as they passed by.

Zoe looked at her nearly empty drink and didn't comment.

"You live around here?"

She shook her head. "Wisconsin," she lied.

The smile that attempted to manifest for half a second quickly became a flat line between his lips.

"So you're here on vacation?" As he asked the question, the leggy blonde walking by caught his eye.

Zoe took great pleasure in delivering her next lie. "Missionary work, actually. Where do you go to church?"

The bartender set down his drink. He tossed a bill on the bar, downed his beverage in one swallow, and stood. "Great talking with you . . . uhm . . ."

They hadn't exchanged names.

She let him out with a smile. "Great talking with you, too."

He walked away, and a deep chuckle beside her diverted her attention.

~

"This is the third bar we've been to."

"This didn't used to be so hard," Luke said.

Wyatt waved a beer in the air as he spoke. "I'm practically married and you're not available."

"I am very available," Luke protested with heat in his voice.

"The tipsy woman at the pool hall?"

"Drunk, not tipsy."

"The blonde at Shiners?"

"Blonde," he said, as if the color of her hair explained everything.

Wyatt narrowed his eyes.

"She wore a ring on her right hand. Newly divorced or stepping out. I don't want that."

"What's wrong with newly divorced?"

Luke wasn't sure, so he went back to his original dislike. "Blondes never did anything for me."

Wyatt glanced around. "What about her?" He pointed his beer at a brunette passing by.

Somewhat attractive . . . kinda short. Luke shrugged.

"Not available. Your head isn't in the game."

Luke turned back to the bar and signaled the bartender. "My head is very much in the game. It needs to be in someone's game."

Wyatt laughed. "Your head is in Texas."

Luke had the bartender's attention and skipped his first thought of another beer. "Jack straight up."

Wyatt lifted his eyebrows.

Even with the noise in the bar, the silence that followed between him and Wyatt sounded like an iceberg in the Pacific.

Luke waved his hand a second time once he downed his first shot of whiskey.

The bartender shifted his eyes between both men and walked away once Luke lifted his glass. Images of Zoe danced behind the mirror in the bar.

"My head is not in Texas," Luke said.

Wyatt ordered another beer.

The jukebox shifted gears from country to classic rock.

"I know I'm breaking the man code here . . . but I call bullshit on that."

The liquor in Luke's head did a tiny tap dance and reminded him he wasn't a teenager any longer.

"I'm not thinking about her."

Wyatt set his beer on the bar and squared his shoulders to the back mirror. Looked like the two of them would be speaking through the thing.

"What I don't understand is why you're not with her."

"She left." Luke didn't need to say who she was . . . didn't need to pretend with Wyatt that Zoe didn't exist. "I'm over it." He drained his drink.

"You may have *been* over it. But after the reunion, you stopped *being* over it."

Their ten-year class reunion brought Zoe back to town. She'd stuck around long enough to sizzle his world with memories and desire, only to leave when all the festivities ended. Then, when Melanie's daughter was in the hospital, she'd come back. The two of them had a couple of conversations that made him think maybe . . . just maybe.

Then she left again.

And she didn't return.

"She's in Texas. I'm in Oregon."

"And?"

"It wouldn't . . . it isn't . . ." It wouldn't work. She lived in Texas. And more importantly, she'd walked away. Yeah, they'd both been young. Too young to be talking about forever, but he hadn't ever truly gotten over her. He'd wanted to . . . God knew he wanted to, but every damn time he saw her it was as if time sucked him into some kind of vortex he was unable to avoid, and he was right back in the summer of his senior year in high school, planning his future with the girl of his dreams.

Only his teenage dreams were just that. Adolescent, hormone driven desires for the sexiest girl in school. As much as he wanted to convince her to stay and make their life work, she left, and he realized how powerless he was. He mourned her leaving for a season and then drove her memory away with every girl he could. It wasn't long before that didn't work and the trips out of town became less and less frequent.

He watched the recorded episodes of *Warring Chef*, the show where Zoe had won the second-place spot, the show that had given her a zillion opportunities. As his eyes caught her tucking her long hair behind her ear on the screen, he'd remember capturing her hair and pulling it back to kiss her neck.

When the culinary show played out in a sensual series of images in his head . . . he turned off his recordings and drove to Eugene for the night.

"Can I tell you something?" Wyatt pulled him out of his thoughts.

"Free world."

"I think you owe it to yourself to give that a second chance."

Luke twisted in his bar stool. "What about 'she's in Texas' did you not understand?"

Wyatt closed his eyes and shook his head.

~

"Perrier with lime? I would never have thought that would work if I hadn't seen it."

He was tall, thinly built, wearing a business suit. The slight twang to his voice said he lived in Texas, but his lack of boots and a hat told her he wasn't a native.

Zoe lifted her vodka tonic and took a drink. "It could be sparkling water."

"*Could* would be the key word."

She liked his smile. "Zoe," she said, extending her hand.

"Raymond." He shook her hand and waved his left in the air. "Married."

"Not married." Zoe waved back.

"I'm guessing you're not a missionary either."

"Nowhere close."

"I would imagine a woman as beautiful as you has to come up with new lines to derail men all the time."

"Quick wit isn't needed when they're drunk . . . but yeah." She looked beyond him and noticed another couple talking. "Where's your wife?"

"At home." His smile left his eyes. "And no, I'm not hitting on you."

She didn't feel like he was. Still, she had to ask . . .

"You're in a bar on a Friday night while your wife is at home . . . what, with the kids? Highly suspicious, Raymond."

He didn't elaborate. "You're in a bar, drinking . . ." He picked up her drink, sniffed it, and set it back down. ". . . vodka, and lying about it to avoid getting picked up. Highly suspicious, Zoe."

Zoe picked up on Jo's laugh from across the room.

Her BFF was getting her groove on with a man twice her size with biceps that belonged on a boxer. Ink peeked out from the sleeves of his T-shirt and desire stared down at Jo from under his well-worn cowboy hat. *Go, Jo!*

"So you're babysitting your friend?"

Zoe almost choked on her drink. Laughing, she said, "Jo does not need a babysitter."

"I don't know. That one is a player." Raymond nodded toward the man picking Jo up.

"So is she." Zoe turned around and placed her attention on her drinking buddy. "You must come here a lot if you know the clientele."

He didn't comment. Instead, he ordered a round of drinks for the both of them.

Chapter Four

Sunlight shot pain deep inside Luke's brain. His tongue stuck to the roof of his mouth and cotton sat like a deep knot in the back of his throat.

He waved the fly away from his closed eyes and attempted to roll over.

"Wake up."

Wyatt's voice, along with a tapping on his forehead, made him crack one eye open.

The fly was an envelope that Wyatt waved in the air.

"What the hell?" It was early . . . too early for this.

Wyatt tossed the envelope on Luke's chest and stood. "You have two hours."

"Two hours? For what?"

"Your flight boards in two hours."

The sheet dropped to his waist when he sat up in bed. "Flight? What flight?"

"The one to Zoe."

Luke rubbed the sleep from his eyes. He needed an aspirin or a shot of whiskey . . . he wasn't sure which.

"Start from the beginning."

"I bought you a plane ticket . . . it's nonrefundable, so don't even think of throwing it away."

"I don't remember saying I wanted to go to Texas."

Wyatt stood and tossed Luke's overnight bag on the bed. "C'mon."

Luke's heart pounded in his head with increasing speed.

He swung his feet off the side of the bed and dropped his forehead into the palms of his hands.

Zoe.

"You need to do this, Luke. Last-ditch effort. When you come back, you need a direction. This limbo isn't working for you."

"What about getting the car home for Mel?"

"You can drive it when you come back. Now move your ass." Wyatt looked at his watch. "One hour, fifty-five minutes."

Luke was buckled in and cruising at twenty-two thousand feet before he had an opportunity to process what he was doing.

What the hell was he going to say to her?

The jingle of keys and the click of her front door unlocking brought Zoe's attention away from the paper she was reading on her tablet.

Jo tiptoed in, shoes in hand, and closed the door behind her.

Zoe stood and leaned against the door frame of the kitchen with a cup of coffee in her hand.

"Oh . . . the walk of shame never looked so devilish."

Jo jumped and started laughing before turning her head toward Zoe.

What makeup Jo had worn the night before was all but gone, her hair was a bit disheveled, and the grin on her face spoke volumes.

"That good, huh?" Zoe was almost jealous.

"Holy shit, that man had energy."

Zoe laughed and turned back toward the dining table she'd been sitting at. "I have coffee."

"I love you."

"Yeah, yeah." She poured the coffee and sat down for the obligatory recap of the night. "Did you get his name?"

Jo nodded . . . then turned said nod into a shake of her head.

They both laughed over the brims of their cups.

Hours later, they stood on the massive porch of a colonial two-story with the Realtor, who was spouting off details of the neighborhood, the schools, the lack of a crime rate.

"There's no such thing as a lack of crime," Jo told the real estate agent.

He placated her with a smile.

Zoe watched as Jo tilted her steel-rimmed sunglasses that should have identified her as a cop, but had somehow managed to slip by Anton. "What are the square miles of this crimeless zip code? And what is the population?"

He blinked. "I can get that information if you need it."

"You do that."

Zoe stepped forward. "What do you think of the house?"

Jo moved past Anton and back inside the front doors. "Very formal."

Yeah, Zoe wasn't sure about all that formality. "It has an amazing kitchen."

"I don't think it's you."

Zoe sighed. "Onward."

~

"You're back?" Raymond was dressed a little more like a local on Saturday.

"So are you."

This time Zoe really was drinking Perrier. She tilted the green bottle toward the other side of the bar, where Jo was once again flirting with Mr. No Name.

"Ahh, I see."

Zoe glanced around. "Still no wife?"

He took a seat beside her and removed his cell phone from the back pocket of his jeans. He found what he was searching for and handed her the phone.

A woman in a wheelchair stared back at her. It appeared as if, along with a physical disability, there was something missing in her eyes. "Car accident three years ago."

Zoe felt sucker punched. "This is your wife?"

Raymond took the phone from her fingers. "Almost lost her." He scrolled through his phone again, handed it back. This was a picture of the two of them at obviously better times. He was kissing the top of her head, and she was laughing as they stood on the shores of some beach. "She's beautiful."

"Yeah." There was loss in his voice. "I recently had to put her in a home. The accident took away her ability to walk and left her brain a mass of scrambled eggs."

Zoe couldn't imagine. "How long were you married before the accident?"

"Three years."

"That's awful."

He shrugged. "Her parents told me I should divorce her . . . move on with my life."

Zoe felt her heart dip. She understood on a practical level why they'd suggest such a thing but couldn't imagine taking that step.

One look into Raymond's eyes told her everything. "You still love her."

He offered a single nod. "Hard to move on with someone new when you're still in love with someone else."

She placed a hand on his arm. "I'm sorry."

Jo slid between the two of them, placed her arm over Zoe's shoulders. "I'm going to take off."

She rolled her eyes and pushed Jo away. "Go, you slut."

"I'll be back before noon."

It was good to see her friend smiling.

"Get his name," Zoe said as Jo walked away.

She was rewarded with Jo's back and a middle finger flying in the air.

When Zoe stopped watching, her eyes drifted to a set of eyes staring at her.

Air rushed into her lungs and her heart took off.

Raymond placed a hand on her arm. "Are you okay?"

"Luke."

Raymond twisted in his chair, and Luke turned to walk away.

Zoe jumped to her feet and wove through the dense crowd.

She caught him at the front door. "Luke!"

"This was a mistake."

"What are you doing here?"

He ran his hands through his thick hair. "I don't know."

Someone bumped her as they left the bar.

Zoe moved outside, where the humidity lay thick in the air. She grabbed Luke's shoulder.

For a minute, they just stared at each other.

She was reminded of the first time he'd kissed her. They'd ditched school and met outside of Grayson's farm. She knew she was meeting out there for a kiss but had no idea she'd fall in love. He looked just as nervous then as he did now.

For years after she'd left River Bend, she'd imagined him showing up like he had now. She'd dream of him showing up on set, in her kitchen with his too-long hair and sexy grin.

Leaving River Bend had been one of the hardest and smartest things she'd ever done.

Now the part of her she'd left behind was watching her as a thousand memories passed through her. She watched and waited for him to spell out what he was doing in Texas, in her neighborhood, at her bar.

"What are you doing here, Luke?"

"I—I . . . I needed to see you." He looked back through the open door. "I see you're with someone."

Confusion marred her brow. "Raymond?"

Luke forced his attention back to her. "His name is Raymond?"

"Oh, my God, you're jealous."

He put his hands in the back pockets of his jeans and rocked back on his heels. "I am not." Luke studied his shoes for several seconds.

"You're such a bad liar."

"I keep hearing that."

"It's been eleven years, Luke."

"I know." He looked at her now as noise from the inside ramped higher and a live band started to play. "I was over it. Then you came back."

All the pain of that first year apart tore at her heart.

"I had to leave, Luke. You know I couldn't stay in River Bend." They'd had this conversation one time before. The night she said goodbye. She'd cried and he had been angry. He told her not to leave one time, then let go of her hand as she pulled away.

"I know that, Zoe."

"If you know that, then why are you really here?"

A couple burst from the door, arm in arm, laughing.

Luke grabbed her hand and pulled her to the far end of the deck. Once he was happy with their location, he dropped her hand and leaned against the post. "I went to Eugene with Wyatt to hook up."

She swallowed. She'd thought as much when Jo had told her about the drive to the airport.

"And?"

"Wyatt pointed out how picky I am."

She avoided smiling. "You didn't hook up."

A short shake of his head had her lifting the edges of her lips.

"Wyatt woke me up with a plane ticket and told me to fly here."

"And since when do you do what everyone tells you to do? Where is that self-assured, confident guy who makes his own decisions that I spent time with?"

There was alarm in his eyes. "I don't know. But I want him back, Zoe."

"You flew here to find him?"

He ran his hands through his hair again. "I did." Unhappiness filled those two tiny words.

Zoe half sat on the railing and placed both hands at her sides. "How can I help?" Seeing him miserable had never been her goal. Escaping misery, on the other hand . . .

"I need to move on."

It was her turn to stare at her shoes. "I never meant for you to stay stagnant."

"I didn't think I had. Then everyone returned last year for the reunion and . . . I don't know . . . I never left. Now I feel like I'm in limbo, waiting for something to shift."

"A lot of kids don't leave. You never talked about leaving."

"Neither did you, until you did."

Yeah, it had taken a bottle of tequila and a hangover to slap her head into the reality of her future if she'd stayed. "Are you saying you want to leave home?"

He stared at her as if her suggestion was a foreign concept.

"I don't know what I'm saying, Zoe."

She loved how her name rolled off his tongue.

Noise filtered out of the bar, breaking the spell Luke had placed on her by simply uttering her name. "Where are you staying?"

He glanced around the parking lot. "I rented a car."

She chuckled. "You really didn't plan this."

Luke pulled his shirt away from his chest as if trying to capture a cool breeze with the effect.

"You can stay with me."

His eyes lit up.

"I have a spare room," she blurted out. "I doubt Jo will be using it."

"Jo . . . shit, I completely forgot she was here."

"She's not . . . well, she is, but she found a tatted up hottie. Then there is always the couch."

He laughed. "Good for her."

"When is your return flight?"

"Monday morning."

"Stay with me until Monday. You'll remember all my annoying habits that you don't miss and be ready to hook up when you fly into Eugene."

He tried to smile. "You don't have annoying habits."

Yeah, she did. "C'mon." She pushed away from the rail and dusted her hands on her jeans. "Let's go find a bottle of tequila and remember old times."

Luke took a deep breath and offered his arm.

Her belly twisted as she looped her hand through and walked the few short steps to their cars.

Luke woke to his tongue tasting like elementary school paste. He preferred not to think about how he knew what paste tasted like.

He cracked an eye open and took stock of where he was.

The plush couch cushioned his back. A large-screen television hung on the wall across the room.

Zoe's!

He let his head fall back and his eyes close.

Unlike when they were kids, they drank the tequila until tipsy, not until shitfaced. He'd crashed on the couch in case Jo snuck in sometime in the night. He didn't want to scare a woman trained to take down men twice her size when she didn't realize he was in her designated sleeping space.

His bladder prompted him to lift his lazy ass off the couch.

When he was finished, the crack in the door leading to Zoe's room asked him to try out his skills in voyeurism. Powerless to stop himself, his little finger moved the door ever so slightly.

She was sound asleep, her hair disheveled on the pillow, her full lips parted in her sleep.

He'd missed her.

The quiet moments . . . the laughter . . . his ability to say and do just about anything and not scare her away.

She'd left anyway, but not because of him.

In Texas, she had a life she never would have obtained staying in River Bend.

Luke eased the door closed and slowly made his way down the hall.

A gasp stopped the movement of his feet.

"Holy shit."

Jo held shoes in her hand and shock on her face.

"Shh, she's sleeping." He glanced over his shoulder to the closed door.

"What are you doing here?" she asked in a rough whisper.

He realized then what it looked like . . . him half dressed, walking away from Zoe's room.

Luke took two steps and pulled Jo from the hall. "I slept on the couch." He pointed to the blanket and pillow.

Jo kept staring. "You were in Eugene."

"There's more than one plane in the air, Jo." He didn't elaborate and turned toward the kitchen. "Coffee?"

"Holy shit," he heard again, only this time with meaning.

Chapter Five

"A three-story house is a lot of up and down."

Zoe slid a glance to Jo when Luke voiced his opinion.

They'd left her apartment two houses ago without her having the opportunity to talk to Jo privately.

Anton had taken one glance at Luke, smiled, and made sure he was by his side as they breached the doors of the homes Zoe was considering buying.

Her Realtor's reaction to Luke's good looks answered a few questions Zoe had about the man's sexuality.

"No more or less than Miss Gina's Bed-and-Breakfast," Zoe said.

"This is a home, not an inn."

"Okay . . . it's a lot of square footage. Are you planning on your mother moving in? Maybe Zanya and Blaze?" Luke asked.

Zoe swallowed hard. The mere image of her mother anywhere near Dallas made her cringe. Would her family think that was an option? Moving to Texas and staying with her?

"Maybe it is a little large."

Jo nudged her arm. "The houses we looked at yesterday were bigger."

"I didn't think about my family."

"Is your mother elderly?" Anton asked.

"No," Zoe sighed. "Just needy."

"Your mom wouldn't leave Oregon."

Zoe knew better. Much as she liked to believe that her mom wouldn't try and interrupt her life, she wouldn't put it past her. And Zanya wasn't exactly rolling in money with any real options. She realized how selfish her thoughts sounded in her head.

What a bitch. Maybe she should be looking at larger homes . . . homes to house her family.

"Don't go there, Zoe," Jo exclaimed.

"They have so little."

Luke edged closer. "Life choices, babe. We've talked about this for years. Nothing has changed. You enable your mom now . . . your sister, even Zane, and you'll be taking care of them their entire lives."

They were right.

"I hate that you both know what I'm thinking before I do."

Luke and Jo smiled at each other.

"Perhaps something a little smaller would be a better option," Anton said.

"It wouldn't hurt."

They were eating a late lunch at 15 Coins. Zoe knew the head chef, who personally stepped out of the kitchen to greet them and suggest what they should order. The hospitality was a norm in River Bend but unexpected in Dallas. Even among the accents and the smiles, the metropolitan atmosphere stood out above everything else. And with metro anything, smiles and simple greetings were about as far as people went.

"It feels a little fancy for shorts and a T-shirt."

"Look around, Jo. There aren't a lot of dressed up people in here."

Jo and Luke glanced around the busy restaurant and agreed with a "huh" and a nod.

"I can't believe the size of everything we looked at today," Jo said. "It's like everyone here wants a huge electric bill to combat all this heat."

"It's Texas. People like their space here. Closets the size of New York apartments are the norm. I'll find something that suits me. Just need to keep looking."

"You're going to need a big closet for all those shoes you have stacked up in the spare bedroom."

Zoe had the good sense to be slightly embarrassed by her collection. "It's part of my on-screen wardrobe."

Luke grunted. "I've seen you cook. You don't use your feet."

The thought made her cringe.

Jo laughed.

Zoe felt a tap on her shoulder and looked up. "Felix."

"I thought it was you. Nobody wears jean shorts with a silk blouse quite like you."

Zoe accepted her director's hug and glanced behind him. "Are you with someone?"

Felix puffed out his lower lip. "Alfonzo ditched me for a pedicure."

She smiled. "Pedicures are important."

Felix winked and looked at Jo and Luke. "Let me guess, out of town friends."

Zoe pointed to Jo. "Felix, my fashion consultant, my friend . . . and occasionally he tells me what to do on set. This is Jo."

Recognition flashed in his eyes as he stuck his hand out. "The posse?"

"I use Sheriff, but posse works."

"My goodness you are beautiful. A little glowing around the eyes."

It was fun to see Jo blush. She wasn't used to compliments.

Felix turned his gaze toward Luke. "Oh, let me guess . . ." He tapped a finger on his chin and then glanced at Zoe. "Is this him?"

She knew she'd talked about her friends back home, but didn't think she'd revealed any secrets to Felix over the years.

"This is your Luke . . . right?"

Luke had opened his eyes wide and wore a smirk.

"I wouldn't say he's mine."

Luke extended his hand. "A pleasure."

It was Felix's turn to blush. "Too bad you don't play for my team. The good ones are always straight."

Luke, the brat, pulled out the lone empty chair. "Join us. I'd love to hear what Zoe has been saying about us."

Translation: he wanted to know what she was saying about him.

"I hate to interrupt."

"You do not!" Zoe almost snorted her response. "Sit down."

"So demanding. See what I put up with?" Felix sat and promptly ordered a martini as a waiter passed by.

For the next couple of hours, Felix did all the talking. Luke listened intently as her flamboyant friend recounted what information he'd gathered about him over the years. Luke was the high school lover . . . the man she left behind. All true, and nothing that wasn't more than an elephant in the room during most conversations. Luke paid close attention when Felix reminded Zoe of a brief affair she'd had over a year before during a filming session in New York. His name was Gary. He was a production assistant infatuated with her, and she was attracted. She didn't often mix business with pleasure, but Gary had been the exception. As Felix pointed out, he resembled Luke in many physical ways.

The affair lasted several months.

When Gary started asking for more, she cut the relationship off.

No matter who she met, she'd always been too emotionally distant for anything long-term.

Felix insisted on paying the bill and promised to "drop by" River Bend the next time he drove through. Considering no one ever drove through, the likelihood of him doing so was slim.

With Felix's arm looped through Jo's as they exited the restaurant, Luke sauntered up next to Zoe and whispered, "So, Gary looked like me, huh?"

She slid her wide rimmed sunglasses over her eyes and stared straight ahead. "We're not discussing this."

Luke laughed and mimicked Felix by tucking her arm in his.

"I can't believe how fast the weekend flew by."

Luke sat back as Jo and Zoe said their good-byes before they moved through security and onto the flight that would take them both back to Eugene.

"You need to ditch that uniform and come here more often."

"The same goes for you," Jo told her as she bent down to tug her duffel bag over her shoulder.

"Tell Mel and Miss Gina I said hi."

"I will." Jo looked over at Luke and said, "I'll see you at the gate."

She left the two of them alone.

When Zoe turned her gaze on him, nerves sat on the surface of her smile.

"I'm glad you came," she said.

"I am, too. I see why you like it here."

"You do?" She seemed surprised.

"Lots going on . . . good friends, great food. Everything you like."

"I suppose."

"And none of your family drama." Which was the real reason she enjoyed Dallas so much.

"They do have a way of reaching me here."

"Not easily," he said.

Zoe glanced beyond him where Jo had disappeared in a sea of people walking through security. "Well, you don't want to miss your flight."

He opened his arms for the obligatory friend hug. She stepped into them as he folded her close. Luke wasn't sure who sighed first . . . him, or her. With a deep inhale he sucked in the feel and scent of her and rested his cheek on the side of her head. He considered telling her he missed her, that he wanted a chance.

He didn't.

With a fortifying sigh, he ended their hug.

Moisture gathered behind her dark, soulful eyes. He wanted to call her on the tears.

He didn't.

It was his turn to pick up his backpack and sling it over a shoulder.

Zoe watched his every move with a forced smile.

"Tell your parents I said hi."

"I will."

"Good-bye, Luke."

Yeah . . . he wasn't about to say those words to her again. Instead, he saluted her with two fingers and turned.

He managed three steps before swinging back around.

Luke didn't give her a chance to back away, didn't offer an out. He dropped his bag at her feet and pushed both hands into her hair before taking her startled lips with his own. If he thought their hug had made her offer a moan, it was nothing compared to the one they both hummed with their kiss.

She was honey on his lips, sweet and savory and open to explore.

He remembered this. The way she bent into his embrace, the way her timid hands fanned on his chest. The way her nails dug deep when she wanted more. He deepened the kiss long enough to make sure she knew he wasn't saying good-bye.

This was hello.

Not the kind of greeting they'd shared when they were kids, but the kind adults who knew what they wanted shared at the beginning of something good.

He tasted her tongue, vaguely aware of those people passing by without comment.

As his body hardened in response to her frame pressed against his, he knew he needed to back away. When he did, her head was tilted up toward his, her eyes closed, her lips slack with wanting.

Zoe's eyes fluttered open and he rested a finger on her lips.

"I'll be back," he told her with a wink.

He wanted her back.

The information took root inside his brain and he smiled.

Before she could utter a syllable, he lifted his bag a second time and strutted as he walked away.

The temperature inside the studio felt as if it were ten below zero, hence Zoe and September sitting at a tiny outside table between the buildings usually reserved for those who smoked.

"You've been awfully quiet these days."

September pulled Zoe from her thoughts of Luke in slow degrees. "Hmm?"

"Man, you are distracted. Is everything okay?"

A feral cat regarded the two of them from several yards away. "Everything is fine."

It registered that September was still talking, but for some reason Zoe couldn't stop watching the gray and white cat long enough to concentrate on what her friend was saying. As if sensing it was on display, the cat stuck its nose in the air as it passed through the sun that gleamed between the buildings before resting in a shady spot under a lone tree.

". . . about a man, isn't it?"

Zoe caught the word *man*. "What?"

September waved a hand in front of Zoe's face. "Hello?"

Zoe closed her eyes and forced herself to concentrate. "I'm sorry. I'm distracted."

"Obviously. I said, this is about a man, isn't it?"

"Yes." There was no use pretending. "First, he shows up like fog on the beach, and then he kisses me. Who does that?"

September smiled. "Is that a rhetorical question? Cuz I think lots of men do that if they know what they want."

"He doesn't want me. I've changed. I'm not the same girl."

"How about we start at the beginning. Which man are we talking about?"

Zoe was sure she looked at September as if she were missing a few screws. "Luke. You know . . . Luke!"

She raised a hand. "Never heard of a man named Luke in your life."

"From River Bend."

"Still have no idea who you're talking about."

It dawned on Zoe that perhaps she hadn't spoken of Luke with September at all. "We went to school together. Took me to prom. We made out in the back of his truck behind Grayson's farm until the sunrise. He was my first . . ." Her first everything.

"That sounds sweet."

"Exactly. Like candy. Yummy, delicious . . . but too much and it will make you fat and stunt your growth."

September's face twisted in a scowl. "That doesn't sound appetizing."

Zoe thought of how he'd walked away at the airport. Full of poise and confidence. The self-assured man she'd known in school. "Oh, he's appetizing. His hair is always a little too long. Doesn't like to shave on the weekends." She touched her cheek, thinking of how that scruff on his face felt against hers when he'd kissed her. How had she forgotten how much she liked those kisses? "Broad shoulders and gorgeous blue eyes. I was the envy of all the girls back home."

"So what happened?"

"I moved away."

"College?" September asked.

"Kinda." She sighed.

"So Mr. McHottie floated in like fog and kissed you after all these years?"

"Yes. Who does that?"

"Someone who knows what he wants and isn't afraid of distracting you to get it."

His parting words sang in her head like a tune. "Then he said, 'I'll be back.' Like he's the Terminator or something."

September simply laughed.

Would he come back?

She could avoid him by not going home, but she couldn't avoid him if he came to her.

And now that Mel was back in River Bend, and Miss Gina called every couple of weeks to ask how to cook something as simple as gumbo for her guests, Zoe wasn't sure she wanted to stay away from the place where she grew up. She could visit more often, soak in the cooler weather during the warmest Texas months.

What was she thinking? She was setting roots in Dallas. Buying a home, for God's sake.

One of the grips poked his head out the back door. "You're wanted on set, Zoe."

Right. On set . . . something River Bend didn't have.

One week later Mel called, giggling like a schoolgirl and talking so fast Zoe could hardly make out her words.

Wyatt had popped the question.

A small engagement party was forthcoming and when could Zoe drop everything and fly in?

Three weeks after Jo and Luke's visit, Zoe was driving out of Eugene, where she'd rented a car through Alamo—the irony didn't escape her—and was taking the two-hour drive back home.

And unlike any time before, she did so with a smile and a little ray of hope.

Chapter Six

Miss Gina's Bed-and-Breakfast looked exactly as it had when she'd last seen it. The throwback from the sixties VW van sat polished in the gravel drive, Miss Gina's baby she'd kept in pristine condition for as long as Zoe could remember.

She no sooner parked her car and stepped out than the screen door on the inn slammed shut and Hope bounced from the steps with her energetic Labrador, Sir Knight, flying by her side.

"Auntie Zoe!"

She knelt down to capture the girl in a hug. "Look how big you are!" Melanie's daughter was eight now, and Sir Knight was less than a year. A full-grown puppy, which meant he was big, bouncy, and uncoordinated.

"Mom and Uncle Wyatt are getting married!"

Zoe petted the dog while encouraging him to keep his overly large paws on the ground and not her slacks. "You'll be calling him something other than Uncle Wyatt before you know it."

Hope had her mother's blonde hair and easy smile. "He says I can call him Dad now."

"Do you?"

Hope shrugged.

Zoe didn't get the opportunity to question her further before the screen door bounced against the frame a second time.

Miss Gina stayed behind on the porch while Mel ran down the stairs much like her daughter had moments before. "I'm getting married!"

She shoved her hand in Zoe's face before offering a hug. "Look!"

It was sparkly and round and sat like a crown on Mel's size six ring finger. "It's about time."

Mel squealed; the excitement in her voice had Sir Knight barking at their feet and running in circles.

"Can you believe it?"

"It would have been harder to believe if it didn't happen."

The wind whipped Mel's hair in her face, which she swiped away in irritation. "Thanks for coming."

"You couldn't keep me away."

Mel passed her a brief look of doubt before looping her arm through Zoe's and walking them up the steps of the old Victorian that had been more of a home to both of them growing up than the ones they slept in as children.

In a tie-dye skirt and a billowing blouse that belonged with the car from the sixties, Miss Gina hugged her with more strength than most women her age. Not that she was old. Probably in her midsixties, but none of them had the guts to ask her. "What is this . . . three times in the past year you've been back? I'm starting to think we don't suck anymore."

"Bite me!" Zoe said without venom.

The floral scent of the parlor, or living room as it turned out, brought back a million childhood memories when Zoe stepped inside.

"Have you been by your mom's yet?" Mel asked, leaving her small suitcase by the stairs leading to the rooms.

"No. Plenty of time for that later."

"Probably good to have some of my lemonade before that visit," Miss Gina said.

The red pitcher sat on a silver serving tray begging for attention. "Let me wash my hands."

From the floral wallpaper to the scented soap she'd expected at the bed-and-breakfast, Zoe smiled into the feeling of home. No matter where she had landed in the past decade, nothing felt like Miss Gina's.

She returned to the parlor and accepted the tall glass of "lemonade." The vodka infused lemonade, or perhaps it was better to call it lemon infused vodka, tasted better than any cocktail at the fanciest restaurant in Dallas. "Is it me, or is this the best stuff ever?"

"It's the best." Mel toasted her glass. "I'm getting married!"

Zoe could see how the weekend was going to go.

"So what is the plan?"

Mel set her glass down. "Wyatt's parents are flying in tomorrow. My dad is coming the night of the party."

Zoe was a little surprised. "Have your parents met Wyatt?"

"We met my mom in Eugene at Christmastime, my dad was here for the . . ." Mel's voice trailed off. She glanced at her daughter, who played with the dog, half listening to their conversation.

Mel mouthed the word *trial*.

The silence in the room became apparent, and Hope glanced up from playing with the dog to find the three of them staring at her. The man who had lured Hope away from the bed-and-breakfast and left her to die on the side of a cliff was standing trial for kidnapping, attempted murder, and murder charges for the death of Hope's father. Zoe knew there had been a pretrial and also knew that it would probably be over a year before the courts knew what to do with the man. He was wanted in London, which was trying to extradite him back to his home country.

The Oregon courts didn't want to risk him going home and slipping through the British system. It helped that Wyatt's father was a high-powered criminal attorney, usually on the defense, but in this case more than happy to switch teams and go for the dirtbag's throat.

The three of them resumed the conversation, omitting any mention of the trial.

"So your dad is coming but not your mom."

"No, she said the wedding would be soon enough to see my dad."

"For God's sake, it's been ten years." Miss Gina slugged back a big portion of the contents of her glass.

"Eleven," Zoe corrected her.

"Even better. Remind me to smack your mom when I see her."

Zoe laughed. "You're gonna have to stand in line, Miss Gina."

"Just do it after the wedding. No drama before."

It was nice to see her friend glowing.

"So what are you and Wyatt thinking? Church, garden . . . courthouse steps?" The last suggestion produced the look Zoe was going for.

"Bite your tongue."

"Well?"

"We'd like a garden wedding . . . but the weather is unpredictable."

"So a church?"

"I suggested a tent," Miss Gina added her thoughts. "If nature wants to sprinkle your special day with liquid sunshine, you have a place to hide . . . if the sun comes out to play, you open up the sides and enjoy the shade."

"I think we need to come up with a guest list before we decide. Wyatt's family has a lot of *need to* invites."

"Half of River Bend will expect to find an invite in the local paper."

"Have you seen my backyard?" Miss Gina added. "There's plenty of room."

It was vast, even with the guesthouse she'd commissioned Wyatt to build last summer. Beyond the few acres designated to the bed-and-breakfast was a lot of open space. The closest home to the Victorian was a mile away.

"We have a lot to consider," Mel said. "Besides, we're getting ahead of ourselves. This weekend is about our engagement. We have time to talk wedding after this first party."

"So where are we holding this shindig?"

Miss Gina rolled her eyes. "Here, of course. I was thinking cocktails, appetizers. I liked those shrimp puffs you made last year."

"Who said I was cooking?"

"Don't start with me, girly. I have the kitchen all stocked with your favorites, and this one"—she hooked a thumb in Mel's direction—"doesn't cook, and everything Sam touches is fried or overbaked." Sam owned the local diner and only real restaurant in town.

"There are plenty of cooks in River Bend," Zoe offered one last argument, not that she'd relinquish her spot in Miss Gina's kitchen for anything.

"Yeah, but there is only one *chef.*"

The No Vacancy sign was posted at the entry to Miss Gina's property and then again on the front door. The rooms slowly filled up with family and close friends the day before the engagement party.

Miss Gina refused payment for the rooms but happily accepted the helping hands of those there for the event.

Hope ran around like the perfect little hostess, happy with the attention bestowed upon her.

Zoe had been in River Bend just over twenty-four hours before she left Miss Gina's to visit her own mother.

It wasn't that she didn't love the woman; she did . . . but as the oldest child, Zoe always felt as if the roles between them were somewhat reversed. She'd been forced to take care of her younger siblings early in life. Helped her mom with a budget, something Sheryl was notoriously bad at, and the cooking and cleaning when her mother worked long hours.

Even now, Zoe sent money home to her mom every month to help pay the bills.

Her mom had made some serious miscalculations in her young life. Education wasn't possible when she found herself pregnant at sixteen . . . the man she married, Zoe's dad, went on to father all three of them, then handled the stress by being a mean drunk who used his fists to get his point across. The day he went to jail for the last time both labeled her and saved her.

Ziggy Brown wanted all of his children named after him. Hence all the Zs in the family. It wasn't until the trial that Zoe learned that Ziggy wasn't even her father's real first name. It was Theodore.

For some reason this thought popped into her head as she left her rental car and walked up the weed-filled path to the front door of the place she'd called home for eighteen years.

Only it wasn't home anymore.

Her hand hesitated as she went to knock. Giving in to both urges, she knocked once and twisted the handle to let herself in.

Scent hit her first. The musty familiarity of worn furniture and the never truly clean carpet layered on top of each other like icing on cake. The added scent of a baby still in diapers reminded her Blaze lived there.

The television blared to an empty living room. Zoe glanced to the left; the kitchen was void of people, too. "Hello?"

She'd called her mom before coming over and knew Sheryl was going to be home.

"Mom!"

"Back here."

Zoe placed her purse on the coffee table, the same one she'd done her homework on as a kid . . . the same one she and the girls had sat around eating pizza and often drinking something they shouldn't have been.

Zoe followed the sound of her mom's voice and found her in Zanya's room, changing Blaze's diaper.

Sheryl wore ill-fitting clothes Zoe was sure she recognized, and Blaze was in nothing but a T-shirt and a diaper when her mom finished the job.

"Look who is so big!" Zoe used a high-pitched voice and settled her eyes on her nephew.

"I was wondering when you'd grace us with your presence." There was jealousy in her voice.

"Oh, Mom." Zoe offered a one-arm hug and kissed her cheek.

Blaze gave her a cheeky smile and kicked his feet when Sheryl sat him up.

"Where is Zanya?"

"Working. She got a job in Waterville at that burger joint." That explained the lack of a car in the driveway.

"It's good she's working."

Sheryl puffed out a breath. "Yeah, but now I'm babysitting."

Zoe could see the stress on her mom's features. The woman had always looked ten years older than she was, but lately it seemed worse.

She reached her arms out to Blaze, who happily took the opportunity to play with someone else. Zoe placed her lips to the top of his head the second she picked him up. He smelled fresh and innocent. Opposite of everything these four walls represented. "Hey, baby boy."

Sheryl took the reprieve and left the room with Zoe following.

Zoe sat on the couch, watching Blaze study her. "You look like your mommy." And he did . . . the dark hair that all of them had, dark eyes and slightly olive skin.

Sheryl spoke to her from the open counter leading into the kitchen. "Let's hope he doesn't get fat like his deadbeat father."

"Mom!"

"What? It's true."

"Yeah, but Blaze doesn't need to grow up hearing that."

"He's too young to understand."

"True, but you say it now and will continue when he's three, when he does understand your words."

"By the time he's three, Zanya and Mylo had best have their shit figured out and be on their own. I'm not doing this forever."

As much as her mom protested, she would never kick them out. She had a healthy fear of being alone.

"If Zanya has a job, she's figuring it out."

Sheryl huffed, unconvinced.

"C'mon, Mom . . . no one understands better than you how hard it is to be a single parent."

"And I thought I taught all of you not to do it."

"Telling people not to have sex is like trying to hold back the tide. Zanya's a smart girl, she'll figure it out."

"Zanya's just a baby and trying hard to fall into my footsteps with the wrong choices. At least I was married to your father."

This was not the defense Zoe expected from her mom. "Great help there! Nothing like getting your ass kicked weekly to remind you who to be loyal to."

"It wasn't that bad."

Words died in Zoe's mouth. How could she say that? "I was there, Mom. It was worse than bad. Zanya is better off on her own than hooking up with someone like Ziggy." She didn't honor the man by using the terms Dad or Father.

"At least he pulled in money sometimes."

"Oh, my God! What the hell?" Blaze must have sensed the rising tension and started to fuss in Zoe's lap. She didn't know a lot about babies, but she had seen people bounce them on their knees, so she started to move her legs in an attempt to calm him.

It worked.

"He put you in the hospital more than once, Mom. None of us escaped his inability to hold his liquor."

"I'm sure all those years in prison have taught him a lesson."

Zoe felt her chest tighten. "What's this all about? We haven't talked about him in years."

Sheryl turned her back to Zoe in the kitchen, fiddled with something she couldn't see. "I don't know. I think Blaze reminded me of when you kids were little. It's either harder now to raise babies or it wasn't that bad then."

"Or maybe you're just done playing mommy. It's okay, ya know. You don't have to take up where Zanya leaves off. It doesn't make you a bad person or anything. Forgetting how bad it was when Ziggy was around is just stupid."

"Are you calling me stupid?"

It always happened like this. They would be having a normal conversation, and when Zoe's logic streamed into the conversation, Sheryl would somehow make it sound like Zoe was calling her names.

"No, Mom! I'm not calling you stupid." Blind . . . forgetful . . . but not stupid.

"Not everyone has it as good as you do."

Talk about a sucker punch to the chest.

Blaze started to cry.

"I work hard to have it good." Like she needed to explain that.

"You cook."

It was her turn to feel like crying.

An automatic swing Zoe had given as a gift to Zanya at her baby shower sat on the opposite side of the couch. Instead of continuing the pain, Zoe kissed her nephew and hooked him in. She turned the motion on and he instantly calmed.

Since sticking around was only going to result in a full-blown fight, Zoe grabbed her purse off the coffee table and hitched it high on her shoulder.

"Where are you going? You just got here."

"I'm going to get some supplies for all that *cooking* I do."

Sheryl stared in disapproval.

"The engagement party starts at five. By all means, bring Blaze. There are lots of hands to hold him and give you the break you obviously need." With that, Zoe turned on her heel and let the door close behind her.

Instead of turning right out of the driveway, which would take her back to Miss Gina's, she turned left and headed into town. She thought about stopping at the station to talk to Jo, but that wasn't where she found consolation when it came to her mom. Yes, her BFFs listened, but it was always Luke who understood.

Miller's Auto Repair had been a cornerstone in River Bend long before Zoe was born.

Mr. Miller was a robust man with a healthy laugh and loving smile. His size could scare a small child, but he was the biggest teddy bear she'd ever known. Mrs. Miller wasn't a small woman either, but neither of them could be labeled as fat. She liked to cook and he liked to eat. It was a marriage made in heaven.

Zoe pulled into the drive and parked beside the only tow truck in town.

The heavy metal thumping inside the garage said Luke was around somewhere. When he wasn't, Mr. Miller was prone to listening to country. The contrast between father and son always made her smile.

Motor oil and the smell of tires brought a flood of memories. She'd seen her share of the inside of garages in Dallas, but none smelled quite like Miller's. There was an old pickup pulled inside with two feet sticking out from under it. Add a pair of ruby slippers and it might resemble an iconic movie. Nikes didn't have the same effect.

Zoe walked inside and bent down to see who belonged to the shoes.

Sure enough, Luke lay on his back, his hands focused on something under the car, grease a part of his uniform. She allowed herself a brief moment of visual pleasure. Strong, lean body, muscles that rippled up his arms and across his chest. Even lying on his back, covered in grime, he was something to look at.

Luke must have felt the weight of her stare.

He didn't jolt when he saw her, didn't immediately scoot away from the car. He offered his seductive smile and said, "Hey."

"Hey."

He lifted a finger, indicating he needed a minute, and turned back to his work.

Zoe rose to her full height and glanced around the garage. She was about to lean on the bench when Mr. Miller poked his head around the corner. "Hey, Luke . . . whose car is in the—" He stopped talking when he saw her. "Well, look who is back in town!"

Mr. Miller opened his arms and Zoe half ran into them.

He lifted her off her feet and spun her in a full circle before setting her down.

He did a quick once-over and said, "Goodness, girl, do you ever eat what you prepare?"

She slapped a playful hand on his chest. "Good to see you, too."

He hugged her a second time while Luke slid out from under the car. "Do I get one of those?" he asked, his arms opened for her to step into them.

"How dirty are those hands?" she asked, not because she cared but because that had been what she'd said all the time when they were in high school.

Luke's playful smile matched his father's. "C'mere."

She did. And when he hugged her close, she didn't feel the need to giggle and scream, she felt the need to sigh.

"I missed you," he said close to her ear so only she could hear.

Before she could tell him she felt the same, he pulled away and looked past her smile. "Is everything okay?"

He could always read her. "I had a fight with my mom," she whispered.

His firm hands gave her a reassuring squeeze before dropping to his sides. "Give me a minute to wash up."

"Okay."

Luke walked into the back of the shop, leaving her with his dad.

"Luke says you're buying a house in Dallas." He turned down the music as he talked.

"If I can ever find something that works."

"Don't all houses work?"

"Let me rephrase . . . if I find something that fits what I want."

Mr. Miller narrowed his eyes. "Let me guess, big kitchen."

"A must!"

"Not too close to your neighbors."

"That would be nice," she said.

"Room for an herb garden?"

She hadn't thought of that . . . but yeah. Zoe nodded.

"Sounds easy enough, what's the problem?"

"Nice neighborhoods equal huge homes. I can find a smaller place in a crappy part of town." She waved a hand in the air. "I'll find something."

"I'm sure you will, baby cakes. You're not working too hard, I hope."

"Of course I am. Isn't that what we all do?"

He shrugged. "I'm glad you're taking time off to visit us. I take it Mel and Wyatt are the reason for the visit."

"I couldn't leave them with pigs in a blanket and boxed cookies for their engagement party, now could I?"

"You're more than just a meal ticket."

She knew that . . . but the food was a bonus.

"I wouldn't have it any other way."

He leaned forward. "Are you making those little shrimp puff thingies?"

Zoe rolled her eyes and patted his belly. "Like you need them."

"True . . . but I'm not getting any younger, ya know. Don't see you all that often."

She loved the feeling of being wanted. "I have ya covered, Mr. M."

He winked, just the way Luke did.

"Are you harassing her, Dad?" Luke had changed his shirt and run a comb through his hair. Even his hands were cleaned from all the grime and grease.

"Just helping her out with menu options."

"Can I count on Mrs. M's banana cream pie?"

"I'll let her know you have a special request. Maybe get a few pounds on those bones of yours."

Such a contrast between Luke's parents and her mom . . . it made her both happy and extremely sad.

Sensing the shift in her mood, Luke took her arm. "I'm taking a coffee break," he told his father.

"You kids have fun. I have things covered here."

Instead of leading her back to the rental car, Luke pulled her toward his bike.

She hadn't been on the back of the thing since she was eighteen.

He handed her a lone helmet and straddled the bike.

Zoe popped on the helmet and tightened the straps without words before climbing up behind Luke.

The bike roared to life and she let her arms crawl around Luke's waist.

As they pulled out of the parking lot and onto Main Street, everything inside her clicked. And for the first time since she returned to River Bend, Zoe felt completely at home.

Chapter Seven

The back of Grayson's farm was a normal hangout spot when they were kids . . . so were the back of the bleachers, the back of his truck, the back of Miss Gina's B and B . . . but the farm was far out of town and away from prying eyes. Also, a wooded spot separated the farm from the cliffs that jutted down to the ocean. The trees kept the wind off the water from being unbearable, and the moisture had always helped Grayson's crops back when the man actually planted them.

Feeling Zoe's arms around him as he drove to a place they were both familiar with warmed him in ways he didn't want to admit.

She was hurting. And true to Zoe fashion, she came to him when she was. At least that was how it had been when they were kids. Even last year, during their high school reunion, she'd broken away from the party twice and needed to bend his ear. She always said he was a good listener. As a kid, he never offered advice on how to fix her problems. How could he? They were just that, kids. He feared now he would have advice she wouldn't want to hear. He'd always wanted to fix her problems growing up . . . now that he was older, he felt like maybe he could.

He brought his bike to a stop and cut the engine.

Zoe didn't move. "It hasn't changed."

"Trees are a little bigger."

She released her arms from his waist, her warmth instantly missed. She shook her hair out when she set the helmet aside.

"Remember homecoming?"

How could he ever forget? He'd planned to go to the dance, then take a trip to the place they were standing . . . he'd even pitched a tent with blankets to offer some protection against the cold if they ended up naked. Then Jo showed up more than a little drunk, her date completely hammered. Mel had driven them and her date was utterly sober. The six of them ended up snuggled in a four-man tent with no one getting lucky.

"You were so mad."

"I was not."

"Were too. Jo was out of control back then. Hard to believe how much she's changed."

Luke glanced up into the thick of the pine trees. "Oh, I don't know. She looked a little more like herself with you in Dallas."

"Her badge is a little like a noose around her neck."

"I've always thought the same thing. She makes a damn fine cop, though."

"Still happy she did it . . . the whole sheriff thing. The alternative would have been bad."

He agreed but didn't want to continue talking about Jo. He wanted to know what was eating at Zoe. "What happened with your mom?"

Luke leaned against a tree while Zoe recounted the play-by-play of her brief visit with Sheryl. He knew how passionate Zoe's hatred for her dad was, so hearing that part of her story gave him pause. The real killer was hearing about Sheryl's complete disregard for all of Zoe's hard work. She took chances, had student loans that put her though culinary school. The woman worked her butt off and deserved more respect than her mother offered.

"You're more than just a cook," he told her.

"I know that. But it hurt. When will her words no longer hurt, Luke? I'm a grown woman."

"And she's your mother. We're all kids around our parents at times."

"What was that shit about Ziggy? It's like she's completely forgotten the black eyes and broken bones."

They hadn't been dating when Ziggy ended up in the state penitentiary. He knew the man was a douchebag but didn't know how bad Zoe and her family had it until after she opened up to him. Even then, Luke was sure Zoe left stuff out of her conversations with him. Luke had always counted the timeline of them dating as a blessing. If Luke saw Ziggy raising a hand to Zoe, it would have been him in jail.

"I know it sucks, but I don't think there is anything to worry about. It isn't like your mom can invite the man over for dinner."

A look of doubt crossed Zoe's features.

"What?" he asked.

She shrugged. "It's probably nothing."

He didn't like the sound of that. "What is it?"

"He's up for parole."

"Isn't he up every year now?"

"Yeah, but . . . it isn't like he killed someone. Fifteen to life in my book means after fifteen years it's all a crapshoot."

"Hasn't it been more like twenty?"

"Seventeen." Her voice wavered.

"You're really worried about him getting out."

She did what Zoe did . . . she tried to blow it off. "Jo says it's unlikely he will ever be free. Prison fights and added time."

That was a good thing. "You still worry." Zoe always worried, even if she hid it from the rest of the world.

"After hearing my mom talk, I'm worried that if he did get out, she'd welcome him back."

"You think she'd do that?"

"I don't know what to think. I've always wondered why she never dated after he was sent away."

"Did you ever ask?"

Zoe shook her head. "No. I asked her years ago if she divorced him."

"And?"

"'Of course,' she told me. But sometimes she tells me things I wanna hear instead of the truth."

Luke ran a hand through his hair, brushing it out of his eyes. "How can anyone stay married to someone like that?"

"I don't know. He gives men a bad name."

Luke remembered all the fear Zoe had early in life. How intimidated she was by his dad because of his size and how long it took to warm up to him. Luke had a brief conversation with his father a few months after he and Zoe started dating. From that day forward, his dad put every effort into making sure that Zoe knew she had a family with them.

"If Jo says he isn't going anywhere, you have nothing to worry about."

Zoe didn't look convinced. "If he did get out, he'd come straight there. It isn't like my mom moved or anything."

He hated the anxiety in her voice, the tense muscles in her neck as she talked. "What can I do?"

She shook her head. "Nothing. Listen, I guess."

"I can do that."

For the first time since they got off the bike, Zoe offered a smile when she looked at him. For a good thirty seconds they stared at each other without words.

"You kissed me," she said, changing the subject.

"I did." He knew the grin on his face said he wasn't sorry. "You kissed me back."

"I did." She sighed. "I haven't decided if that was a mistake."

"It wasn't."

"How can you be so sure?"

He took a step closer. "Because you showed up in my garage."

Zoe tried to blow off her actions. "I needed to talk."

"Your best friends were right down the street. You chose me."

Luke was close enough to see her pulse beating from a vein in her neck. He felt like a vampire who needed to touch his teeth to that very spot.

He placed a hand on her waist.

She didn't back away.

"I don't want to hurt you again, Luke."

"I was a boy when you left. I'm a grown man now."

"I live in Texas. My life is there."

He nudged her closer with a slight tug of his fingertips.

"I know where you live."

Zoe looked up at him; the tip of her tongue moistened her bottom lip. The teasing smile she often wore was all but gone.

The moment he felt her hand find his waist, his world came into focus.

"This isn't smart," she uttered, her lips reaching toward his.

Luke didn't confirm nor deny. He simply removed the space between them and gave the woman what she was asking for.

Unlike the hurried kiss in the airport, this one was slow and soft. A homecoming. She tasted like flowers and chocolate and gentle waves upon the shore. Her eyes fluttered closed and he pulled her in tight. Luke stopped thinking about roses and candy and relished the feeling of her in his arms. She was more assured than when they'd been together before, leading the way by opening to him, tasting him.

When she clawed into his back, Luke matched her hunger with his. Their tongues danced, their bodies rubbed in all the right places.

Her lips pulled away, her breath came in short pants. Luke found the spot on her neck he wanted to taste and gave a gentle bite.

"Oh, God."

When they were kids, he'd back her against one of the trees and make her scream his name. He'd been her first, and that knowledge never left his thoughts. While she wasn't the first woman he'd had sex with, she was the only woman he made love to. The distinction was a clear line in his memory.

Her hand traced down his hip and rounded over his ass.

The space inside his jeans tightened, his cock asking for attention.

Luke took the liberty of filling his palm with her breast. He felt the hardened bud under her shirt and lowered his lips to the fabric covering her. Even through her clothing, she arched into him, her head tossed back.

He smiled as he turned his attention to the other side.

Zoe stopped his assault and brought his lips back to hers.

Luke backed her against a tree but didn't attempt to remove her clothes. He just kissed her until her lips were swollen, his hair tangled from her fingers fanning through it.

When she tucked her hand inside his shirt, he broke away. "We aren't doing this here."

She clawed his skin. "It didn't stop you before."

He smiled, kissed her briefly until she opened her eyes. "We didn't have a choice then. We do now."

Zoe rested her head on the bark of the tree and grinned. "We were reckless."

"Still are." Lord knew jumping back into this fire was a lot like stepping off a cliff into a dark cavern filled with water. Ultimately, you knew you were safe, but the dark drop always made you believe things would turn for the worst.

Luke liked the way she was staring at him.

"How is it possible you look better now than when we were kids?"

He ran a hand down her hair, tucked a strand behind her ear. "Good genes."

That had her laughing.

"I shouldn't be doing this anyway. Mel is going to worry."

Much as his body protested, he knew this wasn't something to be rushed. "Damn maturity."

Zoe laughed again.

"C'mon," he said, pulling her away from the tree. "Before I change my mind."

She patted the tree like it was a thick mattress on a bed. "Lots of fond memories in this spot."

"I can make better ones in a much more comfortable location."

It was her turn to neither confirm nor deny his suggestion. Instead, she assumed her position behind him on his bike and wrapped her arms around his waist for the drive back to the shop.

Zoe hummed while she waltzed around Miss Gina's kitchen preparing a feast of finger foods. If anyone went hungry, it would be their own fault.

Miss Gina snuck in and grabbed an apple from the bowl of fruit. "If I didn't know better, I'd swear you've gotten laid."

Zoe hadn't said a word to anyone about Luke's sudden need to neck with her whenever he had the chance.

"I just like cooking in your kitchen."

Miss Gina wasn't convinced. "Tell that to someone who was born yesterday."

Just to put her off, Zoe said, "I'm sure Mel's having sex . . . even Jo had sex. I haven't in so long I think I've forgotten how."

Miss Gina talked around her apple. "You're getting something."

Zoe rolled the last of the shrimp puffs and placed the tray in the top oven. "You're the one who needs to get some."

"Who says I haven't?"

Zoe twisted around and stared. "Who?"

Miss Gina chewed instead of answering.

"You're full of crap."

"Am I?" Miss Gina left the kitchen as quickly as she'd entered.

Zoe stared at her retreating back. "No way . . ."

"No way what?" Mel interrupted her thoughts as she walked into the kitchen from the parlor.

"Miss Gina just implied she's getting some."

"Some what?" Mel opened the refrigerator and removed a bottle of cold water.

"Sex."

The screen on the back door slammed shut while Mel twirled around to follow Zoe's stare.

"No way."

"Has there been anyone?" Zoe asked.

"Not that I've seen. She drives into Eugene every few weeks, picks up a bunch of stuff at the warehouse store."

"Does she stay overnight?"

Mel placed a hand over Zoe's. "Oh, my God . . . yes. She said she didn't like to drive that much in one day . . . wanted to use the break."

"She is totally getting laid."

Mel slumped into one of the kitchen chairs. "Why wouldn't she tell us?"

Zoe returned to her stuffed mushrooms. "I think she just did."

"That explains the spring in her step."

There seemed to be a spring in everyone's step these days.

"Hello? Anyone home?" The voice was male, and Mel seemed to know exactly who it belonged to.

"William?" She bounced off the chair and darted to the reception area of the inn.

Zoe went back to work and let Mel greet her future in-laws.

The back screen door slammed again, followed by the sound of Hope running through the house.

"Grandpa Bill and Grandma Kay are here!"

The kid whizzed by, Sir Knight running to keep up.

Zoe considered suggesting Hope not run in the house, then reminded herself that she was the aunt, not the parent. Cool aunts added sugar, they didn't bitch about things like messy shoes and dogs.

On the other hand, a dog in her kitchen wasn't going to fly.

Zoe kept on cooking as she heard the weekend guests arrive. About an hour before the party was going to begin, Zoe placed one of the last trays in the oven, removed her apron, and left her post to change.

Mel had wrangled a couple of the young servers at Sam's to help pass around trays during the party.

Zoe slipped up the back stairs and into her room. She rinsed off quickly and slid into a little black dress. She wondered if the lack of sleeves would be a problem, then remembered the sheer number of people that would be mingling all night.

She added a little blush, a splash of mascara on her lashes, and sparkly gloss on her lips. With one last brush through her hair, Zoe tucked her polished toes into a pricy pair of heels that she never thought she'd own.

Instead of sneaking down the back steps, Zoe took the sweeping staircase in the front of the house.

Laughter-filled voices rose from below, and music played in the background.

The front door to the inn opened when she reached the halfway point of the stairs.

Mr. and Mrs. Miller filled the doorway, pie in hand.

Zoe's heart warmed with the sight of them. She glanced beyond but didn't see Luke.

"Mrs. M!" Her name was Audrey, but Zoe always called her Mrs. M.

"Look at you." Mrs. M was all smiles and open arms.

Zoe took the last steps right as Luke walked in.

She hesitated, her gaze no longer on his mom.

Her vision tunneled, and all she saw was him. Decked out in slacks and a long-sleeved button-up shirt, one that stretched across his chest and told her he wasn't afraid of physical labor. The only times Zoe had seen him in something other than jeans was when he took her to prom and homecoming.

Her mouth watered.

Luke's eyes traveled over her like a caress. The room felt hot with his gaze.

Mrs. M was saying something.

Zoe missed it completely.

Luke broke eye contact and took the pie from his mom's hands. "Hey, Zoe."

He'd always played it cool like that. "Mrs. M," she said again, this time giving the woman a warm hug in welcome. "It's good to see you."

"You're too thin."

Zoe hugged her harder. "I love you, too."

She chuckled.

Zoe hugged Luke's father and quickly excused herself to the kitchen, where she smelled her food cooking. Hopefully no one had messed with her oven while she was away.

The parlor was filled with familiar faces she had every intention of seeing throughout the night, but first she needed to put the finishing touches on her dishes and tell the kids what to serve first.

The click of her heels followed her into the kitchen. She rounded the corner and found Luke's arm snaking around her waist and his lips treating her with an unexpected kiss.

She melted.

"You're gorgeous," he muttered after breaking away.

Her thoughts were mush . . . why had she entered the kitchen? "You're distracting."

"Good." Luke patted her ass and pushed her toward the oven.

The oven . . . her oven.

Luke was about to leave when it was her turn to stop him. Zoe grabbed a nearby paper towel and wiped her lipstick from his lips. "Behave yourself," she whispered before taking his lead and patting his ass as he left the room.

Chapter Eight

Mel held a perpetual smile as she floated from one guest to another, Wyatt at her side. The two of them fit like pieces of a puzzle. Zoe knew the moment she met the man that they were destined for this massive step. She couldn't be happier for her.

The photographer in charge of capturing images of the engagement party was one of the track students Wyatt coached. The thinly built sixteen-year-old came equipped with acne, a digital camera, and a lot of ambition. He also came to the party with a sixteen-year-old assistant who sported a D cup.

Jo stood beside Zoe, wearing her uniform since her deputy was out with a stomach bug and she needed to be available to run out if something came up.

"Did our resident paparazzi just grab a cup of Miss Gina's special lemonade?" Jo asked.

She'd already seen the kid grab a red cup and pour it into a soda can. "Yep."

Jo grumbled.

"I have ya covered."

Jo hated playing the heavy when it came to teenagers. A side product of her youth. Zoe didn't mind stepping in so her friend wouldn't have to.

"Is your mom coming?"

Zoe kept eyeing the front door, wondering the same thing. "She said she was, but who knows."

Luke's laughter caught Zoe's attention from the other side of the room. She found herself watching him.

He was relaxed. More than she'd seen him in all the time they'd spent together since she left River Bend after high school.

"What is going on with you two?" Jo whispered the question in her ear.

"What?"

"Luke?"

"Nothing." The knee-jerk denial sounded harsh, even to Zoe.

Jo offered a cold, hard stare. "I was there when you told me and Mel you lost your virginity to that man. And second, I'm a cop. Would you like to rephrase 'nothing' for me?"

Heat filled Zoe's cheeks. "I don't know," she revised. "Nothing *should* be happening."

"But something is."

"He came to Texas."

Jo laughed. "So did I."

Zoe kept staring at Luke. "Yeah, but you didn't take my virginity."

Jo choked on her soda.

Another glance around the room prompted Zoe to take care of the adolescent photographer sooner than later.

She approached the kid with her palm up.

His eyes traveled from her palm to her cleavage, the voyeur. "You want my camera?" he asked.

"Your car keys."

The braces on his teeth flashed as he smiled. "Excuse me?"

Zoe let her eyes dart to Jo across the room.

Paparazzi followed her gaze.

"I've been drinking Miss Gina's lemonade since you were in diapers. Hand over the keys, kid."

He turned a little white and dug into his pocket.

She turned away to find Luke grinning at her. "Beat me to it."

The man made her smile. "Nothing we didn't do when we were kids."

The kid's keys made it into Luke's hand. "You're better off holding on to these. I have no idea what he drives."

"Miss Zoe?" One of the servers came up behind them, asking for help.

Luke dangled the keys. "Go. I have this."

"Thanks. And let him know he needs to take pictures."

He winked as she walked away.

For the next fifteen minutes, Zoe kept her clothes from getting soiled by using an apron over her dress and making sure her help didn't burn what only needed to be warmed up.

When she stepped out of the kitchen for what felt like the hundredth time that day, she heard her sister's voice. Just like Zoe had thought, Blaze was already in the arms of Mrs. M, who was giving her sister a break. It didn't take long to realize that Zanya had arrived without their mother. Zoe wasn't sure if she should be relieved or angry.

"Hey, sis." Zoe approached her younger sister with open arms. "I was hoping you'd come."

Zanya had a few more circles under her eyes and still needed to drop a good fifteen pounds of baby weight from her middle. She looked like she'd aged a few years since the last time Zoe had seen her.

They hugged and Zanya whispered, "Mom didn't come."

"Do you know why?"

"You know Mom. Didn't know what to wear."

Zoe had bought her mother clothes for Christmas and birthdays. She was sure there was something in her closet to carry her through an engagement party. Lack of an outfit was an excuse.

She looked down at her own dress and guilt nibbled at the edges of her thoughts.

"And before you ask, Zane is working. Said he was going to stop by tomorrow to see you before heading into work."

The two of them walked deeper into the room, Zanya waving to Blaze, who didn't seem to have any problem letting someone else hold him.

"Jo says he's keeping his nose clean."

Zoe waited for her unasked question to be answered.

"He's not drinking as much, if that's what you're getting at. At least not that I know of. Comes home to sleep once in a while."

"Is he helping with the bills?"

Zanya nodded, grabbed a napkin full of food from one of the passing trays. "Yeah. Not a lot, according to Mom . . . but who knows. She's been acting odd for the past few months."

Zoe didn't like the sound of that. "She wasn't happy when I came by." Zoe waited for her sister to bring up Blaze and babysitting.

Zanya held a toothpick in the air. "These are really good. Yours?"

She nodded. "How are things with you and Mylo?"

"Working. He wasn't ready to be a dad, but he's trying."

"Does he watch Blaze when you work?" The question was leading, but it didn't seem Zanya was going to offer the answers Zoe wanted without provocation.

"Once in a while. His roommates complain."

Zoe cringed. "Then he should get his own place, don't you think?"

Zanya stared and said nothing for a good minute. "Let me guess, Mom complained about watching Blaze."

The last thing Zoe wanted was to cause strife between her sister and mother.

"It can't be easy on her, Zanya."

"It's not easy on me either."

Not the point!

Instead of saying what she was thinking, Zoe wrapped an arm around her sister. "I know it's not. I just worry."

Zanya offered an insincere smile and captured a glass of sparkling wine as one of the servers walked by. Instead of taking one for herself, Zoe made a point of drinking sparkling water instead. Driving Miss Gina's vintage van to drop off guests was looking like a high probability as the night wore on.

The stress on Zoe's face didn't ease until after Zanya had excused herself when Blaze started to fuss.

Luke was aware of nearly every move Zoe made throughout the night, from taking the keys away from Tim, to disappearing into the kitchen only to return with a parade of food behind her, to toasting the future bride and groom with only a sip of champagne. She wasn't drinking, wasn't eating a lot, and was playing hostess as if the inn belonged to her and everyone was her personal guest.

He tried to offer his help but found her distracting smile and assurance that she had it all handled warding him off.

Slowly the guests at the inn said their good nights and made their way upstairs, and the ones who lived in town found sober rides back home.

Jo had taken a van full of guests home with a promise to return to retrieve her squad car.

Miss Gina took one look at the remaining mess in the parlor and tossed both hands in the air. "Tomorrow is soon enough to clean up this mess," she announced. "I'm going to bed."

"You're a saint." Zoe kissed Miss Gina's cheek good night before she walked out the door.

Mel filled a serving tray with empty glasses and headed toward the kitchen while Zoe followed behind with a tray full of dirty plates.

Luke and Wyatt sat down in the empty room.

"What a whirlwind." Wyatt kicked his feet up on the coffee table and rested his head on the sofa.

"I think it went well," Luke said. "No family drama, no one puked on the carpet."

Wyatt laughed. "Your bar is really low, my friend."

"I have yet to attend a wedding without both."

"Apparently engagement parties don't have the same effect on people."

Zoe and Mel walked in side by side.

Wyatt scooted over on the sofa and patted the space beside him. "You heard Miss Gina . . . tomorrow is soon enough."

Mel didn't argue and hit the couch with a heavy sigh.

Zoe, however, continued to put glasses on a tray.

"You've done enough, Zoe. Don't make me feel guilty for sitting," Mel said.

"I'll just put these in the dishwasher."

Luke lifted himself off his ass and walked behind Zoe. He took the empty glass in her hand away, set it down, and pulled her away from the mess.

She started to protest and noticed everyone watching her.

Much as Luke wanted to pull her into his lap, he directed her to a chair beside his and pushed her shoulders until she was sitting. "There, much better."

"The food was amazing," Mel told Zoe.

"It's what I do best."

Luke could argue that, but didn't. He watched Zoe tuck a finger into the back strap of her left shoe and kick it off. After the right one followed, she slowly rubbed her instep. Without a second thought, he reached down, encouraged her to lean back, and lifted her feet onto his lap.

The woman had beautiful feet.

The first press of his thumb against her instep had her moaning and closing her eyes. "You're hired."

"We're going to have to figure something else out other than you cooking for the wedding. I don't want you working that hard on our day."

Zoe popped one eye open. "You want someone else to cook?"

"I want you to enjoy the day. Besides, you'll be wearing a bridesmaid's dress, not an apron."

Luke found a tiny knot in the arch of her foot.

Zoe nearly groaned. "I can bring in my team . . . oh, God do that again."

Luke did it again.

"You have a team?" Wyatt asked.

"I can round up the right people to prepare what you want. We'll have to figure the menu out early enough so I can get the right people." Zoe spoke with her eyes closed and her toes wiggling.

Luke softened his touch and rubbed each toe before moving to her other foot.

"Everyone was asking about a wedding date tonight."

"I'm leaving that up to you," Wyatt told Mel.

"Why me?"

"Because every man in the room tonight told me to let you decide on date, time, place, flowers, food . . . everything. Saves arguing and aggravation."

"Don't you want to plan it together?" Mel asked.

Luke met Wyatt's gaze.

"I'll plan the bachelor party," Wyatt told her.

Mel frowned.

"That's my job," Luke chimed in.

Wyatt pointed in his direction. "Right. Then I'll just show up wearing the required attire, put a ring on your finger, and kiss you for the camera."

Mel wasn't smiling.

Even Zoe stopped moaning long enough to open her eyes and catch the tension.

"What kind of flowers do you want?" Mel asked.

"Anything but plastic."

"Wedding cake?"

"Chocolate."

"Boring!" It was Zoe's turn to add her opinion.

"We can have more than one layer," Mel said.

"Or a groom's cake," Zoe added.

"Should the invitations be modern or traditional?"

"I don't care."

Luke didn't either.

"What about a wedding date? Don't you want to figure that out together?"

Wyatt leaned over and kissed his future bride. "I don't care. I want you to be happy . . . so if it takes you six months to plan the wedding, great. Three, even better. We're in this together forever, so do what you have to do."

That had Mel smiling and leaning in for a kiss.

Luke looked away and found Zoe watching them with a tiny smile.

When they finished kissing, Mel said, "We should talk about budget."

Wyatt reached over to where his jacket lay over the back of the sofa and into the inside pocket. He removed a dozen envelopes and handed them to Mel.

"What's this?"

"A little help from our friends."

"Seriously?" Mel ripped into the first envelope and pulled out several crisp hundred-dollar bills. "Who is this from?"

"My parents, your dad . . . Great Aunt Minnie."

"I don't have a Great Aunt Minnie."

Wyatt laughed. "Me either. Who cares? People wanna help. Let them."

Zoe lifted a hand in the air. "I agree with Wyatt on this one."

"Add this up and let's figure out what else we need."

"The bachelor party is on me." Luke made sure his donation was in advance and evident.

"Bachelorette party is on me." Zoe had leaned her head back again and was enjoying her foot massage.

"Drinks at R&B's is good enough," Mel said.

Zoe and Luke both laughed.

She opened her eyes, glanced at the happy couple, then looked at Luke. "I'm thinking Vegas."

"I like the way you think," Luke told her.

Chapter Nine

Wyatt and Mel had retired to her room and Jo had dropped off Miss Gina's van before leaving with her squad car and the promise to drop by the next day.

Zoe refused to go to bed with dirty dishes in the sink or crumbs on tables that ants could find by morning.

Luke was removing a few empties from the back patio and turning off the lights.

"You don't have to help."

"Just say thank you."

Zoe smiled. "Thank you."

He tugged a plastic bag out from under the kitchen sink and filled the can. "You really can't leave it until the morning, can you?"

With her hands full of soapy water, she said, "Call it a byproduct of growing up in Casa de Trailer."

It was her quirk that she didn't expect anyone else to understand.

Luke finished with the trash can and rolled up his sleeves.

Instead of putting the clean dishes on a drying rack, she handed them to Luke. He dried them and searched the kitchen until he found the right places to put things.

"I noticed your mom didn't come."

"I noticed, too. Probably for the best." The last thing she wanted was the stress of her mom acting put out. It was always something with her. Zoe wasn't paying enough attention, someone looked at her sideways and whispered. Not to mention she'd always been jealous of Zoe and Miss Gina's relationship. "Zanya tells me Zane's been keeping a job, helping out."

"That's what I hear. I hope it lasts."

"Me, too." Her baby brother had had more run-ins with the law than Jo had before she decided to carry a badge.

"What about your sister?"

Zoe groaned. "I can't place a finger on her. She seemed like she had it together before Blaze was born. Now . . . I'm not sure what she's thinking."

"My guess is she's just surviving."

"Crappy way to live."

"Life's choices, babe. We've talked about this."

They had . . . since she was a teenager. If there was one thing Zoe had on her side, it was the ability to watch the people around her and decide which path *not* to take.

"I can't help but feel like I could be helping more."

It took a minute for Luke to respond. "And how would you help?"

"Send more money . . . send Zanya back to school . . . I don't know, help." Zanya had skirted through high school and dropped out six months before graduation.

"Has Zanya told you she wants to go back to school?"

"No."

"So handing over what you work hard for would do what?" Luke asked.

Zoe watched him put two glasses into a crate Miss Gina had ordered for the party. "Nothing but get her by."

"She has to want it."

From the first open conversation she'd had with Luke, he'd always told her the same thing. The people in her life, from her mother to her father to her siblings, everyone made their own choices. Even when life tossed you curveballs, you had the choice to push away from the base to hit the ball or let it fly by without trying.

"Do you think Zane wants it? That he's figuring out how to get out of that damn trailer?"

Silence had Zoe glancing Luke's way.

He stood with his hand swiping a glass dry with a kitchen towel, his hair falling in his eyes, those same sharp eyes on her . . . "I think you were both raised in the same home, and he sees how life can be. You've shown both your siblings that, Zoe. It's up to them to make life work out for the better."

"Maybe they don't know how."

Luke stepped up beside her, turned off the running water, and took her hands in his. "I know you, Zoe. You've told them both you're there if they need you, right?"

She nodded.

"You've told them you'd help out."

Her head bobbed again.

"You've probably even given money without them putting out their hands."

"Every Christmas."

"It's up to them, now. Their lives . . . the paths they need to follow in order to survive on their own."

Zoe lowered her head and closed her eyes. She saw her baby brother and sister the day their mom had come home from the courthouse after their father was sentenced. The fear in their eyes had matched the joy in Zoe's. As much as they didn't like getting hit, there was an uncertainty that came with the lack of beatings that only survivors living in an abusive situation understood.

Zoe got it . . . but she never looked back. She'd vowed to help her mom out as much as she had to in order to keep them in their broken-down trailer.

"You're their sister, Zoe. Not their mom."

"I've always felt like I was both," she whispered.

Luke lifted one hand to her chin.

When she opened her eyes, she found understanding and support.

"I hate to see you hurting."

It did hurt, more than she cared to admit. "I wish it didn't."

Luke stroked the side of her jaw with the pad of his thumb. "It hurts because you care. If you didn't care, you wouldn't be Zoe. Just don't let it consume you."

"You're right."

He winked and let a cocky smile crack his lips. "I'm always right."

"Humble . . ."

"Bite your tongue."

She bit her lip instead. The touch of his hand on her jaw distracted her, his understanding made her want to fold into his arms and stay perfectly still for hours.

"I should probably go," he whispered.

No! She scrambled to find the words to make him stay. "What if you don't?"

He stepped closer so the heat from his body radiated to hers. "Then I'm taking you to bed."

Yes! A much better idea.

"And in the morning I'll leave early enough to escape the questions until we're ready to answer them."

Zoe wasn't sure she knew the answers herself. "I'm leaving on Monday."

"I know."

"Do we act like nothing happened?" The thought cut through her.

Luke's finger traced her bottom lip, his eyes kept shifting from her eyes to his hand. "No. I'm going to call you, and you're going to take my calls."

"I am?"

"You are. Then we'll see each other."

The image of her crashing into his arms in the rain like some black-and-white movie came from nowhere.

"We'll take it one day at a time."

He released her other hand and placed both on her face.

"What if it doesn't work, Luke?"

He pressed his body against hers, the kitchen counter keeping her from moving away. "We'll deal with that if it happens. Right now, I think we should try."

Zoe rested a hand on his hip, the other gripping the side of the counter. "We never had to try very hard."

"No." He lowered his lips until she felt his breath mix with hers. "We didn't."

His featherlight kiss reminded her of their very first. She'd been so scared, worried that Luke Miller might actually be playing her. How could someone so good-looking want anything to do with a girl from the wrong side of town? But he'd kissed her with such gentle lips, she was the one who pushed in for more. Like now, when he moved away with barely a taste and she reached for him.

She felt him smile under her lips, and she nibbled until he gave her more.

Her heart kicked in her chest, jolting every nerve ending awake. She felt his fingers push into her hair, tilting her head to take a long drink.

Luke's tongue danced alongside hers, the tune familiar but different. They'd both grown up, taken lessons from others in the decade they'd spent apart. This was somehow better. Maybe because they'd denied any desire for so long. Maybe because there was a risk in touching now that hadn't been there when they were kids.

As kids they didn't think about tomorrow.

They'd been careful, always. Condoms, birth control pills . . . Zoe never took chances. Her heart had taken time to become involved, probably because of her trust issues. She knew now, without any real thought, that her heart was at greater risk than when she was a teen.

She pushed thoughts of broken hearts from her head and let herself feel.

Luke was holding her, keeping her from melting into a pool of lava on the kitchen floor. Kissing him was a full body experience. His knee pressed between her legs, his hands stroked the length of her back only to rest in her hair to change the position of her lips.

He was firm, everywhere. And larger than he was in his teenage years. His shoulders, which stretched against his shirt, were full in her hands.

Luke pulled his lips from hers. "You feel amazing."

She nodded her agreement, couldn't find the words needed.

His lips found hers again until she forgot to breathe.

"We should . . ." He pulled away. "Go upstairs . . ."

Zoe smiled and allowed him to lead her out of the room.

They took the back stairs to the second floor, and she rounded the hall to the third. Luke knew his way around the inn but didn't know which room she was in, so she led the way.

She thought of this as the blue room, even though the only blue in the room was the duvet cover on the bed. Much like all the rooms in the inn, this one had a spray of fresh flowers that adorned one of the side tables, fragrant sachets that scented the air with lavender, and a private bathroom so the only time the guest needed to leave the room was to eat. Most of all, it was away from the other guests, which Zoe liked when she was staying at Miss Gina's.

"Ah, the white room," Luke said when they walked through the door. "It's blue."

Luke closed the door behind him, turned on the light. "Everything in here is white."

Zoe pointed to the bed. "Blue."

Luke offered half a smile. "The tiny blue flowers on the bed make it the blue room?"

"The soap in the bathroom is blue, too."

"You're adorable."

Zoe did a full circle. "The candle is blue."

"It is . . . and a single blue candle in a white room makes the whole room blue."

She placed her hands on her hips. "Why are we talking about the room?"

Luke reached out, grabbed her around the waist, and backed her against the slightly blue bed in the middle of the room. "We're not." He kissed her and started to laugh. "It's white."

Zoe turned him around and pushed him onto the bed.

He fell with a grin, caught himself on his elbows. "Forceful . . . I like it."

"I don't remember you being into that kind of thing." Zoe moved between his legs and stood over him.

"A lot can change in ten years."

Oh, boy, did she know that. She reached her arms around her back and tugged on the zipper to unbind herself from her dress.

Luke stared and started to lose his grin. His blue eyes smoldered.

She managed about half the length and the zipper caught.

She tugged, willing the binding free.

It didn't move.

The smoldering behind Luke's gaze turned back into a grin.

So much for my sexy moment.

"Something stuck?"

"And here I wanted to give you a show." Zoe dropped her arms to her sides and started to back away.

Luke leaned forward, and placed a possessive hand on her hip before turning her around.

She grabbed the length of her hair and collected it over her shoulder to give him room.

Instead of reaching for her zipper, she felt Luke's fingers trace the edge of her hip to the top of her knee through her dress. He lingered there, using both hands as he moved back up to her waist.

She closed her eyes and enjoyed his slow awakening of her senses.

His hands felt massive as they spanned her back, his thumbs tracing the edges of the stubborn zipper.

Instead of removing her dress, he used the backs of his fingers and stroked the edge of the fabric before dipping inside to touch.

He was only touching her back, and just barely, but the rest of her body began to hum like a circuit of electricity taking a charge.

Zoe heard Luke lift from the bed, his hands on her arms.

He lifted the strap of her dress and slid it over one shoulder. His touch left a path of tingling skin soothed only by the featherlight touch of his lips when he kissed where he touched. She tilted her head while dropping her hair.

Luke ran his tongue along the side of her neck, his teeth scraping a path to her ear.

She shivered. Memories of their past mixed with the new. They'd watched those vampire movies their senior year, and Luke had vowed to be her personal neck sucker for life.

"Such a sexy neck," he whispered in her ear.

She smiled and bit her lip, waiting . . .

When he caught her lobe with his teeth, her knees started to wobble.

Luke wrapped an arm around her waist to steady her while he rediscovered the places that made her weak.

Zoe gripped the arm that held her close and rolled her head back on his shoulder.

"I missed this spot." He tasted her right behind the ear and kissed his way around the back of her neck to the other side. "And this one."

"Just those?" she asked, breathless.

"There are others . . . but right now . . . just these two." He tugged her hair to the side and bit a little harder. He kissed and licked his way over her shoulder.

Somewhere in all his attention to her neck, he'd managed to tug her zipper free and helped her dress drop to her feet.

She stood in her lacy black bra and barely there panties and wondered what Luke saw. Like him, she'd filled out since they'd last been together. Her hips a little bigger, her breasts a bit larger.

Luke turned her around and scanned her body while holding her hips. "You're so beautiful."

Okay . . . she no longer thought about her rounder parts. "Show me," she told him.

He reached for the buttons on his shirt and fumbled. On his third button, she grew impatient and batted his hand away to take over. Once his shirt was open, she fanned her hands over his sculpted chest. The man looked much better than the high school sweetheart she'd left behind.

She touched her lips to his collarbone and returned the favor of tasting his neck. She liked his late night growth of beard as it scraped against her cheek.

His hand found her breast over her bra and squeezed as she licked the edges of his lips. When they finally kissed, there was nothing light in their touch. It was hot and hungry open-mouthed kisses she'd dreamed about for more years than she cared to admit.

Luke struggled out of his shirt, one arm at a time, without letting her go.

Zoe reached for the clasp on his belt and became distracted by the bulge competing for space inside Luke's slacks. She ran her hand over his length and heard him cuss under his breath.

She gripped him harder and he had to stop kissing her. With slack lips hovering over hers, he released a long-suffering moan. "You're destroying me."

"Is that a good thing?"

The answer lay in a kiss that brought them both to bed in a tangle of limbs.

As soon as his pants met the floor, Zoe draped one long leg over his hip and pressed close.

They kissed with swollen mouths and shattered breaths.

Zoe squeezed his ass and pulled his boxer shorts away. The length of him sprang into her hand with a mind of its own. The silky feel was hot and heavy and everything she remembered. She wanted a taste . . . something she'd been shy about in their time before. That was the old Zoe, the young, inexperienced girl. This was the woman, and she planned on making sure Luke knew she'd grown up.

She pushed him onto his back and kissed a path down his chest. Her teeth lingered over a taut nipple, her tongue made it harder. She moved lower and felt Luke's abdomen flex the moment he figured out where she was going.

Fingernails scraped over his hip and down his leg as she made her way to what she wanted.

Luke squirmed, his hips pushed forward.

She kissed his navel, felt his erection against her chin. The tip of her tongue darted out to taste, and Luke's hand found the back of her head. He didn't push her closer, didn't pull her away. When she looked up, she found him watching her with a lidded gaze.

With eyes locked, she pulled him into the warmth of her mouth. She wasn't sure who moaned louder . . . him or her. Probably him, but she loved his response and took him deeper.

"Jesus, Zoe."

She hummed and kept moving, letting her hands grip what she couldn't take.

Both of his hands were in her hair . . . she felt him tug her away, then push her back for more. Finally, he stopped her pursuit. "Another time," he moaned, pulling her higher on the bed and rolling her onto her back. "Finish that another time."

"I plan to," she told him.

He wiped her lower lip with his thumb and kissed her.

When he pulled at her lace panties, she lifted her hips to help them leave her body. His fingers fanned her belly and buried into the heated folds of her sex.

She whimpered, ready for whatever Luke wanted to do with her. "I want you inside of me, Luke."

He wiggled his fingers. "I am."

She hit his chest with her fist. "Not that part."

"Impatient minx."

"Luke," she warned.

He kissed her snarl before reaching over the bed to find his pants. He unearthed a condom from his wallet and handed it to her.

With his erection in her hand, she covered him quickly and lay back down.

Luke nudged her legs apart and settled between them.

Their eyes locked as he sank into her one inch at a time. He stretched her sex and filled her. They both stilled, alone in their thoughts, but one with their bodies. Luke gave a slow, knowing smile and started to move. And when he reached down to kiss her, emotion clogged Zoe's throat.

He whispered sweet words as he claimed her body as his. The slow, fiery build drew tiny squeaks from the bed. Soon she could only hear the thump of her heart and their quick breaths as they moved closer to release. When her muscles tightened, ready to explode, she wrapped her legs around Luke's waist and willed him closer. She shuddered in her orgasm, his name on her lips, and knew her life was never going to be the same again.

Chapter Ten

Luke walked into his bedroom right as the sun was starting to peek in the window.

Leaving Zoe's side was one of the hardest things he'd done in years. The glow of her smile and weak push as she told him to leave were evidence she was just as affected as he was.

His wallet was empty of condoms and the muscles under his skin were sated.

They'd managed about two hours of sleep before making love one final time.

He had promised himself sometime in the night not to overanalyze what was happening between them. Never once did he think it was just sex. With Zoe, it had never been all about the sex. Yeah, when he was a teenager getting anything had been a priority. If he were being honest with himself, the first time he really noticed Zoe, it had been his dick that stood to attention first. He'd been gone most of the summer, shipped off to his grandparents on his mother's side, just outside of Seattle. He hadn't wanted to go, but as the summer wore on, his parents probably had to book his ticket for their own sanity. That was the year he'd really discovered girls, and much to his delight, they discovered him, too. Those months in Seattle had proven one of the best summers ever. Mainly because of the girls who flirted and *then some* with the kid who wasn't going to be around to tell their steady boyfriends once school started in the fall. Luke enjoyed the *then some* with the girls most likely to put out. When he returned to River Bend, his ego had grown along with his confidence he'd get what he wanted.

He distinctly remembered a hot August day when he'd heard that Jo and her posse were going to hook up at the river with a fifth of whatever liquor she could get her hands on and go swimming. There was only one real swimming hole on the river, and all the kids knew about it.

Luke rounded up Baily and Mike and headed to the river to spy on the girls.

They'd parked far from the swimming hole and walked the long way around to stay hidden, hoping the whole time that one of the girls had forgotten her bathing suit.

They hadn't.

But watching girls in bikinis was almost as much fun as watching them naked. Especially Zoe. Luke had done a double take when his eyes rested on her. She'd always kept herself hidden under big sweatshirts and heavy sweaters. Ugly clothes that didn't fit and only called out negative attention. Even the bathing suit she'd worn that day hadn't suited her well. It had been way too small. Her breasts spilled out from the edges of the fabric and the bottoms did a crappy job of hiding her ass.

Luke was bewitched.

They'd sat in the trees watching the girls swim for half an hour before he accidentally on purpose rolled a half-empty can of beer down the bank and gave their location away.

Jo had been the first to notice and start cussing.

Mel ducked under the water.

And Zoe . . . Zoe placed both hands on her hips and stared them down.

By the time they left the river that day, they'd polished off the fifth and the six-pack, they'd sat around a campfire counting stars, and Luke had gone so far as to hold Zoe's hand.

Yeah . . . it was that big a deal.

He'd gone from getting it to hand holding for the better part of the next year. He'd never looked back.

Luke looked at his bachelor home and small kitchen. Zoe had never cooked there, but he could picture her demanding fresh basil or thyme—whatever the hell that was—while he scrambled over to his parents' to raid his mother's garden. Or maybe he should plant one for Zoe.

What was he thinking?

They'd just hooked up for the first time since before he was old enough to drink in a bar.

He smiled at the memory and decided he needed a shower more than a few more hours of sleep. He had some planning to do.

"You do know the blue room is right above mine, right?"

Zoe blinked several times, her mind scrambling for an explanation . . . then decided a lie now would be heartache later. "Luke said it's the white room."

Mel rolled her eyes. "The bedspread is blue."

"I know, right?"

Mel grinned. "So is there something you need to tell us?"

Zoe, Jo, and Mel sat on the back porch of Miss Gina's inn, looking over bridal magazines and picking out all the crazy crap one picked when planning a wedding.

"What is she getting at?" Jo asked, oblivious to what was obvious.

Zoe picked up her iced tea and said over the rim of the glass, "Luke spent the night with me last night."

Jo's eyes drifted from the satin and lace gown on the page. "Spent the night."

"Platonically slept in the same space?" Mel asked, knowing full well that wasn't the case.

Zoe started to nod, then slowly shook her head. "We screwed like bunnies until about two, fell asleep . . . and he left around six."

"Five thirty," Mel corrected. "After another round."

"Jesus, Zoe . . . what does this mean?" Jo asked.

Zoe dropped her hands in her lap. "How the hell do I know what it means? It means we like sex and we're good at it."

"It's Luke."

Zoe found Jo's eyes. "I know."

"It's more than sex if it's Luke," Mel chimed in.

Jo's eyes stared in judgment.

"He came to me in Texas. Talked with one of my neighbors to find the bar we were at that night."

"This can only end badly," Jo stated Zoe's deepest fear.

"Who said it needs to end at all?" Mel asked. "Luke and Zoe belong together."

"I live in Texas, Mel."

Little Miss Optimism with her shiny new engagement ring and wedding bells ringing wasn't thinking about a probable breakup and fallout.

Jo obviously was.

"Did you guys talk about this before it happened? Or did it just happen?"

"A little of both."

Jo ran a hand through her hair. "I almost had to arrest him last year when you left after the class reunion, Zoe. He has a weak spot when it comes to you."

This was not something she wanted coming between her and Jo, but she needed to solicit her BFF's support. "I know you worry, Jo. I'm more than a little confused myself. But ever since Luke showed up in Dallas, I haven't been able to get him out of my head. Being here makes it even harder to think about anything else other than how it once was with us."

"You leave in the morning," Jo argued.

Jo was torn. How could she not be when she had been the one here to pick up the pieces after Zoe had left?

"But you're going to come back . . . a lot." Mel was playing middle child, mediating.

"And Luke can get on a plane to visit me."

"Did he say that?" Jo asked.

"He alluded to it."

Mel waved a hand between the two of them. "Oh, my God. Stop it, you two . . . this is awesome stuff. Zoe and Luke getting back together is like Sandy and Danny from *Grease*. It's epic and wonderful."

"I think Jo's concerned about a Romeo and Juliet outcome."

Jo nodded. "Not the perfect ending."

"So melodramatic. No one is going to kill themselves." Mel shoved Jo's knee and broke the tension. "So how was it?"

A slight lift to Jo's lips told Zoe she wanted details.

"Is it possible his dick grew over the last decade?"

Mel squealed and Jo glanced at the sky as if contemplating the question.

For the next hour, they talked about makeup sex. Engagement party sex . . . and sex with a nameless man Jo had while in Dallas. Nameless only because she refused to gather the details and save herself the effort of looking the man up in her database. A byproduct of her job, she told them. His tats alone told her he had a history, but damn, the man had been good in bed.

According to Jo in any event.

The conversation switched only when Wyatt and Hope returned to the inn with Wyatt's parents around lunchtime.

Zoe's phone buzzed in her pocket while she baked homemade snickerdoodles for Miss Gina and her guests.

Luke's number popped up on her screen.

I don't know the last time I felt the need to nap on a Sunday afternoon.

I'm shot, myself.

Did anyone see me leave?

Zoe settled against the counter and enjoyed this new way of communicating with Luke. When they'd dated in high school, she couldn't afford a cell phone. They were probably the only kid couple who hadn't shared naked pictures when they were young. Zoe suddenly felt fortunate that there weren't those kinds of recorded pieces of crap out there for someone to exploit.

No, but Mel and Wyatt took notes from the room below us.

Oh, boy . . . twenty questions?

She set her phone down when the oven timer rang. After pulling her cookies from the oven, she returned to her text.

Luke had placed an impatient question mark in its own text when she hadn't returned fast enough.

Sorry, baking. Yes 20 Q's. Jo is worried. Mel is excited.

It was Zoe's turn to lose patience when a dot, dot, dot didn't turn into words quickly enough. Finally his text came. Listen to Mel. I'll talk to Jo.

Zoe stared at her screen for a full minute. Are we doing the right thing?

His reply was instant. It doesn't feel wrong.

No, it didn't.

He told her he'd be by after dinner to take her out to R&B's for drinks or whatever she wanted.

Zoe counted the hours and decided a nap might be the perfect way to pass the time while waiting for Luke to pick her up.

Chapter Eleven

Zoe stood over the stove with the dinner rush in full swing.

The fewer shifts she took at Nahana, the busier her nights were. The owners announced when she was in the kitchen and the reservations poured in. With only two weekends a month on the calendar, Zoe thought she'd have it easier. It didn't feel that way at the end of a shift.

Her mind worked five steps ahead of her hands, and when the kitchen buzzed like it did now, she forced everyone around her to work just as hard. She wasn't a hard-ass as a head chef, but she didn't suffer any slackers. "Why is this salmon still in my window?" she shouted to whoever could hear her and make sure the meal was delivered before it was too cold to serve.

She looked up a second time and the salmon was gone.

She sampled her sous chef's garlic sauté before pouring it over her signature vegetarian pasta. Zoe set it next to a filet and a roast duck on the same order and gave a quick shout to the headwaiter, who whisked away the finished meals.

A new set of orders littered the screen of the POS system, drawing a moan from more than one chef.

"They know you're here, Zoe."

Oliver was her second in charge and nearly as talented as she. "Remind me not to take any more vacation time."

"I don't think that will make a difference."

The next two hours were nothing but a blur. It was close to ten before the orders started to slow.

Zoe took the time to check on the pastry chef and randomly sample the dishes she'd approved. She nixed the raspberry topping on the crème brûlée after popping one of the berries in her mouth and finding it too tart. The upset was small, but she respected the twenty-dollar-a-dish dessert choice and the people who paid that kind of money for it too much to serve something less than perfect. Because she was who she was, Zoe slipped from behind the doors of the kitchen and into the restaurant. The headwaiter took her to a party of six, where three had ordered the dessert she removed from the menu.

She introduced herself and apologized for the inconvenience.

It always astonished her how recognizable her face was to the foodies who went out of their way to dine at Nahana.

Zoe moved around the tables, asked how everything was, and happily posed for two pictures before the manager waved her back into the kitchen right on cue. The patrons would keep her talking for hours if she let them.

By the time Zoe left the restaurant, it was past one in the morning. She'd gone over the menu selections for the next week based on the availability of seafood, fresh vegetables, and Texas beef from a local farmer. She was scheduled to work three nights that week and a Sunday brunch. Filming with Felix was wrapping up the following week, with a trip to New York scheduled at the end of the month.

All she could think about was how to get back to River Bend or find time to squeeze Luke in. He hadn't said he was going to visit, but he hadn't said he wouldn't.

Zoe tossed a handful of mail on her kitchen counter and pressed Play on her answering machine. Anton's voice touted three new listings she just *had to see*. Her talent agent, Suki, had a list of opportunities she needed to say yes or no to before they met in New York at the end of the month . . . and then Luke's voice soothed all the stress of the day with a simple hello.

"Hello, Zoe. I remember you saying you don't check your cell phone when you're in the kitchen and I didn't want you calling while driving. Call if it's not too late . . . and by not too late, I mean . . . call."

He picked up on the first ring. "Hey, baby."

"It's one thirty in the morning."

"Only eleven thirty here. How was your shift?"

Zoe settled into her sofa, curled her legs under her butt, and cradled the phone to her ear. She told him about her crazy night and asked about his.

"The cars in River Bend are running smooth."

She grinned. "It sounds like you own them all."

"It sometimes feels like I do."

"Does it get old . . . working on the same ones time and time again?" She couldn't help but wonder if Luke's day job bored him like algebra did back in high school.

"There are a few I'd just as soon blow up with a truckload of TNT."

"I remember you once saying a car had to be really far gone before you'd consider it a contender for the junkyard." He'd said that about her mother's car, growing up. Then again, he was probably just being polite at the time since Zoe's mom couldn't afford a replacement.

"This from the woman who made leftovers taste like a gourmet meal."

"I wouldn't say that."

"I would. How is everything in Texas?"

She liked this, the ease of conversation, the back and forth. The familiarity she hadn't had with any man since Luke.

"My real estate agent has more houses to show me."

"Oh?" He didn't sound excited about it.

"I'm torn about what to do."

"Because of us?" he asked.

"That's part of it. The restaurant is nuts when I'm there, and my agent, Suki, has a half a dozen guest spots available to me."

"You mean TV shows?"

"Yeah. They dangle some serious money and make it hard for me to pass."

"What do you like better . . . the filming or the restaurant?"

"I like to cook, Luke. I can do that with both. The stress of the kitchen is starting to weigh on me. Felix suggested I open my own place to take my brand to the next level."

"Your brand?"

"My name. Eventually every celebrity chef opens their own place."

"Sounds stressful."

She started talking numbers, the profit potential. She knew how much Nahana was bringing in because of her position. "I'm always trying to figure out how to stay on top so I won't always have to work this hard."

"It sounds like that's what you're doing."

"I'm so wrapped up in it I haven't even asked myself if I'm happy doing it."

"And all this has something to do with looking at homes?"

She stifled a yawn. "I landed in Texas. It was never a place I thought I'd live. Felix and his team came to me, but I film in New York and Los Angeles all the time."

"Are you thinking of moving?"

"To LA or New York?"

"Yeah."

"Lord, no. They both have their qualities, but I wouldn't want to live there."

"I thought you liked living in Texas."

"I do. I mean . . . I've grown used to it. I'm close to the airport, I have lots of opportunity here."

Luke sighed. "By opportunity, do you mean chef positions to choose from?"

"Yeah."

"You could get those anywhere."

"I don't know."

Luke laughed. "Hon, you're Zoe Fucking Brown. You can go anywhere and restaurants will fall over themselves to hire you."

She felt her cheeks heat. "I don't know about that."

"Ha!"

"What?"

"I have a confession to make."

This should be good. "I'm listening."

"I've followed your career a little more than the next guy since you left River Bend."

She forgot about how tired she was and sat up. "What do you mean by followed?"

"When *Warring Chef* hit the air and River Bend started weekly Zoe nights in front of the televisions all over town, I sat at home and watched on my own. I listened to the newscasts on the Food Network and had Google send me messages when your name popped up online or in the paper."

"If I didn't know you, I'd accuse you of stalking me."

"Oh, I stalked you. I made myself a little crazy with it, even when I was doing my best to get over us. You know what I learned?"

"That stalking is a felony in several states?" she said, laughing.

"I learned that every time you pushed to another level, it proved you had to leave this town to get there. And as much as I missed you, I was proud that you were doing it."

Zoe placed a hand to her chest. "Oh, Luke."

"I mean it, Zoe. We were kids, and you needed to do this to find yourself. And if you're sitting there at close to two in the morning questioning if you're good enough to find a job in bumfuck anywhere . . . then you haven't paid attention to just how big of a celebrity you really are."

"I'm not—"

"Yes, you are. You're wicked talented. You're stunning, and if you haven't noticed, a lot of your counterparts look like crap on film . . . and you're genuine."

"I'm not—"

"You are! You have options, Zoe. Lots of options."

She waited to speak. "You're good for my ego, Miller."

"You're not exactly bad for mine, Brown. Now tell me what you're wearing."

He made her laugh. "Nothing sexy."

"Then lie to me."

For the next fifteen minutes, she did . . . about her attire, in any event. And when she crawled into bed, she decided to test Luke's theory in the morning and see where it could lead.

Zoe met Felix at a taco shack that served amazing steak tacos and ice-cold beer. She decided to corner her friend outside of work to avoid anyone overhearing their conversation.

Felix wore dark sunglasses and a fedora. She wasn't sure if he was trying to hide his face or stand out in a crowd. He certainly managed his share of stares before they found an empty table with a red and green shade umbrella that warded off the Dallas sun.

"Very incognito." Zoe touched the brim of his hat as he sat down.

"You said you wanted to meet in private. I don't get those invitations very often." He lowered his sunglasses and winked before looking around. "Not from beautiful women, in any event."

He twisted off the top of his beer and did the same for the one sitting in front of her before taking a drink. "So what's so important it couldn't wait until next week?"

The beer cooled her throat going down and helped her open up. "I was talking to Luke last night—"

"Mr. James Dean?"

She nodded.

"He's hot!"

"Hands off," she warned without heat in her words.

Felix once again lowered his glasses and studied her over the rims. "Looks like someone is getting a little somethin', somethin'."

Instead of confirming his suspicion, she offered a sly smile and continued, "Luke said something that I'm not sure is true."

Felix pushed his glasses high on his nose and sat back. "I'm listening."

"He said I could get a job anywhere if I wanted to."

Felix sipped his beer. "Uh-huh . . . what else did he say?"

"Uhm, that's it . . . that I was enough of a celebrity to get a job in bumfuck anywhere."

This time when Felix unveiled his eyes, he set his glasses on the table and stared. "This is news to you?"

She blinked. "Well, I know I'm popular, that people go out of their way to visit the restaurant when I'm in the kitchen—"

"Zoe, darling . . ." He leaned forward. "If you wanted to relocate to France, Belgium, or Tallahassee, you'd have restaurants willing to redesign their kitchens to have you in them. Your name brings money to everything you touch. Hasn't your bank account shown you that?"

She thought of her account, of the savings she'd been socking away since her first paycheck showed up after *Warring Chef* started to air. "It could all blow up tomorrow."

"Who told you that?"

"I did, years ago. There are no guarantees."

Felix reached over and touched her hand. "Do you know why you're so popular in this world of foodies and networks dedicated to pasta soufflés?"

"Because I can cook."

"No! Lots of people can cook. It means something to you. You're down-to-earth and charming in front of that camera. Your story charmed the average American when *Warring Chef* hit the air and had plenty of them up in arms when you didn't win."

"Sebastian was better than me. He deserved to win."

"That may be . . . but you were the girl next door who was determined to take second place and make it her own. Your friend Luke was right, sweetie. If you don't believe me, I'll put out a few calls and let some of our network friends know you're looking for bigger and better avenues. Slaving away in Nahana can't be good for your complexion."

"It's a great position."

"It's a stepping stone."

"They pay me well."

"So does my producer, but if you asked for more, he'd pay. Don't tell him I told you that!" he quickly added.

Zoe looked down at her foil wrapped tacos and started to open one. "Thanks, Felix."

"Anytime." He leaned in again. "And if you ever decide to relocate, do it outside of this damn state. I'm sick of wearing cowboy boots."

She glanced down at his loafer-clad feet.

Chapter Twelve

"Mel picked a date."

"Well, don't keep me in suspense." Luke sat over an open bucket of fried chicken in Wyatt's backyard.

"Last weekend in August."

"That's only three months from now."

"I know. But if we wait any longer, the window for an outdoor wedding at Miss Gina's fades. Hope is out of school and can go down to the bay area with my parents while we honeymoon."

"And where are you guys going?"

"I have no idea."

Luke bit a chunk out of a chicken leg and waved the bone in the air. "When do you want the bachelor party and who do you want me to invite?"

"You're still thinking Vegas?"

"I am. I'll talk to Zoe and coordinate."

"I think bachelor parties aren't supposed to involve the bride."

"It won't. We'll be on one side of the strip and the girls will be on the other. Outside of getting there, we probably won't see them at all."

Wyatt frowned. "What if I wanna get laid?"

"Then you sneak out like me and hook up with your woman without telling anybody."

That had Wyatt smiling. "How is everything with you and Zoe?"

"Strange. We talk every night, text during the day. Feels like I'm a kid again."

"So you plan to see her in Vegas?"

"I plan on all kinds of things."

"Oh?"

Luke put the chicken down and wiped his hands on the napkin on the table. "I'm going to Texas next week."

"That's going to get expensive in a heartbeat."

Luke thought about the interviews he had set up. "I'm thinking about moving."

Wyatt stopped his hand midway to his beer. "To Texas?"

He shrugged. "I'm going to see what's out there."

"But you have a home here, a job with your dad."

"Aww, Wyatt . . . I didn't know you cared so much."

Wyatt rolled his eyes. "This is all about Zoe."

"Zoe started it. I won't deny that. I'll be thirty in September . . ."

"And?"

"I don't know. I haven't done a whole lot with my life."

Wyatt sat back, ran his fingers over the condensation on his longneck beer. "I hear ya. I knew I didn't want to live in the city. When I found River Bend, I knew this was where I needed to be. If you've only ever been here, you might not know you belong."

"I'm trying not to overthink . . . go with my gut."

"And your gut is pointing toward Texas?"

"My gut is pointing toward Zoe." Something he never considered denying.

"Are you sure that's your gut talking?"

"I felt like I was in stagnant water before Zoe and I got back together. I've never hated my work, or this town. Still can't say I do . . . but with her back in my world, it just feels fuller. She's a pretty big thing out there."

"Doesn't mean she can't come to you," Wyatt said.

"I'm not so full of myself to think I can't consider going to her."

"Wow, you've given this a lot of thought."

Luke shrugged. "No, I've just given it *some* thought. I'm going to Texas to consider other options."

"I'd hate to see you leave, but I get it."

He didn't think asking Zoe to return was an option. "So, Vegas . . ." Luke changed the subject.

They decided a mid-July trip would give everyone time to play and plan. If the women didn't think it would work, they vowed to keep the date anyway. They were six beers in when they made their dedication, and both knew they'd change their tune if two of the three guarantee players backed out.

Luke walked home, not willing to test Jo's friendship after drinking with Wyatt most of the night.

It was going to be a hard enough week for one of his best friends.

The anniversary of Jo's father's death fell on the week of the annual high school reunion for the second year in a row. He made a mental note to be around to help her get drunk or stay sober. Whatever she needed.

He flipped on the lights and opened the window in his kitchen. He didn't need another beer, but he grabbed one anyway. He rang Zoe's cell phone, knowing she'd be just walking in the door after a late shift.

"Hey, baby."

"Richard?"

For a minute, he paused. "That was mean."

Zoe laughed.

"I'll get you for that."

～

Jo stood on the sidelines of the annual high school reunion, watching the familiar ritual of perpetual lying.

"You haven't changed a bit."

"You look better than when we were kids."

"I made a killing on the stock market."

No one made a killing on any stock market in years. Yeah, the bullshit factor ran high when the alumni tried to impress their old friends.

Jo's eyes scanned the crowd, determined to see something out of the ordinary.

"What has your attention so keenly focused, Sheriff?"

Jo jumped when Luke walked up from behind her. "Sneaking up on an armed woman isn't wise, Miller."

Luke gave her a wink and a grin. "You wouldn't shoot me. I fix your car."

"Ha!" She willed her pulse back to normal and turned her attention to the high school gym.

"Seriously, Jo . . . what's up?"

She didn't want to talk about how she'd been keeping an eye on any and all alumni who trickled through town in hopes of finding some clue as to who was responsible for her father's death. She was convinced that if anyone had information, it wasn't someone who still lived in River Bend. So watching the town visitors had become the norm for her every year.

Instead of saying anything to Luke, she kept up with the half-truths being passed around the graduates of a decade past. "I'm wondering which of these yahoos are responsible for the toilet paper dripping off my trees this year."

Luke's slow chuckle turned into a full-blown laugh.

"It's not funny."

"Sure as hell is. Looks like whoever did it managed an even better job than last year."

She'd woken up that morning with a sea of white flowing down from every tree in her yard. Seemed the reunion at River Bend High was accompanied by TPing the sheriff's house for the second year in a row.

"Took nearly six months for some of that crap to get out of the pine tree last year," she mumbled.

Luke scanned the crowd. "I don't see any suspicious toilet paper sticking out of anyone's back pocket, Jo. You might just have to stay up late next year to catch the culprit."

Problem was, the previous year the toilet paper slaughter of her front yard had taken place the night of the reunion, and this time it had happened the day before.

"What is the sentence for toilet papering a front yard these days, Sheriff? Fifteen to life?"

Jo shoved his shoulder and scowled at his laughter as she walked away.

She was half convinced her team of friends was responsible for the stupidity dangling from her house.

Luke moved around the shop, returning his tools to their proper places and putting extra effort into clearing off the workbench.

"I'm starting to think you're getting ready to leave here for good." Luke's father stood in the doorway leading to the office, a shop towel in his hand.

Luke glanced up before returning to the task of separating the metric and standard sockets into two different drawers.

"It's just a few days."

"A few days here, a few days there. How is everything with Zoe?"

Hearing her name made him smile. "Zoe's great."

Fred Miller took up space beside Luke and looked down into the toolbox. "Your mom and I have always liked that girl."

Luke didn't need his parents' approval, but it didn't suck to hear. "She likes you, too."

Fred took a socket from the pile of metric sizes and tossed it into the standard box.

"Do you think things are going to work out with the two of you?"

His father never talked about his relationships, but then again, Luke hadn't had many since high school.

"I'd like to think so."

"The geography isn't ideal."

"Which is why I'm going to visit her."

Fred stopped looking in the box and stared long enough for Luke to stare back.

They were silent for a good minute.

"I remember the first time you climbed under a car with me," his father said, taking a trip down memory lane.

"Your old Chevy . . . and it was a truck," Luke reminded him.

"I was the luckiest father in this town. You didn't cause us any problems, you willingly greased up your hands with mine."

Luke wasn't sure where this was leading. "I like cars. Lucky me you knew how to keep them running."

Fred sighed with a nod. "Yeah, but I never pretended that you'd stay here forever. River Bend isn't a big place."

"What's this all about, Dad?"

His dad looked away. "Oh, I don't know. Your girl lives in Texas. She doesn't have a lot of family love here."

"Zoe has a ton of friends who care."

"I know that. But her blood drove her away once. It would be hard to get her back."

Which was why Luke was exploring other options. "It's just a visit."

Fred winked. "You should know that I'm capable of running this place on my own, son. In case you thought otherwise."

Equal parts warmth and sorrow washed over him with the meaning behind his father's words. "Trying to get rid of me?"

Fred shook his head. "Just making sure you're following your heart and dreams and not sticking around here for mine."

Emotion clogged Luke's throat. "I've never felt stuck."

"I know. And I don't want you feeling it now."

Luke moved in for a hug, and felt his father hold on longer than he had in some time. "Love you, Dad."

"Love you, too, son."

Chapter Thirteen

Zoe stretched her legs until her pointed toes reached Luke's. "I can't believe you're here."

He wrapped his arm around her back and pressed her naked frame against his. The sheets were still damp from the last hour of lovemaking.

"Hope you don't mind a roommate for the next few days."

She traced a finger over his chest. "The benefit package that comes along with a lack of bed space is workable."

He chuckled and kissed the top of her head.

"Seriously, though, if you'd told me you were coming, I could have arranged some time off."

"I think it's a better idea to spend time with each other when we're in our normal routines."

"There's nothing normal about my routine. Thinking about you sitting around doing nothing stresses me out."

"I'm sure I'll find something to do while you're working. Besides, I plan on crashing the set tomorrow."

Zoe wasn't sure if that would be more stressful or not.

"If you distract me . . ."

He slid a knee beside hers. "What do you mean, if?"

"Felix likes you, but he'll kick you off the set if I can't concentrate."

"It sounds like you don't want me there."

Zoe glanced up. "I've never had a guest on set."

Luke's eyes widened. "Never?"

"Not a personal guest. I've had producers, other chefs . . . friends in the business, but not . . ." How was she supposed to quantify who Luke was to her? *Lover* didn't sound right. *Friend* was an understatement. *Boyfriend* sounded adolescent . . .

He must have caught her distress, because he leaned down and kissed her softly. "You won't know I'm there. I promise."

Not only did she know he was there . . . so did everyone else on set.

Felix set up a director's chair beside his and forced Luke to sit next to him, behind the bright lights.

The set had holiday decorations, including Christmas lights, and a tiny, decked-out tree.

The team had already measured and prepped the dishes she was going to make, leaving the actual cooking to her.

Makeup took a little more time. Felix asked that she glitter her eyes to add to the festive feel of the shoot. They had her in a fitted red sweater, black leggings, and three-inch heels. The air conditioner in the studio blasted out a steady sixty degrees, making everyone other than her frozen.

"Okay, Zoe . . . let's do this in as few takes as possible." Felix moved around the set, pushing colorful bowls of sweets a little to the right, a tad closer to the cameras. "It's cold in here."

Zoe pulled her sweater away from her skin. "Speak for yourself."

September moved beside her, handing over a giant glass of ice water while the other hands scrambled to clear the kitchen.

She felt Luke's eyes on her as she took her position behind the counter.

He lifted his hand in a silent wave.

She smiled and directed her attention to camera two and the teleprompter that would cue her opening before she improvised the rest of the segment.

Felix waltzed back to his chair, his words traveling throughout the studio. "Now you get to see your little lady in action. You're in for a treat, Luke."

Zoe rolled her eyes at the *your little lady* reference.

"I've already seen her in action," she heard Luke say.

Several people in the room laughed. Zoe's cheeks grew warm.

She shot him a warning look and pointed a finger in his direction. "Don't start rumors."

He made a motion as if he were locking his lips together and winked.

"Okay, everyone . . . quiet on set. Camera two on Zoe. Camera one, take the profile, and three, be ready to zoom in on her hands."

Zoe glanced at Luke one last time before Felix put her into action.

Eight hours later, Zoe managed to fill five overflowing dessert trays with all the colors of the Christmas rainbow. They would film one dish, then clear the kitchen to film another. She insisted on easy holiday recipes that popped with color and texture and that any homemaker could manage with a little patience.

When she returned from her dressing room after changing out of her winter clothes, she found Luke hovering over the finished goodies with the rest of the crew, sampling her treats.

She caught Luke midbite. "Good?" she asked.

"Oh, my God . . . these are those caramel things you used to make for Miss Gina."

He waved the candy at her. She leaned in and took a bite. "Mmm. Yep."

"They taste even better than I remember."

His praise meant more than it should. "I hope so. I'm a little more talented than when I cooked at the inn."

"What inn is this?" Felix licked part of one of her peppermint shortbread cookies off his fingers.

"Miss Gina's. It's a bed-and-breakfast in my hometown."

September pushed into the conversation. "Isn't that the place you want us to go and help with your friend's wedding?"

"In Oregon, yeah."

"Do they wear cowboy boots in Oregon?" Felix asked.

Zoe stopped chewing and narrowed her gaze at her director.

Airport good-byes were starting to weigh her smile down. Luke felt the gravity of him leaving on the drive into Dallas Fort Worth International.

"When I get home, I'll book the hotels in Vegas," he said from the passenger seat of Zoe's car.

"I plan on getting Mel a lap dance. So make sure you guys are far away."

"I'd like to see that."

"Stand in line."

"When will you be back in town?"

It was her turn to visit, and with the wedding to plan, she had more than one excuse to go. "Two weeks. Now that the holiday filming is over, I need to renegotiate my contracts, which only leaves the restaurant." The restaurant she was seriously considering leaving. Saying it out loud, even to Luke, felt permanent. She wanted to wait for some kind of sign that she was doing the right thing. What happened if the ratings on her holiday specials didn't do well? What if her film days were behind her? She might need the day job.

How had she become so cautious? She'd jumped when she was a kid, now she dipped her toe in the water slowly to measure the temperature before taking a step.

"I have a confession to make," Luke said.

She looked over the rim of her sunglasses.

"While you were working yesterday, I interviewed at a couple of shops."

"Interviewed? Here?" She had to force her eyes toward the road.

"There's a specialty motorcycle garage in Cedars and a domestic shop downtown looking for help."

Oh, damn . . . that wasn't what she expected to hear. She had no idea how to respond. "Luke, I . . ."

"You don't like the idea."

She hid behind her sunglasses. "It's unexpected. I thought your dad would retire and you'd take over his shop."

"My dad is years away from retirement."

"But you live in River Bend."

He turned to stare out the window. Her reaction had upset him. "Never mind."

"Luke . . . it's . . . we just got back together."

He leaned his head back.

"Moving to Texas is a huge step."

"I'm testing the waters, Zoe. Relax. I haven't put my house on the market."

She hadn't heard the hint of anger in his voice for a long time. Hearing it now, and knowing she was the cause, made her heart ache.

They were silent the few remaining miles to the airport. He suggested she drop him off at the curb, but she parked the car instead.

They sat looking out the parked car window in quiet agony. "Luke, I—"

"You don't have to say anything."

"Yes I do. You're mad."

"I thought you might be excited."

She forced a smile. "At seeing you more, of course . . . but moving here for me . . . for us. It's too soon, Luke. What if you hate it? What if we don't work out?" *What if I suck at long-term? What if I'm the wrong woman for you?*

"What if I don't . . . and what if we do?" He turned her words around.

Fear rolled over her skin in waves. She glanced at her hands and noticed them shaking. "I can take a lot of hits, Luke, but you changing your whole life for me isn't something I want to be responsible for. Not yet."

He reached over and covered her hands with one of his.

She felt tears in her eyes. "Please don't hate me."

Luke lifted one of her hands and placed it to his lips. "Hating you isn't possible."

She looked at him now. "Can't we just enjoy what we have for now?"

"For the summer. But after Wyatt and Mel's wedding, we're revisiting this subject."

The summer. A little less than three months. "Okay." A lot could change in three months.

Once Mel picked out the colors she wanted, it was only a matter of dress style for Zoe and Jo's bridesmaid gowns. Even though Zoe had a fair amount of education in fashion, she never missed an opportunity to take Felix with her when it came to expanding her wardrobe.

"Tell me about this wedding." Felix flipped through a rack of semiformal gowns with a salesperson standing by.

"It's at the inn."

"Miss Gina's, right. You told me that. She sounds like a gem, this Miss Gina."

Zoe picked up an off the shoulder three-quarter length silk and held it to her waist.

Felix titled his head in consideration. "Might work for you, but your friend Jo doesn't have your rack."

Zoe turned to the side. "She does, she just hides it."

"Why on earth would she do that?"

"It's the cop in her."

Felix took the gown from her and handed it to the saleslady. "We'll try this one."

They kept looking.

"This inn, does it have a big kitchen?"

"State-of-the-art. Miss Gina updated it the year before I graduated. I encouraged her to take out an old butler pantry to make room for the bigger stove and second prep sink."

Felix found a strapless gown with a beaded bodice and placed it over his arm.

"Will all the cooking for this wedding happen at the inn?"

"Last-minute stuff. Sam's kitchen is commercial. My guess is he'll close the restaurant for the day."

Felix looked like he didn't believe her. "That still happens in this world?"

"It does in River Bend. Main Street closes down for the Fourth of July, and the town pulls together to decorate the town square for every holiday."

"Everyone knows everybody?"

"Almost. The outskirts of town have grown a little, which is probably for the best or River Bend would have emptied out years ago."

"What about an industry . . . jobs?"

"Mom-and-pop stuff. There's a farmers' market that brings out the crafters in town, and there is always someone trying to lure in small retail shops to keep the town going year-round." Zoe found a cap-sleeved dress that stopped at her knee.

Felix shook his head. "Too young."

She thought it was cute, but probably not for a wedding.

"So what keeps the town alive?"

"The schools. We have the local high school that pulls in from surrounding towns. Waterville has the county seat, so we don't have the politics that most towns have. There's a diner and a couple of fast food kind of places. Just enough retail to keep you from leaving town to buy a nail or a can of oil for your car."

"And an auto shop?"

Zoe smiled. "Miller's Auto has been there for as long as I remember."

"It sounds charming." Felix found another strapless dress and handed both to the woman waiting in the wings. "Why did you leave?"

She took another sleeved gown off the rack, glanced at the price tag. She turned it around and showed it to Felix. "Because I would never have been able to afford this if I had stayed."

He couldn't argue that.

"Tell me more about Miss Gina's kitchen. Can we bring a film crew in?"

Zoe dropped her hands to her sides. "What are you getting at, Felix?"

"I hate this state. And I think the industry can use another hometown cooking show. If we brought the world to the kitchen you grew up in—"

"The kitchen I grew up in was a dump," she interrupted.

"Okay, the kitchen you learned to love cooking in . . . I think we could have something there. A bed-and-breakfast is more intimate than a big urban restaurant. Plenty of charm."

She stopped shopping and stared.

"I've already blown the idea past Newton."

Newton was the producer of her current show and the man she and Suki negotiated with on an annual basis.

"You did what?"

"Don't sound so stressed, darling. He liked the idea but made it clear he'd film you wherever you wanted to cook. He did suggest you consider a bed-and-breakfast cookbook if we filmed in River Bend."

"A cookbook?" Was she hearing all this straight?

"Why not? You're a chef. It's a natural."

The saleslady took the dress from her hands. "Are you ready to try any of these on?"

"A cookbook!" She imagined the inn on the cover, her picture on the back.

Miss Gina would have guests lining up.

The thought of the cookbook paying back the woman for all she'd done for her over the years dwarfed the idea of it doing something for her own career.

"A cookbook."

Chapter Fourteen

It was easy to spring for a suite in Vegas when Zoe knew many of the celebrity chefs in town.

She and the girls took a room at the Venetian, while the men parked themselves at Caesars. The hotels weren't that far apart, but with thousands of guests walking around, it would be close to impossible for them to cross paths.

Mel's brother, Mark, flew down from Seattle to join Wyatt and Luke.

A welcome basket of fruit and wine sat on the coffee table in the sitting room of their suite, compliments of Chef Owen, whose name was given to one of the restaurants on the canal linking several of the casinos together. Along with the wine was the offering of dinner and drinks, complimentary, of course.

"It's crazy," Zoe said, setting aside the note that came with the wine. "When I couldn't afford a meal, no one was willing to pay, now that I can, everyone wants to treat me."

Jo pulled a fresh strawberry out of the mix and nibbled the end. "I like your friends."

Mel stood before the open blinds overlooking the Vegas strip. "This view is spectacular."

Zoe pulled up space beside her friend and draped an arm over her shoulders. "After the year you've had, you deserve it."

Mel placed her head on Zoe's shoulder and thanked her without words.

Jo slipped in, a hand on Zoe's other shoulder. "So what are we going to do first?"

Zoe turned and removed the bottle of champagne chilling in the bucket. "A toast."

She ripped the foil from the bottle and gently pulled the cork, not spilling a drop before filling glasses.

"To Wyatt and Mel?" Jo asked.

Zoe shook her head. "No, there's time for that next month. Tonight is about us." Zoe lifted her glass and the others followed suit. "We didn't do too bad. I have a feeling the best is yet to come."

Jo clicked her glass to Mel's, and Zoe pushed in.

"To us!" Mel drank first, then let out a huge squeal. "We're in Vegas!"

"This is going to be so much fun."

Zoe glanced at her watch and set her glass down. "Okay, ladies. Our day is about to begin. Grab your purses."

Jo looked at Mel. "Where are we going?"

"The spa! Duh!"

Mel squealed again and beat them to the door.

"I'll take the couch." Mark dropped his bag on the floor after walking past the two double beds in the room.

Luke offered a weak protest. "You don't have to. I can—"

"Bad back. It's better for me."

Wyatt shoved his bag on a bed and opened the minibar. He pulled out three beers and handed them around. "I haven't been here in years."

"I can beat that!" Luke had always wanted to go but never found the time or the playmates. He opened a basket on the side table that had his name on the tag.

"What's that?"

He dug through the wrapping and found a bottle of Irish whiskey, several bags of nuts, and gourmet crackers along with a note. *Zoe tells me you've never been to Vegas. Here is a card to get you into the players club. Tell them Felix sent you. And remember, it's not Vegas if you're sober. Drink up!*

"I like Zoe's friends."

Wyatt removed the whiskey and ditched his beer. "Now we're talking."

"What's on the agenda, gentlemen?"

Luke lifted the *get into the club* card. "Gambling or strip club?"

Mark's eyes lit up. "Yes and yes!"

"Oh, my God! This is amazing." Mel's muffled words drifted through the room where all three of them lay facedown on massage tables while masseuses removed all the tension of their flights.

"Miss Gina needs to offer this at the inn."

Zoe lifted her face long enough to glance at Jo. "That's not a bad idea."

Zoe's technician found a knot under her shoulder and she moaned.

"This is my first professional massage," Mel told them.

"That's a shame," Jo's tech said.

"Mine, too."

"That's just not right." Here Zoe had less than of both them growing up and more experiences with some of the finer things in life than either of them.

"Where do you ladies live?"

Jo and Mel said River Bend at the same time.

Zoe explained in plain English. "Nowhere-ville Oregon."

"I have to go to Waterville to get a pedicure," Mel told them.

"I don't bother," Jo said.

"Pedicures are the best."

"Only when you're wearing open toed shoes," Jo reminded her. "I wear boots."

"Not this weekend, you're not. Pedicures are next, and if you don't have shoes, we're going shopping."

Jo huffed.

"I don't want to hear it. Little black dresses and men we don't know buying our drinks."

Zoe's tech spoke up. "Sounds like one of you knows how to do Vegas."

"They'll learn."

"Men slip shit into drinks," Jo warned.

"You let them pay for drinks, Jo . . . but you don't let them hand the drinks to you." Zoe had been around the block a few times. "Besides, you're the only one of us bound to pick up someone tonight."

"I wanna see that," Mel said.

"You should have seen the guy in Dallas. He was hot," Zoe told her.

"He certainly was!"

Jo had them laughing and talking about dick size.

The technicians snickered and kept their comments to themselves.

～

"Remind me to thank this Felix guy when I meet him." Wyatt was doing what every self-respecting bachelor did at his bachelor party weekend in Vegas: he was glossy eyed and well on his way to passing out.

Luke slipped water into Wyatt's mix to keep the man sober enough to enjoy the night.

Felix's name had managed to not only get them into the players club, but also secure them two long-legged, beautiful women wearing nothing more than bathing suits in high heels serving them drinks and tutoring Luke on the game of craps. Wyatt tried to teach him, but he kept losing his concentration. Didn't stop the man from earning a little money, however. Mark made his way to a roulette table while Luke took the best man position and kept an eye on Wyatt.

The man at the head of the table tossed the dice and everyone cheered.

"Did we win?" Luke asked Cici, his scantily clad escort, compliments of Felix.

"You did."

"Should I leave the chips there?"

She shrugged. "I would."

He narrowed his eyes. "Do you gamble?"

"God, no. I work too hard for my money."

He found himself laughing.

"Of course . . . I live here. I think once in a while might be okay."

"I'm not your boss, sweetheart. I appreciate your honesty."

She batted her fake eyelashes and smiled.

The crowd at the table cheered again.

"Still winning?"

Cici winked, leaned her boobs into his arm, and whispered so only he could hear, "I'd consider leaving while I was ahead."

Luke pulled Wyatt from the table, both of them up five hundred dollars . . . how the hell that happened, he had no idea. He made sure

Cici and her friend were tipped well, with the promise of returning the next night.

The three of them made their way out of the casino in search of food. It was full dark and at least eighty-five degrees. At least there wasn't any humidity making their shirts stick to their bodies.

The bright lights of the strip added heat to an already hot night. Street vendors sold ice-cold water at a buck a pop while questionable men passed out tiny cards with naked women on them promising a good time. There were homeless people sitting beside cups saying they needed to eat, and parents pulling kids away from the women wearing nothing but pasties over their privates and suggesting a tip for a picture.

"This place is crazy."

"More so as the night wears on, my friend." Mark obviously knew his way around.

Luke wondered how the women were doing and stopped himself from removing his phone from his pocket to ask.

Mark guided them to a big meal, which helped pull some of the alcohol from Wyatt's system. It was just past ten and the night was about to begin.

Zoe didn't give two shits about the myth that what happens in Vegas stays there . . . her cell phone was out and she was doing her level best to take as many pictures of Mel's red face and laughing lips as she could.

The early twentysomething man wiggling his thong-covered ass in front of the bachelorette was worth every bill she shoved in his face. Or thong, as the case stood. The revue was known to mimic the themes seen on a popular movie franchise, and Zoe made sure Mel was front and center as a team of men did their best to act out sex on stage.

The women in the audience cheered and tossed money like it was weeds from a garden.

The men on stage flirted shamelessly and strutted around like peacocks.

"We have got to come back," Jo yelled above the crowd.

Zoe bumped fists with her friend and snapped another shot of Mel for future use.

The woman on the pole managed to twist her legs so far up that she stretched her torso, lifted her hands, and they still didn't reach the floor.

Luke couldn't help but wonder how her tits stayed inside her outfit.

The men watching were just as enamored as he was . . . most silent, with a few shouting out cheers. The music kept thumping and the women on stage had no trouble letting men slip bills into the small space between their thongs and their asses.

"Are those real?" Luke asked.

"I doubt it," Mark said at his side.

When the fiery redhead on stage slipped off her top and nothing moved, the fact she'd spent time at a plastic surgeon was proven. Not that it kept him from enjoying the show.

Loud music filled the after-party, along with wall-to-wall bodies dancing.

Zoe kept an eye on Mel, who'd had more to drink than all of them. She laughed on the dance floor and accepted the water Zoe kept handing her. "You're the best."

"Just don't puke."

Mel slapped a hand on Zoe's shoulder. "I'm not that drunk."

The man dancing by her side heard her and turned with a smile. "She's engaged," Zoe said.

He didn't seem to care. "Can I buy you a drink?"

Zoe pulled Mel away and moved to another part of the bar so they could dance.

~

Somewhere around three, Luke dragged Wyatt and Mark into a restaurant and had them eating breakfast. After, they stumbled into their room and didn't stir until housekeeping knocked on the door around noon.

~

"I wonder how the guys are doing?" Mel wore dark sunglasses and sat under the cabana by the pool.

"I doubt they're even awake," Zoe said, sipping her Bloody Mary.

It was noon, and the poolside party was just starting.

Jo turned over and let her pale skin see the sun for the first time in what looked like forever. "I'm taking a nap . . . don't let me burn."

Zoe glanced at her watch and made a mental note to cover her friend in twenty minutes or douse her with sunscreen.

Hours later, when the three of them had filled their veins with a loading dose of alcohol and had Mel wrapped in a boa with the fake tiara every bride-to-be deserved in Vegas, Zoe's cell phone rang in her tiny purse.

She ignored it, only to find it ringing again.

Expecting to see Luke or maybe Wyatt checking on them, she was shocked to see Miss Gina's inn flash on the screen.

She turned away from Jo and Mel, who were accepting Jell-O shots like they were teenagers, and answered the phone.

"Hey, lady."

"Zoe?"

The music in the bar was too loud to hear every word. "Is everything okay?"

"Zoe, hon . . ."

She didn't hear a thing Miss Gina was saying, but her tone said something was wrong.

"Hold on."

Zoe pushed away from the crowd and out into the street, which was marginally better this early in the Vegas night.

"What's going on?"

"I don't know how to tell you this."

The hair on Zoe's arms stood on end as she waited.

"It's your dad."

Air escaped her lungs. "Oh, no."

"He's out, Zoe. Zanya called and told me your mom brought him home."

Chapter Fifteen

Jo watched as Zoe slipped out of the bar with a phone to her ear. She didn't think much of it until she returned fifteen minutes later and started pounding drinks. All weekend she'd been pacing herself, making sure none of them got wasted. A nice break for Jo, since that was normally her role once she took the badge.

Only now she watched Zoe accept her first Jell-O shot of the night and follow it with a round of tequila.

There was something different about her friend's smile. She flirted with the guy who'd been trying to capture her attention since they'd walked in.

Jo took a moment to text Luke.

Have you talked to Zoe?

There were plenty of bodies between Jo and Zoe. Mel was talking with a group of other women celebrating the same thing they were.

Luke answered. Not since we dropped you off at the hotel.

When Zoe grabbed a second shot of tequila in the time it took to text Luke, Jo knew something was seriously wrong.

Jo told Luke where they were and suggested the men head over.

If he questioned her, he didn't do so with a text.

The next time she glanced at her cell phone, it was a message from Deputy Emery.

Ziggy Brown is back in town.

Jo's arm reached out and stopped Mel from taking another swig of her drink.

"What?"

Jo flashed the message on her screen in Mel's face.

They both twisted around to lay eyes on Zoe.

The thing about drinking when you were an adult was the unique ability to sober up in a heartbeat when needed. There was always that point where you were too far gone . . . but most of the time, unless the sky had fallen, you could pull yourself out of the fog to focus.

It helped that Luke had been pacing himself, since the headache he woke with that morning wasn't something he wanted to repeat. The flight back home wouldn't treat his seatmates well if he overindulged. He left that for Wyatt and hoped that when it came time for him to celebrate his last days of being a bachelor, someone would look out for him.

Instead of telling Wyatt where they were going and why, Luke did what he'd been doing all weekend: he directed.

The taxi drove them to the hotel that housed the nightclub. Jo had told him where they were. Zoe was a beacon . . . her dark hair flowed down her back, her laughter sounded animated in a room full of music and plenty of overindulging adults.

It was obvious to him the man by her side was doing everything he could to get her drunk . . . it seemed to be working.

Luke caught Jo's eyes, and she nodded toward her friend.

Mel jumped out of her seat and into Wyatt's chest. "Hey, sexy."

Luke moved aside as Wyatt grabbed his future bride and pulled her into his arms.

Zoe caught the scene and looked around.

Her eyes landed on Luke, and she blew past the man working to get her naked and wrapped an arm around him. "What are you doing here?"

She was one drink shy of stumbling. "I need my girl." He let the lie sound good.

"Hey, dude." The guy at her side stepped in.

Zoe started to laugh, and Jo took that moment to slide between them. "Don't."

The guy took a step forward, and Luke saw Jo remove something from her purse.

"Whatever, man."

Jo turned with a nod in Luke's direction and tapped her cell phone in her hand.

"Buy me a drink," Zoe told him.

Luke lifted his hand to capture the bartender's attention.

"Have you ladies had a good time?" As he asked, he removed his phone from his back pocket, hoping there would be some clue as to why Wyatt and Mel were staring at them like the earth had just shattered and he was oblivious.

"It's fabulous. Mel needs to get married every year."

"I don't think that's the plan."

Jo's message was quick and to the point.

Ziggy Brown is back in River Bend.

Suddenly everyone's expressions made sense and Zoe's lack of sobriety was understood.

Instead of calling her out, Luke ordered a round of drinks and stuck by Zoe's side the rest of the night. Reality would crash in the morning. He'd be there to help pick up the pieces if she let him.

~

The girls' suite at the Venetian was twice as big as theirs.

Luke was fairly certain Zoe was oblivious to the fact that she was shitfaced drunk while everyone else had sobered up and was talking in a separate room while she slept.

"How the hell did this happen?" Luke voiced the question to Jo, not that it was her fault that Ziggy had managed to get out of jail.

"I don't know. I'll be on the phone Monday to figure out what kind of shit he pulled to get out."

"Fifteen to life . . . doesn't that mean he's there forever?" Mel's question hung in the air.

"Obviously not, hon." Wyatt held her close.

"Ziggy is one mean motherfucker," Mark chimed in. "I remember him pulling Sheryl out of Sam's by the hair one night, yelling that she hadn't made him dinner."

"I don't remember that," Mel said.

"You weren't there. Dad looked at me and told me he was the reason you couldn't go to Zoe's house to play when you were in grade school."

"What the hell is Sheryl thinking, bringing him back in the house?" Wyatt asked.

Luke glanced at the bedroom door and thought of Zoe sleeping off the effect of the news. "He better not hurt her."

Jo stood before the open drapes, staring out at the lights of the Vegas strip. "He already has."

~

Jo held Zoe's hair back as she gripped the edges of the toilet and regretted the last three drinks from the previous night. "Fuck me." She emptied her already empty stomach once again.

"You're not my type."

"I'm too old for this."

"You're not even thirty."

Zoe's clammy skin made her feel a hundred.

"What the hell was I thinking?"

Jo patted her on the back and spoke in soothing tones. "You have your reasons."

Zoe had ignored the stares the night before, but at ten in the morning, with her pores reeking of alcohol, she couldn't deny the truth. "Miss Gina called you, didn't she?"

"Deputy Emery."

Zoe sat her butt on the marble floor and accepted Jo's cold washcloth. "This wasn't supposed to happen, Jo."

Jo pulled up the vanity bench and rested her hands on her knees. "I don't get it. My contact told me he was slated for the next six years if he kept his nose clean."

Zoe had followed the news enough to know the prison system was overcrowded and they were releasing inmates left and right.

"Hey?" Mel stepped into the bathroom with a chilled bottle of water.

Zoe took it but didn't bother drinking it. She placed it to her forehead and closed her eyes.

"I can almost get the fact he managed to get out of jail. But my mom . . . what the hell?"

Mel took the edge of the small seat Jo sat on. "Aren't they divorced?"

It turned Zoe's stomach to think about it. "She said yes, but who knows."

"I can check the county records, find out."

Zoe blinked Jo's way with a little nod. Much as she hated asking her friend to do that, she wanted to know the facts so she could deal with them. Her mother's lies tended to affect everyone around her. "Has anyone spoken with Miss Gina?"

"I did. She said Zanya called her to ask when we were coming back."

"I've got to get her out of there. And Blaze . . . that's no way to grow up." Much as Zoe wanted to let her sister get on with her life and make her own decisions, she couldn't sit back and watch her childhood repeat with her nephew.

"One day at a time, Zoe."

Mel, the forever optimist, asked, "Could he have changed? Maybe he's—"

Both Jo and Zoe stared at Mel until her words died off.

Zoe took a chance, opened the water, and took a tiny sip. "Where are the guys?"

"Packing their stuff. Luke is changing his flight and booking yours for later."

She looked around the bathroom in search of a clock. "Isn't it close to checkout?"

"Don't worry about it. We arranged a later checkout for you."

"We'll get back and gather as many details as we can before you get there."

Zoe's stomach started to protest the intrusion of water. She leaned forward. "We were having such a good time."

"I had a great time, Zoe. I'm not letting your deadbeat dad ruin this whole weekend for us."

Zoe attempted to smile even as her stomach rejected what she'd put in it.

The girls tucked her back in bed, and when she woke, Luke sat beside her. She curled next to him and let him stroke her head.

~

News traveled fast in small towns.

Jo stripped out of her civilian clothes the second she stepped in the door of her home and slipped into her uniform. Her sidearm was a welcome relief on her hip. Something she planned on keeping within arm's reach until Ziggy Brown left town on his own or was back behind bars.

She'd read her father's reports on the man.

He was a piece of human dirt who had little respect for his own life, let alone those of his wife and children. Even though Zoe was coming back to town to sort out some of the pieces of this broken puzzle, Jo couldn't help but hope that her friend would go back to Texas so whatever was going to play out did so without her being there.

She stepped into the station after six.

It was Sunday, and normally Glynis had the calls forwarded to either Deputy Emery or Jo after five. The town wasn't Mayberry, but the crime rate didn't warrant a twenty-four/seven staff unless there was someone in the holding tank. Most of the time they shipped out their temporary incarcerated guests to Waterville, where they had a much bigger force. While Jo's jurisdiction covered a lot of miles, the population wasn't that dense. Her town felt suddenly smaller with Ziggy Brown out of jail.

Glynis straightened in her chair when Jo walked in.

"What are you still doing here?"

"I knew you'd be by."

Jo kept her cool, looked around the empty station. "Anything I need to know about?"

She shook her head. "Nothing you haven't been told. Been a little quiet ever since . . . well . . ."

Jo didn't let Glynis stumble over her words. "I appreciate your attention. Go home. I have it from here."

Glynis stood, pulled her purse from behind the desk. "How is Zoe?"

"Upset. But she's tough."

"I have no doubt. Good night, Jo."

"Good night, Glynis."

Jo sat down at the radio and dialed in to Emery. "I'm back. What's your twenty?"

"Enjoying a little downtime on a back country road, Sheriff. Wouldn't mind a break."

She read between those lines. Before leaving the station, she'd packed up all the files she had on Ziggy Brown and planned on learning everything she could about the man she never thought would step foot in River Bend again.

Chapter Sixteen

It was late when Zoe and Luke drove into town. The later flight, coupled with a flight delay, meant they weren't going to confront anyone that evening.

Not that she knew what she was going to say.

The thought of coming face-to-face with her father had her hyperventilating and scratching her skin like a crack addict in need of a fix.

She hadn't seen the man since her mother had originally dragged them to the penitentiary after he was sent away. It didn't take long for Ziggy to move from the medium state lockup to a maximum state penitentiary. When that happened, they shipped him closer to Portland and too far for her mom to swing the gas and time to drive up.

Or so Zoe thought.

Luke and Zoe were about a half hour outside of River Bend when some of the questions swimming in her head started to come out. "Do you think she ever divorced him?"

Luke drove his dad's truck, which they had left at the long-term airport parking while they were in Vegas.

"She never remarried."

"I don't think she ever dated either. I always thought it was because she was afraid of men. But now I wonder."

"I never knew your dad."

"He's mean. And yet so few people saw that about him until right before he was arrested the last time. I remember him telling my mom about all the women who wanted him . . . how he could be with anyone, and she needed to remember that." The memories of him in the trailer growing up had filtered in and out of her thoughts all day. "I was just about to go into junior high . . . Zane was in third grade, and Zanya was in what, first grade?" She asked the question to herself, searching for the data she knew was in her head. "He'd lost his job at the plant outside Waterville."

"The one that builds RVs?"

"Yeah. He worked there for about a year. I remember thinking how great it was that we had enough money to turn on the heat in the winter."

"Jesus."

"Money was tight. As aware as I was about how tight it was, I was also aware that most of the kids at school had no idea that heat cost money."

"My dad would bitch about leaving a window open and tell me I wasn't born in a barn," Luke said.

"This was different. He'd come in the house, tell us he wasn't made of money, and turn it off. Didn't matter if it was twenty degrees and snowing. He'd drink himself into a sweat while we huddled under a pile of blankets. My mom would turn on the heat when he left the house, just enough to pull the chill out of the air, and turn it back off before he came home. I'd pin up an extra blanket over the window to try and keep the cold out of our room. Most the time it didn't work, but sometimes it did. One night he came home and knew the heater had been on. He forced all of us to sit outside so we 'knew what cold was.' It was raining. The next week we were all sent to school with the flu. Mom wasn't about to take time off of work when we were ill." Zoe had all but forgotten that memory. It was probably best buried. Then again, Zanya and Blaze lived in that house . . . even Zane, although Zoe was certain he had a few options that her little sister didn't. The thought of Ziggy forcing Blaze into the cold made her angry.

"Once your dad was in prison, did your mom turn on the heat?"

"Not at first. I think she was afraid he'd walk in the door. While he sent us out in the cold, he wasn't opposed to hitting her to make her *understand*." How she hated the word *understand*.

You don't *understand*, I'm doing this for your own good.

You'll *understand* when you're a parent.

If I don't discipline you now, you won't *understand* the rules.

And all that was when he was on his good behavior. If he'd been drinking, or just didn't care, he'd come in yelling, throwing stuff . . . swinging his fists.

"I know he battered your mom around . . . did he . . . ?"

Zoe noticed Luke gripping the steering wheel. "All the time," she said without shame. It wasn't her fault the man was abusive. "He was smart about it. Made sure the marks he left weren't visible in normal clothes. I always thought he wouldn't get away with it if we lived in a warmer state." Once again, she felt herself drifting into her own thoughts and memories. "He always had a line . . . why we were sick . . . why we were bruised. Slipped and fell. Rope on the swing broke. Ice on the drive . . . I don't think anyone ever noticed that our drive was gravel." She leaned her head back and kept talking. She hadn't thought about all of this or wanted to talk about it for years.

"Right before he held up that mini-mart, he'd started showing his true self. He stopped being polite to people in town. He'd keep us home from school to avoid anyone knowing there was a problem. In sixth grade, I'd missed about three weeks of school before the winter break. The counselor, Miss Jennings, came to the house right before Christmas break to check on me. I remember her black slacks and polished shoes . . . not sure why the shoes mattered, but I remembered them. She stood in my living room. Dad wasn't there, he'd told me to stay home and watch Zanya, and he went out to 'find money.'" She huffed out a laugh, understanding what that meant now. "Miss Jennings stood with polished shoes on our worn carpet. She asked me why I wasn't at school. I was scared to answer. I don't think I did."

"What happened?"

"I met Jo's dad, formally. I knew of him, of course. But he came over the next day to check on us. I found out later that Ziggy had made a scene in town and the teachers were talking." It helped to know that people were aware and finally willing to step in. "I had just started to stop by Miss Gina's on the way to school . . . she never said anything, but I think she had something to do with Miss Jennings coming over that day."

Zoe looked over to see Luke's carefully controlled jaw, his tense hands on the wheel. "You probably don't want to hear this."

Luke pulled in what seemed like a painful breath and reached over to grasp her hand. "I hate that you went through all that . . . but I absolutely want to hear it. When we were kids and you said your dad was an asshole and in jail, I knew on some level that meant he'd hurt all of you. I heard a few things over the years, but I didn't really know much of anything."

Zoe squeezed his hand back. "I told Mel and Jo years ago how bad it was. I made them swear to not say a thing to anyone."

"Even me?"

She nodded. "It wasn't until I was in my twenties that I wasn't embarrassed about my dad . . . my childhood. In a way, I still am."

"You can't help who you're born to."

"I know that."

Luke pulled off the main road leading out of town and toward his house. "Unless you object, I'd like you to stay with me tonight. I can take you to Miss Gina's—"

"No. I'd much rather . . ." She kissed the back of his hand. "You make me feel safe, Luke."

He gripped her hard. "I won't let him hurt you, Zoe."

"It isn't me I'm worried about."

It was pouring down rain the next morning. Zoe drank her coffee black and stared out Luke's kitchen window. Tiny drops fell off the gutters and onto the back deck. The small pools of water would give the birds plenty of places to bathe once the rain stopped. She wondered if Luke had birds that showed up on his back step. She leaned over the sink to take a better look at his outdoor space. He didn't have a bird feeder.

A back porch needed a bird feeder.

The floor squeaked behind her, taking her attention away from theoretical birds.

Luke slid his arms around her waist and leaned his head into hers.

"You smell nice," she told him. Fresh from the shower and clean-shaven.

"So do you."

He stood holding her, both of them looking out the back window.

"I've never been in your backyard."

"You can go out there now . . . might get a little wet."

She chuckled and hugged his arms around her.

"How are you feeling this morning?" he asked.

She hadn't slept well, tossing and turning with memories and stress. Somewhere around four, she turned her pillow around for the hundredth time, found a cool spot, and drifted off.

"I'm sorry if I kept you up all night."

"I slept."

"Liar. But thanks for trying to make me feel better."

He kissed the top of her head before backing away. "Is that coffee I smell?"

"It is."

Luke removed a clean coffee cup from his cupboard and filled it.

"I tried to find cinnamon to brew with it. No luck."

"You're lucky you found coffee. I don't always bother until I'm at the shop."

She found her smile. "I noticed it's a little lacking in here."

He turned, leaned against the counter, and took a sip with a grin. "Consider it an empty canvas. Feel free to paint it up."

"But it's your kitchen."

"And?"

She glanced around. "Rearranging your kitchen . . . I don't know. That's a big step."

"It's a kitchen." Luke looked at her over his cup.

"Have you forgotten who you're talking to?"

"It's a kitchen. I could give two shits about where things are."

She pretended shock.

"Now if you wanted to talk about a drawer in my bedroom . . . we might have a problem."

She put a hand in the air. "Wait . . . I can move everything around in here, but no panties with your boxers?"

He was trying hard not to smile, but he wasn't fooling her. "We would have to negotiate that."

"And what kind of negotiations are we talking here?"

He held his cup with both hands and kept it close to his face. "For starters, if you have panties here, I have boxers at your place."

"In Texas?"

"Do you have a home somewhere else?"

He'd lowered his cup, and his smile made his eyes crinkle. This was the second time he'd alluded to taking their relationship to a new level. What if it didn't work out? What if it did? She felt like she'd had one of her best friends reenter her life, and she didn't want that going away.

"Tell me what you're scared of so I can shatter it." Luke's words shook her out of her head.

"A shotgun isn't going to destroy my fears."

Concern replaced the humor in his eyes. "I don't think I said anything about weapons."

She studied her pedicure, wondering how her thoughts turned so violent. "I live in Texas . . . everyone has guns."

She heard his coffee cup touch the counter and looked up when he placed both hands on her arms. "When you're ready to tell me what your fears are . . . I'm here."

At that exact moment, there were so many fears she couldn't name one for him to wage war on.

Zoe leaned into his chest and rested her head on his shoulder. His arms wrapped around her and held her tight.

"I'll make space in my panty drawer if you make space in yours."

He chuckled, held her tighter . . . a long while later, he said, "I don't have a panty drawer."

Jo had gone home an hour after the lights in the Brown home had turned off. Her alarm woke her by five. By six, she had another stack of paperwork to study, a fresh gallon of coffee . . . and yes, a pastry that she wouldn't call a donut, but came painfully close, was at her side.

Ziggy Brown was put away during her father's reign as sheriff. On the previous evening, she'd looked through her father's reports . . . documentation of unproven and proven domestic abuse in the Brown home. He'd filed official reports from business owners who wanted to file a report but didn't want to press charges. These reports did nothing but add to Ziggy's lousy character reference when he went to trial.

He'd held up a mini-mart in Waterville at gunpoint. He'd beaten the clerk, stolen what money was in the register, and fled with a case of beer. The car he'd used to drive away was seen on a surveillance camera across the street from the mini-mart. Because he wore a ski mask and gloves, the clerk wasn't able to positively identify him in a lineup. The case was won when the clerk's DNA was found in bloodstains on the steering wheel of Ziggy's old Chevy.

The viciousness of the attack on the clerk and the fact that he used a gun to hold the man up were what put him away for so long. He'd had a laundry list of misdemeanors including two DUIs, driving on a suspended license, and several assault charges. A felony assault had given him a sentence for six months, of which he served only three.

Jo flipped through her father's reports and watched the timeline of the last six months that Ziggy was a free man. He'd been in jail the summer before the reports from the schools started showing up. Apparently, his time in prison made him meaner, and when he was released, he turned his mean onto Zoe and her family.

On two occasions Jo's father quoted Zoe's words.

Each time made Jo's heart ache so many years later.

The school nurse had called him in when she found a welt over Zoe's back.

Sheriff Ward: "How did you get that mark on your back, Zoe?"

Zoe Brown: "The rope swing broke when I was on it and the rope hit my back."

Sheriff Ward: "Did you fall off the swing?"

Zoe Brown: *Answered with a nod.*

Sheriff Ward: "When you fell, how did you land on the ground?"

Zoe Brown: *The child waited for thirty seconds and started to shake.* "I don't remember."

Sheriff Ward: "Did you fall on your bottom? Your knees? Did you catch yourself with your hands?"—*Note: Her hands were not scraped. Child was wearing long pants and a long sleeve shirt.*

Zoe Brown: "I don't remember."

Sheriff Ward: *I ended my questions when the child started to cry.*

The report indicated Jo's dad went to the Brown home to find Ziggy Brown alone. He'd questioned Zoe's dad, who came up with an identical answer. "The rope swing broke and hit her on the back."

When asked which tree the rope swing had been in, Ziggy pointed to an old pine. Upon investigation, there were no marks or evidence of a swing ever being in the tree. Ziggy explained they hadn't had it long.

There wasn't much he could do with the report other than watch for more possible home violence. There was a side note stating that Zane's teacher asked if he ever had a rope swing at his house and the child answered no.

Still, there wasn't anything Jo's dad could do without more evidence and an actual complaint of domestic violence.

Jo sipped her coffee from the front seat of her squad car, her eyes drifting toward Zoe's childhood home. They'd all shared some great times there once Ziggy was put away. Jo remembered her father wouldn't let her go anywhere near the Brown home when he lived there. That didn't mean that Jo and Zoe hadn't been friends. Back then Jo was focused on her own world and not paying attention to Zoe's. It wasn't until junior high that Mel, Jo, and Zoe had really hooked up and formed their forever friendship.

The house hadn't changed much . . . well, it had morphed a little. Lack of maintenance and attention seemed to make the left side of the house dip into the earth. Or maybe that was just the weeds swimming high on the foundation. The rut-filled gravel drive housed the old Pontiac Sheryl drove, and occasionally Mylo's beat-up old truck. Zane was riding a motorcycle most of the time, but it wasn't anywhere on the property.

Lights inside the Brown home flickered on in the back bedroom.

Jo rolled down her window, ignored the drizzle falling from the sky, and heard Blaze crying.

Jo straightened up in her car when the front door opened and Zanya stepped out of the home with Blaze in her arms. Dressed in a bathrobe, she bounced a cranky Blaze around in what appeared to be an effort to calm him down. She spoke to him in a quiet voice with words Jo couldn't make out.

When the door opened a second time, Jo's hand was on the car door handle, ready to step out.

Sheryl's head peeked out, along with her hand, which held a bottle.

Zanya took the bottle, popped it in Blaze's mouth, and turned to walk back in.

That was when Sheryl looked above her daughter's head, and her gaze caught Jo's.

Jo was lifting her hand to wave when Sheryl's expression shifted from surprise to annoyance.

Zanya glanced over her shoulder and offered a weak smile before Sheryl pushed her through the door and closed it.

"Shit," Jo cussed at the universe. The division in the family was already in full swing. The adults would take sides, leaving some with Ziggy and some on the street.

A curtain on the back bedroom shifted enough to know that someone was looking out.

Instead of driving off, she decided to hold out until Zoe showed up.

Jo knew her friend wasn't sleeping in.

No, Zoe would be picking her words carefully and figuring out the best time to show up and confront the whole sordid mess.

Chapter Seventeen

Zoe watched the trees as they drove closer to the house. Each one felt like a countdown, a ticking clock to doom. It was just after ten in the morning. Early enough to ensure that everyone would be home, and late enough to know she hadn't pulled anyone out of bed.

The thought of her mother sleeping beside her father made her physically ill. She silently prayed to find evidence of someone bunking on the broken-down couch.

The last quarter mile to the house, her head lifted, and she saw Jo's squad car off the side of the road.

She attempted a smile.

Luke pulled alongside Jo and stopped.

Jo lowered her wire-rimmed sunglasses as she spoke. "You ready for this?"

"No."

"You don't have to—"

"We both know I do." Zoe stared at the double-wide and felt like it was foreign to her. It might have stopped being her residence a decade ago, but now it didn't even feel like a place she was welcome. And she'd yet to breach the front door.

"Do you want me to go in with you?"

Zoe shook her head. "Luke is coming in." She wasn't about to go in alone.

Bringing Jo in might prove grounds for all kinds of confrontation simply because of her uniform.

"I'm right out here."

Zoe's gaze skirted away from the house and to Jo. The weak smile on Jo's face matched hers. She placed her hand on Luke's thigh. "Let's get this over with."

The rain had let up, but clouds still filled the sky, and fog closed in the edges of the property. Fog always had a way of making the place look cleaner than it was.

Why that thought sprang into Zoe's head as she stepped out of the car, she didn't know.

Luke walked around the front of the truck and reached for her hand. She took it with more force than she expected.

"I'm right here."

They walked up the steps in slow motion. She hesitated before knocking on the door. Before that moment in her life, a knock would always be followed by letting herself in.

Not today.

The curtains to the right of the door moved before she heard the doorknob rattle.

Zoe held her breath.

Zanya answered in silence. Zoe would have liked to say she saw something, some kind of communication in her sister's eyes, but there was nothing.

Behind her baby sister, on the sofa that was older than dirt, Zoe's eyes collided with her father.

Her heart skipped a beat, and physical pain threatened to cripple her knees.

The desire to hit the man ran side by side with her desire to turn and walk back out.

She didn't do either.

Her mom stood at the edge of the couch in worn blue jeans and a white T-shirt. "You don't have to knock," she told her.

Zoe couldn't look at her mom. Instead, she took in the man who stood as the poster child for deadbeat dad. He looked like the devil to her, but to the unknowing observer, he appeared handsome. Prison had given him gray hair and a trimmed beard. The lines on his face were soft as he stared, his eyes occasionally shifting to Luke. He'd stayed in shape in prison, not surprising when he had nothing better to do while locked away. He hadn't aged. In fact, he looked healthier than when she'd last seen him. Forced sobriety was probably to blame. In contrast, her mother looked just this side of homeless. Hard living with no sure way of making it better had done that to Sheryl.

"Why are you here?" She directed the question to Ziggy.

"Well hello to you, too, sweet pea."

Zoe swallowed hard, narrowed her focus. "You shouldn't be here."

"Zoe!" her mom warned.

Ziggy sat back, placed an arm on the back of the couch. "This is where I live."

"Not in over seventeen years."

"That's part of my past, little girl. I'm a changed man." He opened his arms. "Now come here and give me a proper greeting."

Zoe stepped closer to Luke's side and finally looked away. "What is he doing here, Mom? Help me understand."

Sheryl opened her mouth, but Ziggy spoke for her.

"This is my house."

Zoe refused to look at him. "Mom?"

"This has always been his house."

"You told me it's in your name."

Sheryl looked between Zoe and Luke.

"The house is mine, little girl. Your mama is my guest."

Anger flashed. "I'm not a little girl, Ziggy!" She made a point of using his name and setting boundaries. He may have intimidated her as a child, but she wasn't about to put herself in the role of victim ever again. "And my *mama* has been holding this place together since before you went to prison. You have no right to—"

"Show some respect, little girl." Ziggy's smile pushed into a thin line.

"Is this his house?" she asked her mom one final time.

Her mother nodded.

"I gave you money to help with the mortgage. A mortgage I thought belonged to you." To think all these years she'd been somehow putting money in Ziggy's pocket hit her like a wrecking ball.

"I suppose I should thank you, baby doll."

"Don't talk to me. You have no right."

"A man's home is his castle, and I don't appreciate your tone."

Zoe glanced at Zanya, who'd stood in silence during the conversation. "Fine! Mom, Zanya . . . pack up." She'd take them back to Texas, find another place in River Bend . . . anything. If Ziggy held them there because he'd somehow been able to keep the piece of crap trailer in his name all these years, then he could have it.

Zanya didn't move and Sheryl sat on the arm of the couch.

Ziggy snaked an arm around her mom's hips and pulled her into his lap. When her mother didn't resist, a piece of Zoe's heart tore into pieces. "What are you doing? Let's go. You don't have to stay here. I'll take care of everything."

No one moved.

Ziggy sat with a fucking grin on his face.

Zoe wanted to slap it off.

"Mom!"

"Your dad has changed, honey. I know you don't understand—"

"Oh, my God. You did not just say that. He's a piece of crap who beat the shit out of you."

"That's an exaggeration," Ziggy said.

Zoe released Luke's hand long enough to toss her palm in the air. "I was there, Ziggy. I know what I saw. I know what it felt like to have you whip on me and have me lie to my teachers, my friends. Well, those days are long past. I don't know who you charmed to get out of prison, but you're not going to have the opportunity to hurt my family again."

"You were always a willful girl."

Zoe took a step closer, wanted to show him just how willful she could be. Luke clasped his hand to hers, kept her close, and spoke up. "Sheryl, Zanya. I have room at my place. You can stay with me while we figure this out."

The heat of Luke's frame and warmth of his voice as he volunteered his home to her family filled her heart.

"You're the Miller boy, right?" Ziggy asked.

Luke didn't bother looking at her dad.

"C'mon, Mom." Why was the woman sitting in Ziggy's lap? Had he already threatened her, found a way to force her to stay?

"You leave my wife alone, little girl. She belongs here, with me."

The word *wife* made Zoe cringe. She stared at her mother. "Mom?"

Ziggy kissed the side of her mother's cheek and bile rose in Zoe's throat.

"Son of a . . . you didn't divorce him, did you?"

"You don't understand."

"I don't. You're right. He's a felon, an abuser, a piece of shit father—" She was yelling now.

"Zoe, enough." This time it was Sheryl cutting her off. "We will talk about this another time. You're upset."

"He beat us up, Mom. You stayed with him all those years and watched him get drunk and use his fists on us kids. How can you even let him touch you?" Zoe purposely didn't look at her dad or even acknowledge him being in the room.

"Discipline is a fine line these days," Ziggy said. "So many people want to cry abuse. I might have been a little harsh with you, but I did not beat on you, little girl."

Zoe swung her head around and glared. "I am *not* a little girl. I'm not your sweet pea . . . I'm not your anything. You are dead to me."

"Zoe!" The warning came from her mom. "Please."

It was obvious her mother wasn't going anywhere. Worse, it didn't look like she was being forced to stay. Zoe turned to Zanya. "Grab Blaze. We'll figure something out."

Zanya shook her head. "It wasn't that bad, Zoe."

The air in Zoe's lungs rushed out. The desire to scream and recall in painful detail every beating she'd experienced under the hands of her father came out in a manic laugh. "Unbelievable."

"I think you should leave," Ziggy said.

"C'mon, Zoe." Luke squeezed her hand and tugged her toward the door.

She turned to leave and stopped cold. Her eyes reached her mom, her sister. "He will hit you again."

In the back room, Blaze started to cry.

In Zoe's head, she promised herself that if Zanya allowed her son the abuse they'd suffered as children, she'd step in with legal help to keep him safe.

Luke kept an arm around her, and her frame shook as they walked to the truck. He helped her into the passenger seat without words and climbed in to drive.

As they pulled away from her childhood home, Zoe vowed to never return.

～

Jo arrived at Miss Gina's in uniform.

A lack of sleep circled under her eyes, making Zoe wonder if her friend was sleeping in her squad car instead of her bed.

Zoe threw together a simple dinner and encouraged Luke to spend time with Wyatt or his parents . . . or someone so she could talk in private with her friends. Not that she was keeping secrets, but talking candidly while figuring out where her head was at with everything revolving around Ziggy's appearance called for alone time with the girls.

The clouds had opened up and rain was falling in deep sheets. The inn was free of guests, making it easy to dominate the parlor without worry of interruption or eavesdropping.

Mel wrapped a blanket over her lap as she curled up on the couch with a portion of cheesy chicken and rice casserole on her plate. Zoe tucked her feet under her butt and settled in while Jo removed her cop belt, gun included, and placed it on the coffee table.

"So she never divorced him," Mel said as she filled her fork. "That's stupid crazy."

"Why did she lie?"

"What would she have gained by telling you the truth?" Jo asked between bites. "You breathing down her neck to get a divorce?"

Zoe played with her portion of food. "Probably. She lied about everything. If Ziggy owned the house, she could have told me, I would have helped her move."

"If there is one thing I've learned since putting on this uniform, it's that some people don't want to be helped. Alcoholics don't want to get sober, thieves don't want to get a job so they don't have to steal to make a buck, and battered women don't want to leave their abusive husbands for fear of being alone."

"But she's been alone for seventeen years. She hasn't had to dodge a fist or sit out in the cold for years." It made no sense to Zoe. None whatsoever. "And what the hell is wrong with my sister? Has she forgotten what an ass he is?"

"Zanya is a lot more like your mom than you are. She's looking for someone to take care of her and Blaze. Maybe your dad—"

"Don't call him that, Mel."

Mel lifted a hand in apology. "Maybe Ziggy promised the world."

"I promised the world and they both know I can deliver."

Both of her friends shook their heads in disbelief.

"We're just going to have to wait and see what happens. I don't care what the system says, animals like Ziggy don't change their stripes. The man is on parole. One drink and I'm bringing him in . . . one step outside the line. Then, when he's back on the inside, we can figure out this mess."

Zoe attempted another bite. Even her comfort food wasn't doing its job. "I don't want to wait for him to screw up. I need to know if he is holding something over my mom."

"And if he isn't? If she's making a mistake and doesn't care who it hurts . . . what then?" Mel asked.

"Then I walk away. I don't want that stress in my life."

"You say that now, but if she showed up bruised and broken, you'd pull her in," Jo countered.

"Then I'm counting on you two to talk me out of letting the cycle continue. I don't know if it's a lost cause yet . . . but when it becomes painfully evident that I'm wasting my tears on the situation, you both need to remind me of this night."

"What do you want us to do then?" Jo's stoic expression told Zoe she was listening hard.

"Tell me to walk away. Remind me she'll just fall for him again. If she is stupid in love with that bastard and is willing to go through all that crap again, let her have it. I'm no longer a kid and don't have to stick around to watch." The thought of her own mother picking Ziggy over everyone else left her broken on the inside. What parent did that?

Who was she kidding? Sheryl had done that most of her life.

From the way she comfortably sat on Ziggy's lap, she seemed willing to do it again.

Mel put her fork down. "Pisses me off. I feel like we just got you back, and now your family is pushing you away again."

"Oh, Mel . . . I'm not going away." Only she couldn't imagine running into her family on a daily basis with Ziggy holding everyone in tight control.

"I want that in writing," Mel whined.

"Let's talk about something happy," Jo suggested. "So, sex with Luke . . . better than before?"

Zoe felt an instant smile on her face.

Chapter Eighteen

Luke had walked Zoe over to Sam's the next day, and then continued around the block to the police station. He was hoping Zoe having a private word with Sheryl would end with some kind of resolution. She hadn't been able to sleep since they returned from Vegas. She wasn't eating either. For the first time since they'd gotten back together, he thought it might be best for her to return to Texas to get her mind off of her family. She was too close to the players to clear her mind and focus. In three weeks, when she returned for Mel and Wyatt's wedding, she'd have some time behind her to let the reality of her father returning sink in.

Who knew, maybe Ziggy would screw up in those three weeks and end up back in jail.

Luke entered the station and waved at Glynis as he walked past. "Jo in there?" he asked, pointing toward her office.

"Yep."

He winked and kept walking.

"Hey, Luke?" He turned around.

"Yeah."

"Try and get her to eat."

What was it with the women in his life not eating? "I'll do that."

Jo's desk was mounded with open folders and empty coffee cups. "Looks like someone is running on caffeine."

"Hey."

"What's all this?"

Jo placed a hand over an overstuffed folder. "This is the life of Ziggy Brown, illustrated by the Department of Corrections for the past seventeen years." She slapped her hand on a file a quarter of its size. "This is the life of Ziggy Brown, illustrated by my dad and a few of his colleagues in Waterville." She pointed to the far left corner of her desk. "River Bend Unified School District records of the Brown children . . . and last, but not least, Sheryl Brown." Jo tapped her finger on the smallest pile in the stack.

"Who would Sheryl's file be illustrated by?"

"My dad and the state of Oregon."

Luke sank into a chair. "Your dad?"

"He tried to gather enough evidence of neglect to bring Child Protective Services in without any risk of the case being thrown out."

"Too bad that didn't happen."

"According to the state of Oregon, Sheryl Brown has been the wife of Theodore Brown, aka Ziggy, for twenty-eight years."

Luke tilted his head in thought. "Sheryl and Ziggy married after Zoe was born?"

"Yep. I'm not sure if Zoe knows that fact."

"If only Ziggy wasn't her biological father." He couldn't help but envision what that would look like. The thought was fleeting, however, since Zoe had a striking resemblance to the man.

"I doubt that."

"Me, too . . . but it was a pleasant thought for a second."

"No, more likely Sheryl ended up pregnant, and it wasn't until after Zoe was born that Ziggy stepped up. Not that she was better off for it." Jo paused, then asked, "Where is Zoe?"

"Confronting her mom at the diner. She didn't want company."

"I have a feeling Sheryl isn't going to tell her what she wants to hear."

Luke didn't think so either. "I'll never understand why people stay in abusive relationships."

"We're all able to take a certain amount of pain for love."

He thought of his own love life . . . therefore he pictured Zoe. "True, but not when it comes to putting your kids in danger. I blame Sheryl for that. I want to like the woman, but it's becoming harder by the day."

"She's not on my list of favorite people. Never has been. I always saw her as selfish and using. Her hand was out all the time once Zoe started making a name for herself."

"Zoe is kicking herself for giving her anything to support that home."

"She wouldn't have done it if Sheryl told her it belonged to her dad."

"What is it you always say, believe none of what you hear and only half of what you see?" Luke asked.

Jo nodded.

"That fits this whole situation. Sheryl lies about the house, the divorce. The powers in the penitentiary said Ziggy was in for another few years . . . even that was bull."

"He did his time." She tapped the biggest file on her desk. "Cleaned up the fights the last year . . . started to get friendly with those holding the keys. He also managed a consistent visitor."

"Let me guess, Sheryl Brown."

"Bingo."

Luke sat forward, glanced at the names scribbled on the files on her desk. "So what can I do, Jo? We all know Ziggy is going to screw up. Do you know what his parole conditions are?"

"The standard stuff. No alcohol or drug use. Staying away from known criminals or criminal activity. His license was suspended, so he can't drive. Although he might get that privilege back within a few months."

"I don't see him staying away from liquor."

"Me either. And I doubt he'll find a local job, but who knows. The RV plant is hiring."

"Which leaves him right back to 'finding' money off unsuspecting people." Luke used Zoe's words for her father's days as a thief.

Jo glanced at her watch and pushed back from her desk. "I've put Josie on notice if he shows up at R&B's."

If there was any trouble to be found, it would be at R&B's. It was the only real bar in River Bend and close enough to the highway to attract caravanning motorcycle groups several times a year. "Buddy is still working in the kitchen there, right?"

Buddy had corralled him and Wyatt into a bar fight the previous year. He'd been a drifter until he found himself useful in finding the man who was behind Hope's abduction. He was as big as a house and had several priors leading up to the fight, so the fact that he'd helped in finding Hope's abuser shocked many of them. Apparently Buddy was tired of the life he was leading and decided to make a few changes. Working in the bar he'd done his best to bust up had a bit of irony.

"Yep."

"My guess is he's spent enough time with Ziggy's kind to spot them."

"What are you suggesting?"

"Maybe Buddy can keep an eye open. Give me a call if he sees something Josie doesn't."

Jo stepped around her desk, grabbed her jacket off a coat rack by the door. "We can't have enough eyes and boots on the ground. The sooner Ziggy is back in jail, the better for River Bend."

"The better for Zoe." Luke stood and followed Jo out.

"I'd like to think Zoe is back to being a part of this town."

Yeah, he wanted to think that, too.

Zoe watched her mother through the window of Sam's diner for several minutes. Her mom was an attractive woman, more so when she put a little effort into her appearance. Makeup had been a necessity to hide the bruises Ziggy left behind years ago. So it wasn't a surprise to Zoe to see a dusting of foundation over her mother's face. Was it preemptive makeup, something she wanted in place so people wouldn't be surprised to find her painted up once the hits started coming? Or was her mom already catching the wrath of Ziggy's fist?

Zoe wondered how many of the customers in the diner knew the truth about dear old Dad. Right after he'd been sent away, Ziggy had been all the town talked about. Zoe remembered her mother telling her to ignore the gossip and the stares. *People all have issues in the privacy of their own homes.*

As an adult, Zoe translated that to mean everyone had a skeleton they wanted to hide. She'd spent time watching other families and wondering if those dads were hitting their kids. It took a long while to hear someone yelling and not cringe. Even as an adult, Zoe would sometimes freeze when she overheard a heated argument between two strangers.

Her mother must have felt the weight of Zoe's stare. Her eyes lifted from the table she was cleaning off and found hers.

Zoe took the few remaining steps and pushed through the doors of Sam's diner.

The bell announced her arrival and a few heads swiveled her way.

Brenda stood behind the counter, coffeepot in hand. "Hi, Zoe."

"Hey, Brenda."

"I heard you were in town. Stayin' for long?"

Zoe strategically avoided a direct answer. "I'll be in and out. Mel's wedding and all."

Brenda refilled the cup of a customer at the counter. "Don't be a stranger."

Zoe looked directly at her mom. "I won't. Do you mind watching my mom's tables? I need a word."

The diner only had a handful of patrons scattered about. The lunch rush had yet to start.

Sheryl started to protest. "This isn't necessary."

"Really?" Zoe asked, hating the fact that her mom was skirting around the needed conversation. "You don't want to talk in *private*?"

Giving up, Sheryl placed the wet towel on the counter and led Zoe out the back door, away from eyes and ears.

With the grease pit and garbage cans as their backdrop, Zoe gave her mom one more chance.

"What are you doing? Does he have something over you?"

Sheryl wouldn't look her in the eye. "No, nothing like that."

"Then what is it?"

She sucked in a deep breath. "Have you ever loved someone, honey?"

This was worse than she thought. "You're telling me you love that monster?"

"He's not a monster."

"He is! You know he is. We didn't talk about him after he left, but that didn't make what he did to us less real." They'd all kept the past in the past, never really talking about all the crap Ziggy brought with him. They slept better and had far less use for Band-Aids and bags of ice for swollen body parts.

"He wasn't wired for kids, Zoe. You kids were a handful."

Her mother's words soaked in. "You're blaming us."

"No . . . just. It was hard."

"So what's changed? Zanya is still there, Blaze. How long before Ziggy realizes he hates crying babies?"

Sheryl glanced up, only to quickly look away. "Zanya and Mylo are working on getting a place. And your dad doesn't drink anymore."

"He is an asshole even without liquor. You know it, I know it. The whole damn town knows it."

"People can change."

"You're right. People can change . . . monsters like Ziggy, not so much."

Sheryl glared at her now, animosity in her eyes. "I'm sorry you feel that way. But you don't have to worry about him or me . . . you can just go back to your pampered little life and forget all about us."

Zoe didn't think her mother could hurt her more. "My pampered little life?"

With her nose high, Sheryl stared.

"I worked my ass off to get out of this town. To get where I am." Heat filled Zoe's face.

"I guess I didn't do too bad of a job raising you then."

Her mom wanted credit for the good but couldn't take any of the blame for her shitty life decisions that affected them all. "What about Zane? Do you take credit for all the times he ended up in juvenile hall? His lack of graduating from high school? What about Zanya? Do you take credit for her falling into your path of premarital baby making without a way to support her son? Do you take credit for that?"

Her mom scowled. "I did the best I could."

"Sure you did. By staying with the likes of Ziggy, you did your best." Zoe clenched her fists and did everything she could to keep from yelling. "You know, Mom, I always said there is a statute of limitations on how long a person can blame their parents for their fucked-up life. I took that and fell from my family tree and rolled really far down the hill. You did *not* make that happen. I did." She tapped her own chest. "So don't try and take credit for what I've done with my life. If you want to belittle it, fine. But you won't have an audience with me. I came here hoping you'd have a real explanation as to why you're falling back in bed with that man. I guess I got it." And for the first time in Zoe's adult life, she had nothing more to say to her mother.

Chapter Nineteen

Zoe sat on Luke's back porch and watched the final rays of sunshine disappear from the sky. She'd heard his motorcycle announce his arrival after he spent a half a day in the shop.

She was leaving in the morning, and while she hated the fact that she was leaving behind a mess, she understood there wasn't a damn thing she could do about it staying in River Bend.

"Zoe?" Luke called from inside the house.

"Out here."

She glanced over her shoulder when she heard the screen open.

Blue jeans hugged Luke's hips, and a tight black T-shirt stretched over his chest.

She leaned her head back and puckered her lips.

Luke's smile was instant before he reached down to accept her offering. He kissed her, pulled a hair away, and said, "I like this." And then kissed her again.

"How was work?" she asked.

He looked at his hands. "Greasy."

"Dinner is in twenty minutes, if you want to shower."

He pretended to smell under his arms. "Is that a hint?"

Zoe reached for one of his palms. "Yep."

She accepted another kiss before he walked away. "I'm going."

The water in the shower turned on, and Zoe left her perch on Luke's back deck to make the salad.

She'd done everything she could to get her mind off her family. And by everything, that meant she'd cooked.

Luke had a vast supply of sealable rubber containers, which she made good use of. She started with tortilla soup and worked her way into making enchiladas that Luke could toss in the oven to cook on another day. She moved from south of the border to West Texas and a recipe she had for chili and beans. Zoe packed that in the freezer with heating directions taped to the lid. She baked three dozen snickerdoodles and finally placed a small pork roast in the oven for that night. Unable to stop herself, she tossed together a plum sauce for the pork and a carrot puree to go over the potatoes. For the first time in what felt like a week, she was hungry.

She opened a bottle of white wine and sipped while she shredded parmesan cheese for the Caesar salad.

Luke slid a hand over her hip when he walked up behind her. His lips touched the side of her neck. "I could get used to this."

She picked up a crouton, store-bought, unfortunately, and lifted it to Luke's lips. "I leave in the morning."

He crunched on the stale bread and grumbled, "I know."

Zoe missed the heat of him when he walked away and opened his fridge. "What's all this?"

"I can't have you hungry while I'm gone."

He lifted the container holding the soup. "Seriously?"

"I could give it to Mel if you—"

"Hell, no. Mel can get her own." He set the soup back down, grabbed a beer, and closed the door.

She dusted off her hands and reached for the dressing. "Why don't you grab us some plates?"

Luke took a swig and turned to the cabinet where the plates once were.

"One over," she told him.

He gave her a sly smile before he found the plates and put them on his small dining table. They worked together to get the meal on their plates.

She refilled her wine and sat beside him.

"It smells amazing."

"Not something you're going to find at Sam's," she told him.

He used his fork to cut into the tender meat. Zoe watched as he took his first bite.

Luke did an eye roll and moaned. "Oh, man."

"Glad you like it." She took a bite and silently patted herself on the back. She would have liked the tarragon to be fresh, but she did her best with what she had.

Luke filled his fork with the potatoes. "Amazing."

She picked up her wine to help wash down her bite.

"If we get married, will you cook like this every night?"

Zoe felt the wine stick.

Luke was smiling and digging into the next bite.

"If we got married, I'd teach you how to cook."

He waved a fork in the air. "Deal."

He was kidding, she knew he wasn't serious. The dimples in his cheeks etched in from the smile he wore. "What is this?"

"Carrots."

He took another big bite. "I don't like carrots."

She smiled. "Good to know."

He pulled his salad bowl closer. "So how are you feeling about this morning? You look better."

Her morning conversation with her mom weighed on her until about three hours into her cooking spree. Then her mind started to let go. "I'm sure I'll be pissed again tomorrow. But I'm okay right now."

"It's probably good you're going back to Texas."

She knew he hated to say the words, and knew even more he disliked the truth in them.

"I'll be back before you know it."

He moaned over another bite. "Good thing. I'll starve if you don't."

"I saw your refrigerator. You won't starve . . . malnourishment is a serious consideration, however."

Luke shrugged. "I'm not that bad."

"Cold pizza and fried chicken?"

"There's vegetables on pizza."

"Pepperoni and sausage?"

He had the decency to look guilty. "The sauce."

It was Zoe's turn to roll her eyes.

They finished their meal without any more discussion of her mom or Ziggy. Instead, they talked about Mel and Wyatt's wedding and discussed what gifts they should add to the table. He was all about something manly for Wyatt. A beer tap was the brilliant idea in his head. "What about a grill?"

"A barbeque?"

"Yeah," Zoe said.

"He has one."

"What about a wine fridge?"

"Do they drink a lot of wine?"

Zoe lifted her glass. "When I'm in town they do."

"If it will get you to River Bend more, I'm all over it."

She didn't want to think about how much time she'd spend in town with Ziggy residing down the street.

Her heart started to weep at the thought of leaving . . . and it screamed at the thought of staying. Instead of bringing words to her thoughts, Zoe stood to clear their dishes. Tears started to well as she rinsed away plum sauce and carrots.

Luke walked up behind her and removed the plate from her hand before turning off the water.

Without words, she twisted in his arms and let the tears come.

She heard herself sob, and his arms circled hard.

"It's okay, baby . . . let it out."

The sheer anguish in her heart at being let down once again swam like a sea of sludge in her veins.

She muttered obscenities through her tears, cursed the universe in her grief.

Luke let her pound her fist against his chest and blubber all over his shirt.

Tears for a lost childhood morphed into tears she wasn't able to shed when she was battered and broken. Tears for the years she spent away from River Bend chasing a dream . . . for the time she didn't spend with her friends, who were more like family than hers could ever be.

Then those pools of wet spots on Luke's shirt were filled with the loss of what was yet to come. Her father had returned and taken her mother away. Even Zane hadn't answered her calls, leaving her to believe all of her family was gone to her now.

And why?

Because they somehow believed Ziggy had changed. Or maybe they just wanted an excuse to get away from her. She'd worked for years to distance herself from them, perhaps this was the price she had to pay.

By the time her tears had dried up, Luke leaned against the counter and she all but lay on his chest.

He was whispering to her, "You're not alone, baby. I have you."

Even those words kept tears in her eyes.

"I don't deserve you," she uttered.

Luke pushed her hair back, made her look at him. "You deserve the world, if only I could give it to you."

She bit her bottom lip. "I left you." And she wasn't completely sure she wouldn't leave again. The pain in River Bend ran deep.

"Shh." He dropped his lips to hers. Salty tears mixed with the taste of his kiss.

She pushed up, hungry for his touch.

Luke pushed back.

His hunger matched hers, his hands spread in her hair, holding her so she couldn't get away.

Not that she wanted to.

She wanted this. The man who could make her forget about the crazy in her life. The man who could make her feel something other than anguish and hate.

Zoe sucked him in, her hands all over his chest, up his shirt, and down his back. His smooth skin heated along with hers until they couldn't stand the heat and clothes started to find the floor.

Luke's hand dipped over her stomach, his fingers inched inside her jeans.

Zoe unbuttoned her pants and moaned when he found her core. "Yes." She bit his lip when he came back for a kiss.

He curled his finger inside of her and she pushed closer. So good . . . she wanted more.

Working quickly, she pulled Luke's jeans from his hips, used her feet to anchor them so he could step out. All the while he worked her, bringing her painfully close to a powerful orgasm.

"Bedroom," he said in a rough whisper.

She shook her head, dislodged his hand, and pushed him into one of the kitchen chairs. "Here. Now!"

Zoe kicked off her pants, let her underwear follow. In only her bra, she straddled Luke's lap and sank over his erection.

"Holy hell." Luke's expletive matched her thoughts.

He was amazing, perfect, and so damn deep.

She tried to move, and he held her down. "I won't last . . . hold on."
Zoe giggled and tightened the inner muscles surrounding him.
"Damn, woman."

He gave up the fight and lifted her, brought her close again.

Only she had the control, with leverage on her side.

She rode him, hard.

His teeth sank into her breast over her bra, exciting her more. The slick slide of their bodies brought them closer until Zoe couldn't catch her breath and every nerve centered where their bodies became one. She was close, the chair they assaulted creaked, making her think for a moment that it might break. Then her body shattered, clenching Luke in a power unlike any she'd experienced before.

Then she heard his moan and felt the rush of his body as he reached his release.

He carried her lax body to his bed and tucked her into the crook of his arm.

Zoe curled into him, completing his world. "It doesn't get better than that, does it?"

"I don't know how it can," he said.

"We might have broken your chair."

"I'll build a pedestal and make it hillbilly art in the backyard."

Zoe laughed and ran her fingers over his chest. "We left the kitchen a mess."

"I'll clean it in the morning."

"Such a bad habit," she said, her words drifting as the day caught up with her. "Thank you for being here, Luke. I don't know what I would do if—"

He cut her off with a finger to her lips.

She opened her eyes and looked up at him.

"There is no other place I'd rather be."

Zoe kissed him and curled back up.

He felt her breathing even out and her hand grow lax on his chest and knew she'd found her dreams.

As he felt his own eyes drifting closed, he realized two things.

First, he missed Zoe already. She hadn't left, and he was already counting the days for her return. And second . . . they'd failed to use a condom.

Chapter Twenty

Luke stepped into R&B's hours after he left Zoe at the airport. Saying good-bye was starting to become impossible. He'd stumbled out of bed that morning to Zoe cleaning the kitchen.

She'd slept better than she had the night before, but there were still dark circles under her eyes. Probably a byproduct of crying for an hour before they'd made love.

When he brought up their lack of latex the previous night, Zoe assured him she was on birth control pills. He seemed to remember her saying that before but didn't want her feeling alone if something were to happen.

Zoe removed his concern by suggesting they conserve water and shower together. By the time they stepped out of the bathroom, he'd spent his desire inside her a second time and vowed to throw away all his condoms so long as she was the only one in his life.

R&B's was crowded for a Wednesday night. The parking lot full of Harleys indicated a club riding through. Luke wasn't surprised to find clean-cut middle-aged men drinking light beer and playing pool.

He found an empty stool at the bar and waved Josie over.

In her midforties, Josie ruled her bar in Daisy Duke shorts in the summer and skintight jeans in the winter. Today she showed a little midriff when she reached above her head to grab a bottle of Grey Goose from the top shelf. Luke had always thought she was an attractive woman, if not a little old for him. He often wondered why she wasn't married, but not enough to ask.

"Well, look who showed up." Josie reached across the bar and gave him a hug.

"Zoe flew out this morning."

"Oh, God, no . . . no bar fights," she teased.

He deserved that. Zoe leaving in the past had resulted in bad behavior on his part. "She'll be back in three weeks for the wedding."

Josie pulled her long brown hair behind her shoulder. "You look happy."

It was hard not to smile. "I am."

She used the rag in her hand to clean the space in front of him. "What's your poison?"

He ordered his favorite on tap and looked around while he waited for her to come back.

She was back in less than two minutes. The beer felt cool in his throat.

"I heard about Ziggy. That really sucks."

"Zoe is pretty torn up about it."

"I can't imagine. And what the hell is Sheryl thinking?"

"That's the ten-thousand-dollar question everyone is asking."

Someone from the other end of the bar called for her attention. Josie waved a hand in acknowledgment.

"Ziggy isn't welcome here, though I'd be half tempted to serve him and then have his ass thrown back."

Luke lifted his glass. "Not a bad plan."

Josie tapped the bar and moved away.

Luke swiveled around in his chair and searched the room for familiar faces.

Principal Mason and his adult son sat at a small table by the jukebox.

Matt, his partner in bar-fighting crime, sat sucking on a longneck and flirting with a woman who wasn't his wife.

There were a couple of young faces he recognized that he couldn't place names to, kids who were just twenty-one and drinking on a Wednesday night in a bar because they could.

Waterville was starting to reach closer to River Bend, putting faces into the mix Luke didn't recognize. Growth was important, or small towns like River Bend would fold in a bad economy. Considering they'd managed to stay afloat in one of the worst economic decades since the twenties, River Bend wasn't doing too bad.

Places like Josie's bar were busy midweek as a result.

Luke picked up his drink and walked around the opposite side of the bar, toward the kitchen. He watched the window where the waitress or Josie would toss up a food order . . . food being a loose term for the fried menu items R&B's had to offer. Still, he watched until he saw Buddy peek over from his side.

Luke raised his beer. "Hey, Buddy."

"Busy night," Buddy said, placing an order of fries up in the window and ringing a bell.

Considering the man had done his best to kick the shit out of Luke not long ago, they'd managed to be friendly.

"Can I take a minute of your time?"

Buddy looked around the kitchen and nodded toward the service entrance.

Luke set his beer down and met Buddy in a quieter part of the bar.

After the two shook hands, Luke got straight to the point. "Have you heard about Ziggy Brown?"

"Josie brought him up in a staff meeting. Haven't met the man."

Luke fished his phone out of his back pocket and found the picture he'd gotten off his record in Jo's office.

"He's a complete dirtbag. Beat up on his kids, his wife before he ended up in jail."

Buddy wasn't one to get involved unless kids were part of the equation.

"Everyone has a past."

"Maybe. But he's back, and his grandson is in his home. I'd hate to see something happen to the kid."

Buddy was a big man. That, coupled with the heat of the kitchen, had him sweating and wiping his forehead with the back of his hand.

"Grown men shouldn't hit kids."

"Couldn't agree more. I was hoping if you saw him . . . saw anything you thought didn't look right, you'd give me a call."

Buddy narrowed his eyes. "This kid yours?"

Luke shook his head. "No . . . nothing like that. My girlfriend's nephew. She's given her sister an out, but she hasn't taken it yet."

Buddy glanced back at the picture with a slow nod. "Doesn't hurt keeping your eyes open."

Luke shook his hand. "Thanks. I appreciate it."

With a quick nod, Buddy walked back into the kitchen.

Luke moved to retrieve his beer, found something floating on the top, and abandoned it.

He started to leave the bar and found the whites of Zane Brown's eyes. Zane turned around and walked away.

Luke double-timed out the door, skirting around bikers and a few men who'd had one too many drinks before reaching the cold of the night. He scanned the parking lot to see Zane jumping into a car.

Luke managed to get to his side before he could turn the key.

"Zane! Hold up."

A flash of disappointment floated over Zane's face before he offered a half-assed smile. "Hey, Luke."

Luke left a hand on the roof of the car. "How are you doing?"

Zane looked a lot like his dad . . . younger, without the gray hair, but there wasn't any mistaking his DNA. "Good. I'm good. You?"

"It's been a rough week." There was no point in lying to him. "Zoe left for Texas today."

Zane nodded like one of those bobblehead dolls. "Yeah, I heard she was in town. I'm in Waterville most days. Work . . . you know."

It was obvious Zoe's brother wasn't going to come forward with anything about Ziggy, so Luke brought up the elephant in River Bend. "How do you feel about your dad being back in town?"

Zane glanced at his phone as if he was checking the time. "I don't know. Bound to happen at some point. It's not like he murdered someone."

Not yet. "Zoe's worried. Thinks your mom letting him come back is a mistake."

With his hands wrapped around the steering wheel, Zane leveled his gaze to Luke. "Zoe isn't—" He stopped himself. "I get it . . . but my dad . . . he deserves a chance."

Luke felt his hands fist.

"I'd imagine you'd want to see him as a changed man."

"Not everyone has the perfect family, Luke. Some of us grew up with less, and that shit's stressful."

It was obvious Zane wasn't going to hear anything Luke had to say.

He straightened up, removed his hand from Zane's car. "You know where I am."

"Yeah . . . I gotta go."

He did, wheels kicking up gravel in R&B's parking lot.

Zoe ruined four plates and an entire pot of orange sauce for the duck before she tossed in her apron and left her kitchen.

She might be in Texas, but her thoughts were in River Bend. The good parts of her life, the crappy parts of her life . . . all of it. She sat in the break room of the restaurant, ignoring the stares of the waiters who walked in. This wasn't a space she often occupied outside of staff meetings where she discussed the menu and had everyone try new dishes. A half an hour ticked by with her telling herself to get it together.

In the end, she removed her purse from her locker, made her apologies to her sous chef, and stepped out the back door.

En route to her favorite dive bar, she texted Felix and begged an audience. Not that she needed to beg—the man loved to drink.

Still, she sat at the bar with her purse in the seat beside her, waiting for her favorite director and nursing a rum and Coke.

"Hey, I haven't seen you in weeks."

Zoe twisted to see Raymond. She opened her arms for a hug. "How are you?"

"Same job, different day." He glanced at the space beside her. "This seat taken?"

She grabbed her purse. "Soon. He isn't here yet."

Raymond thumbed toward an empty seat down the bar. "It's okay . . . I can—"

"Don't be silly. Sit. Felix is always late."

He sat down, glanced around. "Where's your friend?"

"My friend?"

"The blonde. The one that likes the big guys?"

"Oh, Jo . . . she doesn't live around here."

He lifted his chin. "Out of town friend?"

"Yeah . . . so how are you? How's your wife?"

"Good." He waved at the bartender. "Same, but what can I do?"

Zoe sipped her drink. "I'm sorry I ran out that night."

"It's okay. That looked intense. Hope it all worked out all right."

She smiled. "Seems to be. I've known Luke a long time."

The bartender made his way over and took Raymond's order. "So, Luke . . . does he live close by? I've never seen him in here before."

"No, no . . . he lives in Oregon."

"Oregon? Really, whereabouts?"

"River Bend. Small town—"

Raymond sat up taller. "I know River Bend . . . it's next to Waterville."

Zoe's jaw dropped. "You know Waterville?"

"Yeah. I had family there for years."

"That's crazy. Such a small world. I grew up in River Bend."

Raymond smiled and shook his head. "What are the chances of that? How on earth did you end up in Dallas?"

The answer to that was easy, considering the time in her life that she'd left. "It wasn't River Bend."

Raymond nodded in understanding.

Zoe turned back to her drink and noticed how little was left in her glass.

"Can I get you another?"

"I shouldn't, but . . ."

Raymond laughed and flagged the bartender.

Chapter Twenty-One

"Wild child turned cop . . . what are the chances of that?"

If Jo had ever felt a desire to pull her weapon on a person out of pure spite, it was when Ziggy Brown opened the door.

"Mr. Brown."

"JoAnne Ward . . . spittin' image of your daddy, uniform and all." If Ziggy had left it at that, she might consider his words a compliment. Instead, he let his eyes run down her body, linger back up over her chest, then shift to her eyes.

Jo hiked her sunglasses higher and pretended not to notice.

"Is Zanya here?" Jo already knew the answer but wanted to get the man talking so she could grow accustomed to his voice . . . notice the difference if he was drinking or under the influence of something other than soda.

"She and my adorable little grandbaby are visiting his father."

Jo wanted to heave.

"And Sheryl?"

"I'm guessing you know she's at work. Hard to miss her car in the lot as you pass by, *Sheriff*."

Well, at least he had her title right.

"And how are you doing?" she asked. "Adjusting to civilian life?"

Ziggy Brown ran both hands through his hair. The muscles across his chest flexed. "I am. I learned a lot on the inside. I have your father to thank for that, you know. He had a hand at putting me away."

Jo took an involuntary step back before stopping herself.

The shift of Ziggy's eyes said he noticed her hesitation.

"There's a whole lot of preaching that happens in prison. Did you know that, JoAnne?"

"It's Sheriff Ward, Mr. Brown."

He put his hands to his sides. "Of course. I mean no disrespect. It's just hard, thinking of how you were growing up, running with my daughter. You're both so grown up now. Willful . . . anyway . . . lots of God-fearing men on the inside. I suppose that's to be expected."

"Are you trying to tell me you found God?"

"In some ways I do think I have."

And in others? she wanted to ask but didn't. He was full of shit from the snark-filled smile on his face to the way his arm flexed, holding the door.

The man was attempting to intimidate her.

"Well, Mr. Brown, I'm here to tell you that Oregon's Department of Corrections has informed me of your parole conditions. I'll be in constant contact with your parole officer in Eugene and will accept nothing less than one hundred percent on your part in keeping your nose out of trouble."

Ziggy looked her up and down and made more than one hair on her body stand on end. "Is that right?"

"No wiggle room, Ziggy." For the first time in their conversation, she used the name he went by.

He didn't stop staring. "I'll be the perfect little ex-con, Sheriff." He lifted three fingers in the air. "Scout's honor."

With clenched teeth, she took a backward step off the porch.

It wasn't until she was back in her car that she took a deep breath.

Ziggy stood on the porch, grin on his face, as she backed out of the drive. She made a mental note to have Deputy Emery with her on future visits to the Brown home. If there was one person she expected bad things from, it was Ziggy Brown.

Summer was in full, heated swing in Dallas, complete with humidity that sucked the air out of your lungs the second you left your air-conditioned car. The space between your car and the building you entered was always a challenge.

Even the dogs sitting on front porches appeared too tired to lift their heads and bark. This time of year always ate at Zoe and had her booking trips to Europe or even somewhere in the tropics where she could at least sit on a beach, sipping an adult beverage or two.

As she drove around the neighborhood she'd considered moving to just a few months prior, she thought about how she would escape the heat once she had a home to consider and not just an apartment. Affording to travel wouldn't be the problem, but leaving the responsibility might prove difficult.

The humidity in Oregon, even on the coast, was nothing like that in Texas. Not to mention how cool the nights would get. She thought of Luke's backyard and the open window over the sink.

Yeah . . . that didn't happen in Dallas in the summer. You turned the AC on and ignored the thermostat for months. There were storms that would blow through, some of them cool enough to open a window, but as soon as the clouds parted, the humidity pushed in.

Zoe turned a corner and noticed a handful of kids, not more than eight or nine years old, playing on a front lawn.

A sprinkler connected to a hose was all the entertainment they needed. A dog ran around their heels, barking.

Would her kids run in the sprinklers? Would they have a dog? How could she get a dog if she couldn't stand the heat and left the state for weeks on end?

Where on earth had the thought of kids popped into her head from? She'd be a terrible mother. Lord knew she had an awful example of how to parent a child. Besides, growing up without any family help was no way to live if you didn't have to.

Her grandfather on Ziggy's side was long gone, left her grandmother early enough that Ziggy had no memory of the man. Zoe always thought that was part of her dad's problem. He hadn't had a male role model and didn't know how to be a man without using his fists and the testosterone in his veins. Her grandmother moved around enough to have Christmas cards kick back every other year.

Her mom's parents were still alive. Divorced . . . but that seemed to be the theme in Zoe's life when it came to her family. Her grandfather had remarried, but his new wife wanted nothing to do with them, therefore the Brown children never had a relationship with the only grandfather they could ever know.

Grandma Workman went out of her way to keep in touch with them. She'd send the occasional birthday card and care package for Christmas. Only Grandma Workman lived in San Francisco in a tiny studio apartment. Zoe knew there were times Sheryl hit Grandma up for money, but there wasn't much to give.

Once *Warring Chef* hit the air, Uncle Don, Sheryl's brother, had sent a letter—the kind that required a stamp—saying he was happy for her. Still, the relationship never moved from there.

Zoe had a Christmas card uncle and grandmother . . . that was it. No one else to say they were family.

There weren't many times in Zoe's life that she thought about having children of her own. The thought of bringing them into her life with such screwed-up grandparents felt wrong. So Zoe worked on being an independent woman who didn't need a family to support her for anything.

Only now, with drama once again nipping at the edges of every day, Zoe leaned on Luke, on Jo and Mel. Miss Gina sent her text messages several times a week, asking how she was holding up. Even Luke's mom had shown up right before leaving River Bend the last time to give her a hug and tell her she was there to listen if she ever needed to talk.

She realized she'd been sitting in an idling car watching someone else's kids while all these forgotten thoughts ran in her head.

Zoe dialed Anton's number and waited for him to pick up.

It went to voice mail.

"Hi, Anton, it's Zoe. I'm sorry, but I'm going to suspend my search for a home in Dallas for now. My life is a little complicated to add this to my plate. I'll let you know if I pick up the search again." Zoe drove away from the nameless kids playing and didn't look back.

"I'm flying to New York in the morning."

Luke leaned against the workbench in the garage with the shop phone to his ear. "Are these new plans? I don't remember you saying you were going."

"Spur-of-the-moment plans. I need to see my agent."

He liked when she talked business. The confidence in her voice was a nice change from the defeated woman she was when talking about her family. "Sounds important."

"It might be. I'm thinking of diversifying."

"Which means?"

"Promise you won't laugh."

"Unless you tell me you're joining the circus, I won't laugh."

There was enough silence on the line Luke thought she wasn't going to tell him.

"I'm . . . ah . . . I'm thinking of writing a book. A cookbook."

He grinned. "Why would I laugh at that? I think it's a perfect idea."

"It is, isn't it? I also thought I would do a series of videos . . . maybe web based, or perhaps an actual made for TV spotlight featuring some of the recipes. I was talking to Felix, and we thought up several different angles to do this big."

The excitement in her voice gave his heart a jolt. "So how does this involve your agent?"

"I talked with her over the phone, and she's set up a couple of meetings with publishers. I've never published anything. Since this is new ground for me, I wanted to see these people face-to-face so I know who I'm dealing with."

Luke listened while she told him about one of her contracts where she'd ended up hating the producer and fighting with him every time she was on set.

"It sounds like you're taking a smart approach."

"There's no hurry, so why not make sure I can work with these people?"

"Good plan. I have a hard time wrapping my head around all the decisions you've had to make in the last ten years." It made him even more proud of her when he heard the process she had to go through to "diversify," as she called it.

"In the beginning it was easy . . . if it involved a paycheck, I was in. According to Suki and Felix, I can pick and choose now and ask for more."

"I'm proud of you, baby."

He heard her sigh. "That means a lot, coming from you."

"Can I do anything?"

"Have you ever published a cookbook?"

He laughed. "I haven't even used a cookbook."

Zoe joined his mirth. "How is everything there?"

It had only been a week since she'd left. "Quiet."

"I'm not sure if that's good."

"Me either. Jo's watching . . . everyone is listening. Have you talked with your sister or Zane?"

"I left a message for Zane, he didn't call back. Have you seen them?"

He considered keeping the conversation he'd had with Zane to himself. Instead, he gave Zoe the CliffsNotes version, even though he knew it would hurt her.

"Seems like everyone in that house forgot what a scumbag the man is."

"It won't be long before you can tell them all you told them so."

"That isn't what I want."

Luke switched the phone to his other ear. "I know it isn't. So tell me about New York. Is it like everyone says it is?"

"New York is crazy . . ."

There was a lift to her voice with the change of subject.

By the time he got off the phone, he made her promise to call him at the end of her day when she was in New York to tell him all about the experience so he could live it with her.

He turned back to the car he was working on with a smile.

The trailer was too fucking quiet.

After seventeen years of noise . . . grown men crying, yelling, grunting as they jacked off or moaning as they violated their bunkmates . . . the quiet was killing him.

Sheryl was at that nothing job at the diner, and Zanya and her brat were gone when his wife worked.

Ziggy was making up for lost time between Sheryl's legs, even though she complained about being sore after the first week he'd been back. She knew better than to argue, a lesson he'd taught her before the kids were born.

Ziggy had gone out of his way sweet-talkin' her when he was on the inside.

He had no choice. Intimidation wasn't an option when she could walk away.

He liked having the upper hand, having control. That control was slowly coming back. It was different this time. A quiet control that didn't require him to move too many muscles to gain.

The four walls of his piece of crap home were starting to fold in on him. What the hell did he do with his time seventeen years ago? The guys he ran with used to live in Waterville. One skirted alongside Ziggy in maximum lockup for a good five years, and his other buddy moved north into Montana or some nowhere place.

Ziggy turned up the volume on the TV. Damn wife didn't pay for cable so all he had was fucking soap operas and talk shows all day long. The noise from those shows wasn't enough to fill his head.

What he needed was an occupation.

And that didn't mean work.

No one in River Bend would hire him to pick up dog shit, and Waterville . . . yeah, best stay clear of that town. He had a healthy fear of going back to jail. After he was transferred to maximum, he realized where he'd gone wrong.

Ziggy Brown wouldn't be holding up any mini-marts again. Seventeen years of his life gone for a fucking mini-mart.

Laughter from the other inmates at his weak crime caused many fights. He showed them often how strong he was. Part of the reason he'd been moved around inside the system.

Then he met Axel.

Axel shared the same temper and power behind his fists. They'd fought once, both ended up in their version of the hole for a week, then walked side by side for the better part of ten years. Axel had shown Ziggy how to control his words and actions to appear more calm than he was. It made parole hearings more agreeable, kept the other inmates on their toes . . . and eventually gave Ziggy the ability to leave.

Axel wasn't up to leave for another two years, maybe less.

They'd get together . . . share a few drinks. Consider their options. Ziggy knew he couldn't stay in River Bend. Damn town watched him like he was a fish swimming in a bowl. Especially little JoAnne Ward. It took all his effort not to laugh at that bitch when he saw her. Nose up in the air, hand on her gun.

Laughable.

Completely laughable.

Yet every time he heard a car go by, a glance out the window showed the taillights of a squad car. Thanks to his uppity daughter, who he clearly didn't teach enough lessons to growing up, the only law in River Bend was watching.

While he wasn't scared of the little girl the town called Sheriff, Sheryl and the rest of them were.

Damn, it was quiet.

Ziggy scratched his nuts and looked at the clock. He needed to fuck . . . well, he needed a drink, but there wasn't any alcohol in the trailer. His parole officer set him up with the right people to reinstate his drivers license, all dependent on a drug free cup full of urine.

Once he could drive, he'd work his way into Eugene and fill up.

For now, he was no better off than he had been in jail. Yeah, he could leave the house, but go where and do what?

Just a few more steps and he'd have all the real freedom he needed.

He looked out the window. Where the hell was his wife?

Chapter Twenty-Two

Zoe wore a little black power dress, Jimmy Choos on her feet, and a smile on her face. The view from Bar SixtyFive in Rockefeller Center was out of this world. The martini wasn't bad either.

"You're making the right decision," Suki said.

"I haven't made one yet."

"You're picking between three publishers for the book and have two producers who want to wine and dine you to follow you around with cameras. I'd say you can't make a bad decision. This is all about your gut at this point."

"I want to hear what your literary agent friends say about each publisher. And I do mean everything. Especially the bad stuff. Adversity will happen, how they handle it is going to determine if we can have a good working relationship."

"You're too young to be so wise, Zoe."

"I'm older than my years." Last week she felt like she was sixty. "I want to do this right. Let's keep my income the same, or better, without my time at Nahana."

"You're going to have to travel a little more."

She nodded. "I can do that."

Suki sat back, crossed her legs, and sipped her drink. "So what is all this about, anyway? Are you tired of Texas?"

Zoe looked out the window. "I think I've outgrown Texas."

"So where do you think you'll land?"

Her mind went straight to Luke's house. "Where do successful chefs end up?"

"That depends. Some own their own restaurants in big cities. Some go home to open up a niche boutique setting or teach. I don't see you teaching quite yet."

"Not without a camera. God, I sound like a diva."

"You're amazing in front of the lens. No need to be shy about it."

"There are a lot of chefs on the TV."

"And you're one of them . . . and you're not going anywhere. Tell me what your goals are, and I'll see what I can do to make them happen."

"I told you. I want to stop the daily meal planning and weekend shifts at Nahana."

"What about opening your own place?"

"I don't know about that. Not yet."

"Someday?"

Zoe pictured River Bend. "I wouldn't know where. I think I need to land somewhere and have it feel like home before I can dedicate that kind of time and money."

"Yeah, but shouldn't you plan for the probability of it? If the cookbook takes off and the vignettes on film fill your time, you'll be pulling in some serious money."

Zoe couldn't help but like that thought. "I'll deal with how to spend the money once I'm making it."

Suki lifted her drink and sat forward. "To making it."

Zoe clinked her glass. When her gaze moved back out the window, she wondered if Luke would like the view.

~

Zoe skipped having Luke pick her up at the airport. She needed a car on this trip, so renting one in Eugene and driving into River Bend was a much better option. She rented an SUV so she had room to pack it with whatever, whoever. The whoever started with Felix.

The man traveled like people had in the twenties. From the fedora that covered his bald spot to his loafers, the fancy, pinstriped slacks and button-up shirt, Felix was always ready to find the love of his life. Sorry to say he wasn't going to find him in River Bend.

His suitcase matched the size of hers, and she was staying longer.

"I like this better already," he said as he climbed into the passenger seat.

"This is Eugene."

"The weather, darling. The weather."

"Let's hope this holds out. I'd hate for Mel's wedding to get rained on." Zoe slid behind the wheel and parted ways with the parking lot.

"Tell me again . . . how far is the lot for our crew from the bed-and-breakfast?"

Zoe had arranged space for the crew trailers on Grayson's farm, which sat between town and Miss Gina's. There weren't enough rooms at the inn to house all of them, she told him, ". . . but there is room for the production trailer on-site."

"You're sure the city won't have an issue with us being there?"

Zoe laughed. "You are greatly overestimating the concept of *city*. And no . . . Jo has already talked with the neighbors, and no one holds any issue with 'movie making' in River Bend."

Felix set his head back and closed his eyes. "We don't make movies."

"That isn't what they think."

Zoe's current producer agreed to a segment surrounding a wedding. With his approval came his money and the ability for Zoe to bring in a team of prep cooks and help for Mel and Wyatt's reception.

The only cost to Mel and Wyatt was the actual food. Even then Zoe pulled a few favors and had much of it sent in at a huge discount.

Her thoughts had been on the wedding, the prep for the reception, but her family drama sat on the sideline, waiting for an audience. "I'm going to apologize now for any drama my family causes while we're here."

Felix rolled his head to the side and looked her way. "You don't need to do that."

"I do. From lifestyle choices to looks . . . there is bound to be someone talkin' smack. I'm hoping to avoid the lot of them, but I doubt that will happen."

Felix reached over and touched her hand. "Zoe, m'dear. I've been gay my whole life. I've lived with comments, laughter, and flat-out nastiness from my family. I expect nothing less from yours."

She patted his hand. "Thanks."

He turned back around and leaned back. "So how long of a drive do we have?"

"Two hours."

"Wake me before we drive in . . . I want to experience River Bend at the city limits."

Zoe turned onto the highway and increased the volume of the radio once Felix started to snore.

Maybe this wouldn't turn out ugly after all.

"Now this! This is a kitchen! Zoe, why didn't you tell me how charming this was?" Felix gushed over Miss Gina and the outside of the inn before walking in like he owned the place. "I see great things."

Miss Gina grinned ear to ear. "I like this one, Zoe."

"Oh, has she been bringing other directors around I should know about?"

"Of course," Miss Gina lied. "You don't think you're the only man in her life, do you?"

Miss Gina and Felix were from the same generation . . . or close to it. "I can tell this is going to be very entertaining," Zoe said.

"I think two cameras and one stationary from the pot rack." Felix did what Felix did . . . he muttered instructions, only there wasn't anyone there to make notes. "When is September arriving?"

"In the morning, along with Rupert and the rest of the crew."

They were driving from Dallas and had headed out two days before.

"We might need a wide angle to capture the whole space."

Miss Gina leaned on Zoe's arm. "Is he saying my kitchen is fat?"

Zoe laughed and turned when she heard Hope running in from the backyard, Sir Knight at her heels.

"Auntie Zoe!"

She knelt down and picked up Hope in a hug. "You're getting too big for this."

"That's what Daddy said."

Hearing Hope refer to Wyatt as her daddy warmed her soul. The girl deserved the best daddy ever, and Wyatt fit the bill.

The back screen door slammed against the frame, announcing the arrival of Mel and Wyatt. "Look what the wind blew in." Mel moved in for a hug.

Zoe pulled back. "You look so damn happy."

"Swear jar!" Hope ran out of the room to retrieve the silly thing.

The adults laughed and Zoe made the introductions.

Felix embraced them both as if he knew them and talked about how he planned to make Miss Gina's Bed-and-Breakfast a hit, starting with their wedding.

By the time they moved from the kitchen to the living room, the front door framed Luke.

He stood there watching her; only her.

Zoe sucked in an unexpected breath and held it until she reached him. His arms slid around her back, his lips found hers for a proper hello.

They broke apart when Hope walked down the stairs, saying, "Eww . . . why is everyone kissing all the time?"

"It's in the air," Luke explained, his arm stayed snug on Zoe's hip.

Hope shoved the swear jar in Zoe's personal space. "A quarter for the *D* word."

Zoe rolled her eyes and moved to where she'd left her purse.

"Now that is a very enterprising idea, young lady. Be sure and stick around when we're filming, you're bound to make a ton of money," Felix told her.

"And come out cussing like a sailor," Zoe added.

"I think maybe Hope should stay clear of that." Mel encouraged Hope to sit close to her.

Hope tipped her jar and looked at the coins inside. "I make enough off Miss Gina. She cusses a lot."

Miss Gina's mouth dropped wide. "I do not!"

Everyone laughed except Felix.

While Felix set up production in Miss Gina's kitchen, Zoe directed a team in Sam's kitchen at the diner.

Ernie and Tiffany, her seconds on set, followed her into Sam's diner after two o'clock the following day.

A sign on the door of the diner said they were closed the day of Mel and Wyatt's wedding and for dinner the night before.

Sam met her at the door with a hug. His welcome made her feel at home. "My kitchen is yours."

"You're just saying that because you want a free meal."

Sam patted his overextended belt line. "I can always use a good meal."

Zoe laughed. "Tiffany and Ernie will be doing most of the cooking."

"Any friends of yours are friends of mine."

Zoe did a quick scan of the diner.

Sam lowered his voice. "She has the dinner shift."

For some strange reason, tears filled her eyes. She didn't want to see her mother, and it seemed most of the town knew that. "Thanks."

She led Tiffany and Ernie into the first commercial kitchen she'd ever worked in. Sam had cleaned it. His effort lifted her heavy heart.

"Your shipments started arriving this morning."

Zoe opened the massive refrigerators and found familiar supplies. She went through the inventory with Tiffany and Ernie standing close by, taking notes on what to expect. They went over the menu and discussed capacity of the ovens and storage.

Brenda welcomed her through the window while she tossed up an order. Sam flipped frozen hamburger patties on the grill.

Ernie and Tiffany exchanged glances but kept their comments to themselves. There was a difference between a cook and a chef. Sam had no issues with that. He liked the fact that Zoe Brown's journey from cook to chef had started in his kitchen. Liked it even more when she was in town and helped fill the booths of his diner.

"We should have the fresh herbs in with the shipment, but if something isn't right, let me know. I know a few people in town with gardens who can help in a pinch."

Zoe pointed out issues in the kitchen she knew she'd had problems with in the past. One of the ovens ran hot, and one of refrigerators ran too cold no matter how many times Sam had it fixed. "I don't need frozen romaine."

"Who is going to be here from the staff?" Tiffany asked.

"Sam?" Zoe caught his attention. "Who did you assign to help?"

"Brenda volunteered. As long as she can watch the wedding."

"All the food will be at the inn by then." Or close enough to it.

They talked about when they could dominate the space and the time span for preparation.

By the time Zoe was leaving the diner, it was just before four.

Just when she thought she'd skirt out of Sam's before seeing her mother, the woman nearly knocked down Tiffany as they were walking out the back door.

Sheryl stepped back, instantly irritated. "Who are . . ." Her eyes caught Zoe's and her words stopped short.

Tiffany and Ernie had expectant faces.

Zoe didn't feed them with an introduction.

Anxiety crawled up Zoe's throat. "Hello," was all that came out.

Her mom offered a quick nod and stepped around them and into the diner.

Zoe released a deep sigh and felt dizzy as she exited the building.

"Who was that?" Tiffany asked a few steps away from the car.

Zoe yanked open the door. "My mother."

The lights of Sheryl's car shone into the windows as she pulled it into the drive.

"'Bout fucking time," Ziggy muttered to himself.

His hand was already adjusting his jeans to make room. He'd made Zanya go to her room with her baby hours ago. The smell of diapers never did anything for him. And Zane was due back before midnight.

A little noise, a nice toss in bed, and he'd be ready for something to eat.

Sheryl stepped inside without a whole lot of sound.

"Hey, sugar."

She must not have seen him sitting there, because she jumped, and her hand went to her throat.

"What's wrong, you forgot I'm back already?"

She shook her head, looked around the room. "Didn't want to wake you if you were asleep."

He picked himself up off the couch and made his way to her side.

She smelled like hamburgers and greasy fries. He caged her hips in his hands and ground his groin into hers. "Now you know I can't sleep all pent up." He pushed in closer. "Look what you do to me, sugar." He nuzzled her neck and she tried to pull away.

He didn't let her go far, but looked at her face for the first time since she'd walked in the door.

The black shit she put on her eyes ran in streaks down her cheeks. "Why are you crying?" Who was screwing up his night?

"I'm fine. A little tired." She tried to pull away again.

His cock protested. He had one thing he looked forward to, and her tears were not going to stop him from getting it.

"Fine, then. Let me help you out of those jeans." His hand was already in her waistband.

"Ziggy, please. I'm tired. It's been a long day." She twisted away and ducked out from under his touch.

The muscles on his arms flexed, but he kept his finger loose. "Long day? *You've* had a long day?"

Sheryl had the good mind to hesitate. "Yeah." She moved into the kitchen, set her purse on the counter next to the dirty dishes. "Zoe's in town."

"So this is about that prissy daughter of yours."

"Ours."

He rubbed the side of his groin to keep the anger from affecting his abilities. "You raised her."

Sheryl mumbled something and turned away.

"You have something to say?" His voice rose above the noise of the television.

"I—I said I'd make you something to eat."

Ziggy forced his teeth not to sink into each other and slowly followed her into the kitchen. "Is that what you said?"

Sheryl turned her back on him. Her bony ass pushed out when she opened the refrigerator and reached for a gallon of milk.

He grasped her elbow and put just enough pressure to keep her from picking crap from the fridge. "I don't think that's what you said. Would you like to try again?"

The fear in her face when she looked at him now was a much better image than a moment before.

"Let me cook you dinner."

"I don't want dinner." He pushed her against the counter, made sure she knew exactly what he was going to get before he ate. "And you need to stop lying. You know how I feel about lying."

She lowered her head. "I'm sorry. It's a hard day is all. I'm tired."

"Hard?" He pushed a knee between her legs. "I'll tell you what's hard. Seventeen years with only your hand to fuck, and then when you get out, have your woman telling you she's *tired*."

A squeak behind them had Sheryl looking beyond his shoulder.

"It's okay, Zanya. Go back to bed."

Out of the corner of his eye, Ziggy noticed that Zanya didn't move.

"You heard your mother!" He didn't hold his voice down.

"Mom?"

He twisted around and Sheryl grabbed his hips. "Go on now, Zanya."

Ziggy lifted his lips when Zanya turned away.

"Now, let's talk about how tired you are." He pushed a hand into Sheryl's pants, and this time she didn't push him away.

Chapter Twenty-Three

"I wouldn't go in there if I were you."

Luke passed Mel on the porch en route to the kitchen.

"That bad?"

"She's yelling at Felix."

Luke paused, waiting for the bad part. "And?"

"That's her director."

Luke lowered his sunglasses and winked. "I think I'm safe."

Mel went back to the magazine in her lap. "It's your skin she'll chomp on."

He laughed. "I kinda like it when she chomps on my skin."

"Men!" was all Mel said as he walked into the inn and straight to where all the noise came from.

The smell of something sinfully sweet mixed with bright lights and more people shoved into Miss Gina's kitchen than Luke had ever seen.

"Oh, thank God. Luke, tell her she's gorgeous." Felix nearly jumped on Luke the second he peeked his head around the corner.

"He has to say that, I'm sleeping with him." Zoe glanced around September, who was putting powder on her face.

A few people behind the cameras laughed.

So did Luke.

Instead of giving Felix satisfaction, he stepped over cords and boxes and moved into Zoe's production space.

She was stunning. A little more makeup than he cared for, but he knew the need for it on film. He saw the tired under her eyes, which was probably what she didn't care for.

"Something isn't quite right," he said.

Felix grunted and September stepped aside to give him room.

"I told you," Zoe said over Luke's shoulder.

"Let me see . . ." He dipped his finger in the frosting she was working with, placed a dab on her lips.

"Luke," she gasped.

Then, before she could say anything, he kissed some of the frosting off.

She giggled under his touch. When she tried to back away, he placed a hand on her neck and held her from going too far. Then he licked the rest of the frosting off her lips.

He felt some of her tension leave her shoulders.

Luke sat back, looked at her. "Much better."

She licked the remaining frosting off her own lips and smiled. "You're terrible."

"You're beautiful." He dipped another finger into the frosting before filling his mouth. "This is amazing."

"Okay, let's get this over with," she said.

Felix slumped in his chair. "Finally."

Luke backed out of her space and watched from the edges of the makeshift set.

For the next hour, he stood in place and watched Zoe's world revolve around her. He couldn't feel more pride for the woman.

When they called the filming done for the day, two people Luke recognized but whose names he couldn't recall stepped in and started to put together more of the dishes that Zoe had made for the purpose of filming.

Luke was surprised to hear her say, "I just need to change, I'll be back to help."

"Take your time."

He followed her out of the kitchen. "You have to be tired."

"Exhausted. But we need to prep for tomorrow so everything is ready for Saturday."

He stopped her before she reached the first step of the front staircase. "You're pushing yourself."

"Mel deserves the best."

"And she'll get it. You've thought of everything. Even cut her cost for all of this."

"She'd do the same for me. I'll only be in the kitchen for another hour or so. Then I'll hit the porch for some lemonade."

"I'll hold you to it."

Zoe turned to walk upstairs when the sound of a loud exhaust pulled their attention outside.

They both walked out to find Mel, Miss Gina, and Felix already partaking in vodka infused lemonade. They'd all turned their attention to the drive.

Zane slammed the door of his car, anger on his face.

"Zane?" Zoe took a step forward, but Luke caught her arm, keeping her from going very far.

"Nice going. You couldn't just leave things alone, could you?" Zane yelled.

"What are you talking about?"

"Mom . . . she's been crying all day."

"I haven't seen her."

"She said you ignored her yesterday, and today you sent that letter."

Luke made a point of standing in front of Zoe when Zane inched closer to the steps.

"What letter?"

"Telling her to uninvite herself to the wedding." Zane's eyes skirted to Mel. "Shitty thing to do."

"I didn't—"

"Everything was fine. You just had to come back and stick a fork in him."

Zoe stepped around Luke. "Can you stop yelling for a minute and listen?"

"You think you're better than us."

Miss Gina stood. "That's enough!"

"I didn't send a letter, Zane."

"Dad said you'd deny it."

Luke saw the moment Zoe realized what was happening. He couldn't help but wonder if Ziggy himself sent the letter to turn Zoe's family even more against her.

"Ziggy . . . you're believing Ziggy over me?"

"Now he's pissed and yelling all day. Everything was fine."

Zoe pulled away from Luke and reached Zane in a few steps. "Zane . . . listen, please."

She placed a hand on her brother's arm and everything moved in slow motion.

Zane instantly shoved her away, causing her to stumble in her high heels. She met the ground, breaking her fall with her hands.

Luke flew down the steps and crashed both hands into Zane's chest, pushing him against the car. Adrenaline like nothing he'd ever felt drew his fist back and connected it with Zane's jaw.

Someone caught his arm before he could swing again.

He heard Zoe calling his name, stopping him.

Mel and Miss Gina were helping Zoe to her feet, Felix held Luke's arm . . . and the entire production company was standing in the doorway.

His breath came in short pants.

Luke turned his attention to Zane, who was looking at Zoe with what appeared to be remorse in his eyes.

Miss Gina's voice rose above everyone's heavy breathing. "You're not welcome here, Zane Brown. I don't know who told your mother not to come on Saturday, but if this is what we can expect, she can just stay away. No one is going to ruin Melanie and Wyatt's day."

Zane's gaze moved from the women to the crowd, then to Luke.

Felix pulled him back while Zane jumped behind the wheel and kicked up dirt as he sped away.

All the attention turned on Zoe the moment Zane was gone.

She trembled. "I shouldn't have touched him."

Luke reached her in two steps and took over for Mel and Miss Gina.

Felix waved his hands in the air as he walked in front of them. "Drama is over . . . everyone get that kitchen cleaned up. We have a wedding to prepare for."

Zoe couldn't stop shaking. She'd taken a shower, cleaned the scrapes on the palms of her hands . . . and downed a full glass of Miss Gina's special lemonade. The trembling didn't stop.

"I shouldn't have touched him."

"Stop, Zoe. He pushed you. He had no right." Mel sat on the edge of the bed while she dressed.

Jo hadn't dressed in something other than her uniform in what seemed like forever. "I can bring him in. Just say the word."

"No. Please. Tension is high . . . that's all. Ziggy is spreading shit. My mom is being an idiot."

"Don't justify bad behavior."

Zoe knew how her words sounded. Knew the pattern her mother had taken for years. "If it happens again, you have my blessing. Let this go. He didn't go after Luke when he punched him." She tried to hide the tremor in her hands and failed. "Good God, I feel like I need a Xanax."

Mel grasped both hands in hers. "It's okay. You have a right to be shook up."

"I'm sorry, Mel. I don't want any of this touching you."

Mel looked at her as if she were crazy. "You mean everything to me, Zoe. I hate that this is happening to you. But I'm glad I'm here to hold your hand and talk trash about the whole lot of them."

Zoe pulled her into a fierce hug. "I love you."

Mel hugged her back. "I'm already taken."

The three of them worked their way downstairs together. The voices in the living room faded from whispers to nothing when they entered.

Jo called out everyone in the room. "Could you be more obvious?"

Luke was on his feet and at her side. "Feel better?"

"I'm fine." She took his hand, knew he had to feel her shaking.

Felix winked at her from across the room. "You get the award for crazy family, Zoe."

"Let's just keep Ziggy from showing up."

Jo sat on the arm of the sofa. "I'm already on that."

"Oh?" Wyatt had joined the group and sat beside Mel.

"A couple of my friends from Waterville agreed to keep an eye on things."

Zoe read through those lines quickly. "Not a bad idea. I'm sorry it has to be that way."

"Enough, Zoe. Not your fault. I don't want to hear another word." Mel used her Mom voice.

Zoe bowed out.

Luke pulled her closer.

Felix leaned close to Mel. "How do you get her to stop arguing so easily?"

"Practice."

Chapter Twenty-Four

Waterville was the next closest anything to River Bend. It was three times as big, with a lot more anonymity to suit the needs of Ziggy Brown.

Jo was certain it was only a matter of time until the man pushed his limits and found himself in the town where he'd committed the crime that put him away for close to two decades of his life.

Jo walked into the tractor supply store and straight to where the semi drivers dropped off their shipments.

She wasn't wearing her uniform, something she did with purpose. She was pissed, more than she'd been in a long time, and wearing a uniform would probably set her in the mood to cuff the man she was coming to see. Since she'd promised Zoe she wouldn't do that, Jo left her badge behind.

There was, however, a .38 strapped to her ankle—she wasn't stupid.

Zane Brown wore the light blue issued uniform shirt with the logo of the store and a belt around his waist to help protect his back.

Jo was fairly certain her presence in the employee only section of the warehouse caught the attention of a few people. She also knew that when you acted like you belonged somewhere, people seldom called you out.

She approached Zane, who had yet to notice her walking in.

He was helping a driver stack boxes half his size onto a dolly.

The man inside the truck noticed her first.

That's when Zane's startled gaze found hers.

With one look, she knew he understood this wasn't a social visit.

The truck driver eyed her with a slight smile.

Not gonna happen, buddy.

After a few more stacked boxes, Zane made his excuses and walked toward her.

"Zane."

"Sheriff." He said her title softly enough to avoid anyone else hearing it.

"You have a minute?"

"I'm kinda busy right now."

Jo tilted her head. "You have a minute." She turned and walked out of the warehouse and into the massive parking lot.

It took Zane less than a minute to find her side.

Their eyes locked before he broke his gaze away. "I didn't mean to push her."

"Half a dozen eyewitnesses would disagree."

Zane shoved his hands in the front pockets of his jeans. "How is she?"

"She's hurting, Zane!" Jo pushed two fingers into her own chest. "Right here. I don't know what crap Ziggy is feeding all of you, but he is going to destroy you."

"I won't let that happen."

"Oh? And how are you going to stop it? I have every right to pull you in right now. With your record, you'd be in just long enough to lose this job and meet some new friends who might have bunked with your dad."

Zane had the good sense to look worried before he did a great job of studying the dirt on his steel-toed shoes.

"I need two things from you."

Zane lifted his chin, and she continued, "None of you show up for the wedding. Zoe doesn't need the stress and Mel deserves her day."

He nodded. "And the other?"

Jo glanced around the truck yard. "You have a set schedule here?"

"Late shifts Tuesdays and Thursdays. Early days Wednesdays, Fridays, and Saturdays for shipments."

"Six a.m. Tuesdays and Thursdays."

His eyes narrowed.

"River Bend High on the track." Jo patted his arm, made sure he understood this wasn't negotiable. "Bring your running shoes."

"Excuse me?"

Jo lifted both her palms to the sky and moved them in opposing directions. "Life is full of options, Brown. You meet me at six on Tuesday or I meet you . . . your choice."

Jo turned on her heel and was fairly certain she heard Zane cuss at her as she walked away.

The rehearsal and subsequent dinner went off without a hitch. Even the former Mr. and Mrs. Bartlett pulled it together long enough to get through their first dinner together in eleven years.

Mel made the menu choices and Zoe made it happen. Well, she directed her soon to be overworked staff to make it happen.

And Jo played maid of honor.

Mel didn't want to pick between them for the top spot, but the certificate of marriage only had one line for a witness to sign on the bride side. Zoe backed out to give Mel the ease of knowing she wasn't offended. Besides, Jo lived in River Bend and deserved the honor.

Once the dinner was over and the majority of guests who weren't staying at Miss Gina's had left, Zoe and Mel left the inn to have their final night as single women at Jo's house.

They opened a bottle of wine Zoe had been saving since she arrived in River Bend and paired it with microwave popcorn.

The singular focus was on Mel.

Zoe watched her all night and couldn't help but think she glowed.

They dressed down the second they made it to Jo's house. Braless, with their faces clean of makeup, they turned on music they all enjoyed and curled up in Jo's living room.

"It's really weird drinking in this house, Jo." Zoe looked at the mantel, which held the flag that was once draped over Sheriff Joseph Ward's casket. It sat in a triangular frame with a plaque given to her the day of the funeral.

Zoe would never have considered drinking in Sheriff Ward's home unless invited by his own daughter.

Jo gave a sideways glance at the symbol that reminded them all of her dad.

"I didn't have a problem with that when I was a kid . . . get over it."

Mel laughed and lifted her glass for Zoe to fill.

"I thought wine was safer than tequila," Zoe said.

"God, yes."

Zoe tipped the bottle to Jo's glass next.

"When was the last time we sat around—just the three of us—drinking tequila?" Mel asked.

"Graduation."

Zoe shivered, filled her glass.

"God, I feel old," Jo said.

"High school graduation . . . how is that possible?"

"It's simple. Mel went to college."

"Lot of good that did."

Jo waved her off. "And you moved away as fast as the Greyhound bus could take you."

Zoe set the bottle down. "Ironic, isn't it? I always thought you'd be the one to leave first, and you're the one who stayed."

More than one set of eyes lingered on the flag over the fireplace.

"Do you think about him?" Mel asked.

"All the time."

They marinated in their own thoughts for a brief moment before Mel said, "Can you believe my parents made it through the night?"

"No!" Jo protested first.

"They better continue throughout tomorrow."

Jo pushed her feet under her butt on a side chair. "I think Miss Gina put the fear of God in both of them the minute they hit the door of the inn."

"And if she didn't, I did."

Both Mel and Jo turned to her.

"What?"

Jo and Mel had expectant eyes. "What did you say?"

"I said . . . 'You ruined the night of our graduation, don't screw up her wedding. Whatever issues you might have, deal with away from here.'"

Mel's jaw dropped. "You did not."

"I most certainly did."

"What did my mom say?"

"She told me I was exaggerating. To which I let her know that we went through a half a bottle of Cuervo the night of our graduation, and you puked for hours the next morning."

"You didn't."

"I did. Why not? It was shitty of them to tell you they were splitting when you were handed your diploma. People can split, that's fine, but have some respect for life's milestones."

Jo started to laugh until she lifted her hand in a high five.

"God, I love you."

"Yeah, well, I expect the same of you if I ever get married. My family would be a disaster. I'd be better off eloping."

"Speaking of . . ."

Zoe glanced at Jo.

"Luke? How is that going?"

Zoe bit her lip. "It's . . ." She sighed. "Amazing. I'm afraid to say that out loud." And she was.

"Why?"

"I'm going to jinx it."

Mel sipped her wine. "How can you jinx it? You're already in a divisive situation and you're making it work."

"We are, aren't we?" Her in Texas . . . him here in Oregon. Crazy family, her career.

"You know what I overheard?" Mel was already reaching for more wine.

"What?" Jo asked.

"Felix was talking to that Rupert guy about future features. Have they asked you for more filming at Miss Gina's?"

"Felix mentioned it—"

"Ahhh!" Mel was the excitable one.

"Mentioned, Mel. Directors do that all the time."

A splash of disappointment washed over her face.

Jo called Zoe out. "You're just being cautious."

"Felix likes anything other than Texas. It helps that he just broke up with his boyfriend. I love him, but a couple of weeks in River Bend and the flowery disposition will wear off."

"I like it here," Mel said.

"So do I," Zoe defended. "But Felix is all fancy food and men with the same sexual tastes. How many gay men can we set him up with in River Bend?"

Jo and Mel exchanged glances.

"I got nothin'."

Mel laughed.

"He doesn't have to live here," Jo said. "Come in to film your amazingness and off to Eugene."

The thought had crossed her mind but never went very far.

"One thing at a time."

Mel squealed. "I'm getting married tomorrow."

Both Jo and Zoe sat forward, glasses in the air. "To a long, happy, healthy life," Zoe said.

"To great sex!" Jo added.

Mel flapped her feet like flippers in the sea and they laughed.

Chapter Twenty-Five

For all the events Zoe had managed to be a part of in her life, a wedding wasn't one of them.

Never been in one . . . never catered one. Hell, she never believed in one.

Go time was three in the afternoon. But before Zoe and Jo preceded Mel down the aisle, they had some serious needs to be met.

Two women from Waterville drove down to ensure they all had pretty fingernails and polished toes. Mel sat in the queen chair with Zoe's stylist working her hair into an updo. Something they'd all have before putting on their dresses.

Both Mel and Jo sat with their feet in hot water when Zoe ducked out of Jo's house to check on the staff cooking their lives away at Sam's.

A light dusting of white cloud floated overhead.

With no makeup, her hair pulled back in a knot, and wearing sweatpants that said Juicy on her ass, Zoe ran in the back door at Sam's.

Her impressions came fast. There were four butts cooking in a two-butt kitchen. Pasta boiled on an open flame. Ernie stirred what smelled like a cream sauce. Brenda stood over a prep sink, cleaning vegetables, and Tiffany was yelling out the time.

"I totally won!" Ernie glanced over his shoulder, fist pumped the air, and went back to his sauce.

"Won what?" Zoe asked as she made her way to the ovens, opened a door, and then turned down the heat by a hair.

"They are betting on your OCD tendencies," Brenda explained.

"My OCD what? I'm not OCD." Zoe lifted the spoon in Ernie's work, dipped a finger, and took a taste. "Perfect," she said before moving to another station.

"Yes, you are." Tiffany removed a Styrofoam cup from the window and turned it around so Zoe could read the writing on the side.

Everyone in the kitchen had their name scribbled in ink and a time.

"What is that?"

Tiffany pointed to her name. "I thought you'd be here an hour ago. Ernie was off by five minutes, but the next time is Dell's, and she has you down for a half hour from now."

"That's because I thought she was getting her nails done first," Dell said from the other side of the kitchen.

Zoe rolled her eyes, glanced at the money inside the cup, and pushed out her chest. "Ten bucks a bet?"

"Go big or go home," Ernie said.

"You guys are bad."

Laughing, she finished her rounds and glanced at the time. "Shit, I gotta go."

As she retreated, she heard Tiffany say when she was just out of sight, "Okay, bets for round two."

~

Wyatt and Luke sat on Miss Gina's back porch, watching a team of busy hands setting up chairs, makeshifting an arbor, placing flowers on every possible surface or rock.

"What do you think the women are doing right now?" Wyatt asked.

"I doubt they're watching TV."

Wyatt laughed.

"It looks nice."

"It does. Mel did an amazing job."

The tent for the reception sat on the north side of the property. So far, the weather was cooperating, and it appeared that they'd be able to have the ceremony in the sun and dance the night away in the tent.

Wyatt pointed to a flatbed truck that was bringing in extra tables. "Do you think we should help?"

Luke shrugged. "I think someone will yell at us if we do."

Wyatt swung his feet off the railing and stood. "I could use a sandwich . . . want one?"

Luke nodded. "That would be great. No mayo."

"Gotcha."

Mel, Jo, and Zoe all had their hair up, with tiny flowers woven into the fancy knots.

"I feel like I should take a nap," Mel said, her eyes closed as the stylist dusted her lids with shadow.

"No!" Zoe said, her hand placed in the palm of the woman painting her nails.

"Not unless you can sleep without putting your head down." It had taken nearly an hour to put Mel's hair up, and thirty minutes for

Jo. Zoe, on the other hand, had hers in place within fifteen minutes. The speed came with practice. And since the on-camera team was there, they were pitching in for all the things women did to make themselves beautiful for a wedding.

"I said I think I *should* . . . not that I *would*."

Mel's hand displayed her nerves as it tapped on the edges of the chair.

"Nervous?"

Mel looked at Zoe without moving her head. "Excited."

Zoe's cell phone buzzed, sitting next to her. Carefully making sure she didn't scuff her freshly polished nails, she checked her text messages.

> The reception tent is up, the tables are set . . . the flowers
> have arrived and the florist is spreading them everywhere.
> Tell Mel not to worry.

"Who was that?"

"Luke, he wants you to know everything is on time and set up or close to it."

Mel grinned ear to ear. "Eeek! I'm getting married today!"

Jo blew on her fingers. "You're such a dork, Mel."

There were four of them on the porch. Along with Wyatt and Luke, Wyatt's father sat drinking coffee, and Mark was drinking a beer.

"Is this considered supervising?" Luke asked.

Bill glanced over the paper in his hand, then ducked back to whatever he was reading. "You wanna jump in that and help, go right ahead. When someone shoots your head off for doing something wrong, you'll be back."

"Sounds like too much trouble for me," Mark said.

Wyatt slouched down in his chair and closed his eyes. "Someone wake me by two."

Luke looked at his watch. "I guess that would be my job." Damn it . . . he could use a nap, too. But someone needed to stay awake to get the groom showered and ready on time.

∽

"Do we have everything?" Mel asked.

They had a makeup bag, extra hair spray, and an emergency repair kit in case one of them should break a nail in the next hour.

All three of them were still in sweatpants and button-up cotton shirts. That way they wouldn't mess up anything removing clothes to put on their dresses. Dresses that were hanging in Mel's room at the inn.

"Oh, shit," Jo exclaimed and then ran into her bedroom.

When she returned, she held a holstered gun the size of her palm.

"What do you need that for?" Mel asked.

Jo walked past them and out the door. "Don't worry, it straps to my thigh. No one will know I have it."

Zoe rolled her eyes. "Dork."

∽

Luke swiveled his head when the screen door opened.

Miss Gina poked her head out and motioned toward the sleeping Wyatt. "Don't let him in here."

"Oh?"

"Yeah, the girls just arrived, and Mel doesn't want to see him until she walks down the aisle."

They both glanced at the sleeping groom.

"I don't think she needs to worry."

Miss Gina shook her head. "I'll let you know when it's clear."

It took every effort and muscle under her skin to not leave Mel's side when the trucks arrived with the food.

In their strapless gowns the color of dusty pink with silver sequins adding drama to the bodices, Jo and Zoe stood side by side, taking in the bride.

Mel's eyes sparkled brighter than the diamond drop earrings she'd borrowed from Zoe for the day.

The photographer snapped pictures of Melanie framed by the lace-covered window.

"Spectacular."

Jo nodded her agreement, and someone knocked on the door.

Zoe peeked out, making sure it wasn't Wyatt.

Felicia, Mel's mother, stood in the doorway, holding Hope's hand.

Zoe ushered them in and quickly closed the door.

Hope wore a princess-cut dress in the same color as Zoe's and Jo's. With curls in her hair and flowers in the barrettes, she was a smaller version of the adults. The eyes in the room focused on Hope as she walked up to her mother and placed her hand on Mel's dress. "Oh, Mommy, you're beautiful."

Mel knelt down and placed a hand on Hope's face. "Thank you, sweetheart. And look at you. Did Grandma help with the flowers in your hair?"

Hope glanced at Felicia and nodded.

Another knock on the door announced Miss Gina and Felix, who brought with them the flowers the bridal party was going to carry.

Zoe grinned. "Not long now."

Luke nudged Wyatt awake. "Dude."

Wyatt blinked a few times and stretched from his chair. "Time to shower?"

"Probably not a bad idea."

Wyatt and Luke made their way up the back stairs while Mark and Bill went around the front.

The water pressure in the inn kinda sucked, but at least it was hot.

The mothers left with the photographers, and Hope bounded down the stairs with her newest best friend, Felix.

Zoe just hoped someone had the good sense to tie up the dog far enough away that they wouldn't hear him barking throughout the night. The image of Sir Knight frolicking through the catering trays was nails on a chalkboard in her head.

Jo glanced out to the yard below. "Looks like people are starting to arrive."

"Do you see Wyatt?" Mel asked, several feet from the window.

"Nope."

"He's here, don't worry."

Mel placed a hand to her stomach. "Oh, God."

"Finally nervous?"

Mel shook her head. "I think we forgot to eat."

Luke straightened Wyatt's tie. "You know, you clean up pretty good, Gibson."

Wyatt slapped the side of Luke's arm and winked. "Not too bad yourself, Miller."

Luke glanced at his watch. "Now what do we do for thirty minutes?"

Wyatt pulled at the cuffs of his sleeves. "I say we sneak a few shrimp thingies before everyone eats them all."

"I like the way you think."

Chapter Twenty-Six

Luke always thought it would be him standing in the number one spot and Zoe in white.

His heart kicked so hard when she rounded the corner and walked down the aisle he thought he might pass out.

Zoe Brown dominated the space she carried herself through. Her dark hair was piled high, the bodice of the gown dipped just enough to be classily sexy.

She smiled at familiar faces as she took her time walking up and rolled her eyes at Felix, who dabbed his eyes with a handkerchief.

Then she looked at him and her smile turned radiant.

For the first time in what felt like forever, he knew they were on the same page.

It was Jo's turn in the spotlight, and Luke had to admit . . . the town sheriff cleaned up really well. *Is that cleavage?* He'd never noticed Jo having a rack.

Many of the people in the crowd lived in River Bend, and he was fairly certain they were all muttering the same thing.

Holy, shit . . . that's Sheriff Ward.

Obviously Wyatt wasn't looking at the bridesmaids. He leaned in and whispered, "You have the ring, right?"

Luke let his smile drop and his eyes grow wide.

He knew he gave his friend a tiny heart attack before he winked with a smile.

"Fuck you, Miller," he whispered.

Mark, who stood beside Luke, chuckled under his breath.

"Not my type, Gibson." And Luke's gaze once again landed on Zoe. Her profile, her beauty, her poise. He wanted to call her his . . . like really call her his.

Hope was next, tossing rose petals as she walked a little too fast in front of her mom.

Once Hope made it to the podium, she walked right up to Wyatt.

He leaned down to hear her words.

"I do, too."

There were plenty of *ahs* and *ohs* before the music changed and everyone stood.

When Mel turned the corner, she received the reaction she deserved.

She was beautiful, and blushing, and smiled all the way to Wyatt's side.

Pictures took well over an hour. While Zoe enjoyed the fun and banter of the moment, she couldn't help but wonder how everything with the food was going.

Wyatt had recruited several of the track kids to don black pants and white shirts to serve.

Felix had taken the liberty of directing a cameraman to ensure a proper wedding video as his gift to the bride and groom.

"This is lovely, Zoe. Exactly the kind of thing that isn't being done on any of the culinary shows."

"There is more to a wedding than food."

Felix pointed a thumb over his shoulder. "Say that to them."

The *them* he spoke of were the wedding guests destroying the appetizers.

She'd sampled them herself and knew Ernie and Tiffany had brought their A game. She made a mental note to pay it forward when life settled down.

Thinking of calm had her doing another scan of the guests mingling outside of the tent.

She was the only Brown in attendance.

It pained her at the same time it relieved her. The last thing any of them needed was pushy brothers or ex-con fathers. Her job on this day was to shelter Mel from anything ugly and make sure the food was something River Bend would talk about for years.

Since the maid of honor had a sidearm strapped to her thigh, Zoe figured Jo had Mel taken care of.

Luke snuck up beside her, placed an arm around her waist. "It's killing you, isn't it?"

"What?" She glanced over his shoulder at the catering tent.

"C'mon. They don't need us here any longer." Luke pulled her away from the photographer and toward the reception tent.

Zoe felt her pulse returning to normal the closer she got.

She was vaguely aware that Felix followed and snapped his fingers in the air. At what, she wasn't sure. Her focus was linear.

Check the food.

Was it hot?

Did the cream sauce survive the drive over?

Did they need Miss Gina's kitchen for more than a working sink?

She buzzed around the servers and behind the serving station.

The cream sauce survived . . . it wasn't hot enough outside to wilt the lettuce for the salads.

She sampled everything. When she reached the Italian dressing, she found a problem.

"Tiffany?"

With a wave of a hand, Tiffany was by her side.

"What's it missing?"

They used a tiny, straw-like siphon for Tiffany to sample.

She tasted it twice . . . "Oregano."

"Exactly!" Zoe waved Tiffany to follow over.

In high heels that had no place traipsing around a yard, Zoe led Tiffany to a garden on the side of Miss Gina's inn.

She pointed. "Do what you can with what we have. Better to run out of something fabulous than serve something forgettable."

Tiffany moved beyond the small fence meant to keep the dog from digging up their efforts.

When Zoe turned, Felix and Luke stood beside her, and a cameraman had the lens focused on her, recording.

She looked at both of them like they were crazy. "What are you doing? That dressing needs to get into the kitchen for Tiffany to fix." It was her turn to snap her fingers. "Let's go. We don't have much time."

Jo noticed the moment Zoe pulled away, with Luke and Felix standing over her.

Jo stood to the side, watching over Mel as she and her brand-new husband posed for pictures that would someday make their way over a mantel.

Wyatt lifted Hope into his arms and made sure there were plenty of family pictures of the three of them.

A moment of nostalgia hit her, watching the photographer snap that shot.

Her father had kept a cherished photo of the three of them on his desk. Jo's mom, before she'd died, her dad, and Jo at an age not too far from Hope's.

They'd smiled for the camera . . . a moment frozen in time.

Only someone took that away. Twice.

Jo had to look away, and when she did, she felt eyes on her.

Her senses heightened, and the weight of the gun strapped just above her knee reminded her she wasn't defenseless.

Guests filled the lawn from every corner.

Many were looking at her. Probably because she had a shit-ton of makeup on and a dress that defined her as a woman and not a cop.

She stretched her neck.

She liked the cop on the inside.

The girlie girl all dressed up . . . not so much.

After a successful dinner, the dishes were cleared, and Zoe could finally breathe.

Dessert consisted of piles of tiny delicacies, appreciated by everyone.

The cake was the only culinary taste not created by Zoe and her staff. The pastry chef in charge, however, made a point to deliver the cake herself. When she did, she asked Zoe's opinion and floated with her praise.

Zoe posed for a picture with the woman and couldn't help feeling a little self-pride.

Mel had opted for a DJ. Fog had a tendency to sock in as the day wore on, which would muffle live music and annoy those trying to enjoy the wedding party.

Day slowly turned into night.

Lights that belonged in the local Christmas tree lot in December lit up the space between the inn and the tent.

Inside the tent, there were table centerpieces with candles, lights propped up on the sides, and several massive glowing balls in the center.

For most of the night and pictures, Jo had been paired up with Luke, since he was taking the best man position.

Zoe stood beside Mark, Mel's brother, and smiled.

Yet when Mel and Wyatt had their first dance, and Wyatt showed his father had taught him how to move, it was time for the wedding party to join them.

Zoe glanced toward Mark, who was already grabbing Jo's hand.

She laughed and made her way into Luke's arms. "You planned that," she whispered.

"I'm tired of seeing another man holding what's mine."

Zoe stopped midstride to the dance floor. "What's yours?"

He hesitated, tugged her close. "You have a problem with that?"

With someone other than Luke . . . maybe.

She bit her bottom lip and snuggled closer.

People were watching but she didn't care.

She placed her head on Luke's shoulder and let him lead her through a song she was fairly certain played at their high school prom.

The music shifted and someone tapped Luke's shoulder.

Tickled, Zoe let Mr. M lead her in a dance.

"You did a great job."

"You liked the food?" she asked.

He patted his stomach. "A little of Audrey's, too, I'm afraid."

The excitement of that simple feat wasn't something Zoe could completely describe.

Making things right . . . making people happy was something she'd been born to do. It took leaving River Bend to realize she could and returning to River Bend to make it count.

Mr. M had some serious moves . . . he spun her when others were just swaying to the music.

She laughed and kept up, and when the music softened, Mr. M leaned in close enough so only she could hear. "You're like a daughter to me, Zoe . . . it makes my heart full to see you happy."

Instead of letting the tears that suddenly filled her eyes fall, she rested her head on his chest and let him lead her in a slow dance. When he pulled away, she kissed his cheek.

He walked away, and her eyes gravitated to Luke.

With a sigh, she opened her arms and willed him to fill them.

He slipped out of the house.

Zane had finally left. The kid wasn't acting right. A little too quiet, a little too watchful.

Not right.

Zanya managed to quiet her kid and Sheryl pretended to sleep.

So Ziggy slid out.

He didn't dare drive a car . . . there was more than one person with a badge in this town, and he'd bet money that Deputy Emery sat close by with an eye on his trailer door.

But he knew the back way to the inn.

If only to watch the players and see who still lived in town.

The property surrounding the bed-and-breakfast was dark compared to the light coming from the reception in full swing.

It was late for a small town that normally rolled up its welcome mats by nine o'clock. Yet there didn't seem to be many spaces along the road where people had pulled out to return home.

Keeping out of sight, Ziggy picked out the major players quickly. It helped that the only people formally dressed were the wedding party.

He found his daughter first. She walked around like she owned the place. Her nose sat firmly in the air, even as she danced. When she tilted a tall glass with what he assumed was champagne, his mouth watered.

Everyone, it seemed, held a glass of something in their hands.

And why not? They were adults. He was a fucking adult and yet he was treated like a child, limited to a diet of milk and water.

Ziggy narrowed his gaze when he found little JoAnne Ward.

She didn't look like a cop now. Busty and round enough in the right places to forget the little girl she'd once been.

Sheryl was too thin, he decided. Too easy to climb on and bend.

He needed a challenge. Something to get him living again. Because River Bend was just a bigger jail. A jail with a tiny girl running the joint.

The woman in question suddenly stopped talking to whomever she was with and turned his way.

He sank farther into the shadows and didn't divert his focus until she returned to her conversation.

"The whole town is here," he whispered to himself.

He backed away from his perch and stretched. It was a nice night for a walk, he decided . . . and an empty town was a quiet place to visit.

Chapter Twenty-Seven

Even though they didn't leave the inn until after one in the morning and stumbling into bed resulted in a rush of limbs and kisses and then finally sleep around two thirty, Zoe's eyes opened at just before seven.

Stupid internal clock.

She tried to roll over but Luke's knee kept her pinned to the bed.

She couldn't feel her toes, which was probably part of the reason she woke. Moving a grown man who wasn't awake was a little like pushing against a mule who'd found a patch of green grass.

The push, the nudge, the wiggle . . . none of it worked.

Changing tactics, she ran a fingernail over his bare hip in hopes of tickling him enough to roll off.

His chest rumbled. "Starting something?"

She flattened her hand. "You're awake?"

Luke shifted his hips, and a warm part of his anatomy told her just how awake he was.

"A warm, wiggling, naked woman in my bed has a way of getting me up early."

Her hand brushed his erection. "You're insatiable."

Caging her hips in his hands, he pulled her on top of him.

Her toes started to tingle. "I have morning breath," she offered in a weak protest.

Luke opened his eyes and offered a cheeky grin. "So do I."

Some time later, fresh from the shower, Zoe padded around Luke's kitchen with a steamy cup of coffee. He needed a grinder, she decided . . . and maybe a latte machine.

She chopped an onion to add to the eggs before pulling out a piece of paper and a pen from the obligatory kitchen junk drawer.

By the time Luke joined her, the eggs were cooked, the toast was jumping out of the overactive toaster, and Zoe was on her second cup of coffee.

He nuzzled her neck before pouring a cup for himself. "Good morning," he said into his cup.

"Brat." She laughed and set their plates on the table.

Luke found her list and started to read. "What's this?"

"Kitchen must-haves. Your knives suck and I almost burned our breakfast."

He took a forkful of her eggs and moaned. "If this is burned, don't ever let me cook for you."

She took a bite and removed the list from his hand. The window in front of his sink pushed out just far enough for a few herbs. With the closer proximity to water, Luke would be more inclined to make sure the plants didn't starve.

He glanced at what she'd written and said, "So you rearrange my kitchen and fill it with things I have no idea how to use."

"You have a problem with that?"

"Nope, nope." He took another bite. "Hell to the no."

"So when are Wyatt and Mel leaving this morning?"

"Their flight leaves at noon."

"Did they need a ride? I didn't hear anything about the arrangements."

"No, his parents were flying out around the same time. They're taking Hope to Disneyland before flying back to San Francisco."

Zoe put jam on her toast, took a taste, and then scribbled on the long list of things the kitchen needed. "She'll love that. Take her mind off her parents basking away in Fiji."

"What is there to do in Fiji, anyway?" Luke asked.

She'd never been, but she knew people who had. Zoe pointed to the right. "You eat." She pointed to the left. "Have sex . . ." With a back-and-forth wave, she continued, "Sit on the beach, have sex on the beach, eat a little more. You know, the basics."

"I like the sound of that."

She did, too. "We should go sometime."

His grin told her he liked the idea.

Luke finished his plate and eyed what she'd left on hers. She pushed it his way and he dug in.

"So, the wedding is over."

"Happily ever after," Zoe said. "I think they're gonna make it, too."

"They make a great couple. Mel deserved a good guy."

"I couldn't agree more."

"Remember what I told you I would revisit after the wedding?"

She blinked a few times.

"Me moving to Texas."

The thought didn't hit her as hard, hearing it now. "You like Texas that much?"

"It has its good points." He let his eyes linger over her, making sure she knew what he was talking about.

She thought of her apartment that didn't have a yard . . . the weekend shifts at Nahana she was going to give notice to. The big houses on streets empty of familiar faces. "If you like Texas, you should move."

He narrowed his gaze.

"I probably won't be there, but I can visit you."

"You're moving?"

"Probably."

Luke stopped eating. "Where to?"

"I haven't decided yet."

He tried not to smile too wide. Luke picked up the list again. "A bird feeder?"

Zoe waved a hand to the kitchen sink. "I have to have something to look at out there."

They cleaned the dishes together, and Zoe took inventory of what they had on hand for dinner. The Sunday farmers' market would be setting up in town and would offer a few of the things on her list. She dug a little deeper in the fridge. The wine she'd brought to pair with fish wasn't inside.

She thought of Luke's comment about how Wyatt and Mel didn't need a wine refrigerator and had to laugh. Looked like Mr. I'm Happy With Beer was getting a taste for the good stuff.

With a big hat and a massive canvas bag, she grabbed Luke and headed to the market.

While they didn't continue to discuss where she was going to move, Zoe did notice the space Luke had made in his dresser drawers.

Fog sat low to the track at River Bend High.

Jo sat on the last step of the stands, lacing up her running shoes and checking her watch.

This was so much better than a formal dress and high heels.

She'd never been much of a girlie girl. Probably a byproduct of being raised by a man, and a cop at that.

She learned to shoot at an early age and had skills befitting a Boy Scout by the time she entered elementary school.

At two minutes past six, the sound of a motorcycle interrupted her internal rant about the blisters on her feet created by fancy shoes.

Without words, Zane took a spot next to her and pulled off his boots. "Mind telling me what we're doing here?"

She looked at his feet before standing. "You're bright. You'll figure it out."

She leaned against the bleacher in a calf stretch and moved to the next leg.

"It's cold out here," Zane bitched as he tugged on a worn pair of running shoes.

She lifted her chin and took off before calling behind her shoulder, "Keep up, Brown."

A tiny lift of her lips stayed until he matched her pace. The second lap around the track was when Zane started asking questions. "What the hell am I doing here?"

"Exercise is good for you."

"You should only be running if a cop is chasing you."

Jo couldn't help but smile.

Zane let his lips split in a grin, too.

"Is Zoe still here?"

Jo considered how much to tell Zane. She knew for this to work he'd have to trust her, and that would require a few quiet moments. "No. She left last night."

Zane didn't comment.

"She'll be back."

"She seems to be here a lot this year."

Jo ran for another quarter lap before making a comment.

"There's a lot to bring her around."

It was Zane's turn to wait to talk. "There's a lot to keep her away, too."

Now they were getting somewhere.

"Yeah, your dad coming home has put her back."

Zane gave her a sideways glance and then concentrated on breathing. Breathing that was becoming more and more difficult as the laps accumulated.

A mile and a half into the run, Zane started to drag. "How many do you run?"

Jo picked up her pace and said, "Not cold any longer, are you?"

She'd lost count of her laps and slowed only when she noticed the cars starting to arrive.

Finally, when it appeared Zane was either going to pass out or puke, she slowed them down to a walk for the last two hundred meters to arrive where they'd left their other shoes.

"Holy shit." Zane lowered his head between his open legs and moaned.

Jo shoved cold water from her supply into his hands.

He downed it in one continuous swallow.

A handful of members of the cross-country team made their way from the parking lot.

"Hey, Sheriff."

"Hey, guys."

Zane glanced her way.

"Tim, lead everyone in a warm-up. I don't want anyone bitching about shin splits."

Tim saluted her, and the lot of them made their way to the center of the field.

More than one set of eyes fell on Zane.

"Looks like someone got in trouble," she heard one of the girls mumble.

"What's that about?" Zane asked, nodding toward the group of teens that were starting their stretches.

"Nothing. Good kids, just need a little extra push once in a while."

"Huh!" Zane stood and grabbed his boots. "So we're good here?"

"Until Thursday."

"Seriously?" He turned a little green.

"Six sharp." She didn't give him any room to argue. Jo took off on the track. "C'mon, slackers. We have some miles to run today."

Jo heard Tim grumble.

"And one trip up Lob Hill."

"Why?" one of the girls asked as they all moved to catch up with her.

"I was at the wedding, Tina. I had eyes everywhere." Which they all knew to mean she'd caught more than one of them drinking. And since there wasn't any more bitching, she knew they'd all had a hand in something they shouldn't have over the weekend.

Zane shook his head as he walked away.

~

The first box arrived two days after Zoe left for Texas.

Luke opened the package to find a set of knives and a packing slip that had him looking twice.

He didn't hesitate, he picked up his cell phone and called her.

"Hey, baby . . . I have a package here for you."

"Awesome."

"Am I reading this right? You spent two thousand dollars on knives?"

Zoe hesitated. "That isn't right. Did you look in the box?"

He fumbled with some of the packing materials and removed three smaller boxes with images of the knives inside. "There's three in here."

"Oh, a partial shipment then. I'll call."

Luke flipped the box over in his hands. "Wait, are you saying you spent two grand on three knives?"

"Uh-huh."

"That's crazy."

"Really? What do you spend on a drill set? Hydraulic hoses for the shop? Or, hey, that lift that keeps breaking down?"

Luke put the box down and grinned. "I get it."

"Good. I have more coming, so keep an eye out. I'd hate for the boxes to sit on your porch."

"Because I live in such a bad neighborhood."

"Never mind. I seem to have forgotten there are places you can leave your front door unlocked."

"I wouldn't go that far." But even as the words left Luke's mouth, he knew he'd left his door unlocked more times than not in his life.

"Are you checking on Miss Gina?"

"Every day. I think she's catching on to me."

"Let her catch on. I hate the thought of her being in the place alone."

Luke put the smaller boxes that held the knives on the counter and tossed the bigger one by the back door to take to the trash.

"Brenda is there in the mornings to make breakfast when she has guests until Mel is back."

"Yeah, how is that going to work with her and Wyatt married?"

"Better, I think. Miss Gina has been known to tell people that the inn is at capacity if she didn't like the look of them."

"Mel told me that the inn has been losing money ever since Hope got hurt last year."

Luke drizzled a little water over the tiny plants sitting by his sink as they spoke. "Now that Hope has her own room at Wyatt's, my guess is Miss Gina will get back to normal. Better than normal. This town seems to have filled up in the last few months."

He heard Zoe laugh. "The film crew alone doubled the population."

"I wouldn't go so far as to say that, but there are a few more people I don't recognize in town."

"That should be good for everyone."

"Except maybe Jo."

"Oh, is something going on?"

Luke was quick to backtrack. "No. But a bigger population means more people to police." And he knew for a fact that Jo was spending a lot of her time outside the station ever since Ziggy showed up.

"Then she needs to hire another deputy."

"I think there is only so much in the budget for her."

"I hadn't thought of that."

He didn't want to think of the magnitude of Jo's job. He'd seen her dressed in a uniform for years now, but never saw the cop . . . he almost always saw the chick that went to high school with them.

"So what are you doing today?" he asked, not wanting to drop the conversation yet.

"I'm sitting down with the owners of Nahana and turning in my resignation."

Hope filled Luke's chest like a rush of wind. "You're really quitting?"

"I am. It feels strange. But after I spoke with Suki, I knew I was going to be okay."

The name of her talent agent always made him grin. "What does Suki have to do with the restaurant?"

"We heard back from the publisher I liked. Guess what they are paying me for a cookbook?"

He had no idea. "I got nothing."

"A hundred grand."

Luke felt actual chills. "W-what?"

"I know, right?"

He slumped against the counter. "For a cookbook?"

"Yeah. It will give me an opportunity to walk from Nahana and explore for the next six months."

"Holy cow, Zoe. What kind of money do you make?"

"What?"

He shook his head. "Never mind. It's none of my business. I'm happy for you."

"I have to run. Keep an eye out for my orders?"

"I will, baby. Don't work too hard."

Luke ended the call and lifted one of the boxes holding Zoe's knives. He didn't think he spent two grand collectively on all the stuff in his kitchen.

Chapter Twenty-Eight

Most nights, Jo lived off microwaveable dinners and pasta in a box that didn't require much effort.

Since Ziggy Brown returned, she spent a lot of her time, and money, frequenting Sam's diner.

"Hey, Sheriff," Sam called out from behind the window into the kitchen. "You're back."

"What can I say, Sam? I think Zoe taught you a few things back there."

"I doubt that," Brenda said from across the room.

Jo took a spot at the counter and greeted those she recognized. There were a few faces in the mix that weren't familiar. Something she had noticed happening throughout the summer.

She grabbed a menu, though she was fairly certain there wasn't anything new on the thing.

"When are you going to change some of this?" she called out to Sam.

"You get that friend of yours to move back to town and help me out back here, and maybe you can have something new."

"I don't think you can afford her."

Her banter escaped right as Sheryl pushed through the two-way swinging doors that led to the back.

Her hands were full of a tub of ice.

Jo lifted her chin, made sure a smile was firmly in place. "Hi, Sheryl."

This woman had known Jo since before she had her first period, was her best friend's mother. The lady put her nose in the air and averted her eyes before she offered a weak greeting.

Jo counted it as a win. The last time she was in, Sheryl had completely ignored her.

As winning went, Jo had apparently sat in Sheryl's section, so she had no choice but to talk to her.

"How does the soup look tonight?"

"Same as it has for twenty years."

"I'll skip it then."

Sheryl didn't crack a smile.

"How about an iced tea."

Sheryl put away her pad of paper and twisted around.

Brenda moved behind the counter to grab the coffeepot. "When are Wyatt and Mel coming back?"

"Not for a week."

"I've never been anywhere tropical." Brenda hummed to herself. "Fiji . . . I hope she takes lots of pictures."

"Me, too."

"Think you'll ever go?" Brenda asked.

Jo adjusted her gun belt so her .45 wasn't digging into her waist. "And leave beautiful downtown River Bend? I'm good."

Sam glanced through the window. "You just need a Wyatt in your life."

"I'm too busy for that."

"Ha!" The laugh came from down the counter.

"Grant? Aren't you at the wrong bar?"

Grant had been known to spend a little time in the only jail cell in town for drinking a little too much and yelling at the dogs, the kids . . . and anyone who wasn't drinking with him. The running joke in town was he needed a set of keys to the jail cell like that guy on *The Andy Griffith Show.*

It never really came to that since more serious overnight guests were taken into Waterville, where they had twenty-four-hour surveillance.

Not that it stopped Jo from occasionally making a kid on the wrong path spend the night in her jail. A tactic that had worked quite a bit for her dad.

"I'm on the wagon, Sheriff."

Jo noticed the gloss in his eyes. "By wagon you mean you're pacing yourself?"

"Well, let's not be ridiculous."

Jo couldn't help but laugh.

Sheryl set an iced tea in front of her, pulled out her pad of paper again, and waited without comment.

"I'll go with the roast beef."

Without eye contact, Sheryl scribbled the order and tossed it in Sam's window.

Brenda walked behind Jo and leaned in close. "Don't take it personally."

"Do I ever?"

"I don't know . . . do you?"

Jo waved her off and turned to her drink.

"I have to say, Sheriff, you cleaned up really well the other night."

"Why thanks, Sam. I didn't know you cared."

"I don't remember the last time I saw you in something other than a uniform. You're like a girl under all that stuff." He waved at her as if he were washing away her badge.

"Most people in town already know that." *But thanks for announcing it to a restaurant full of them.*

He winked and went back to the task of cooking.

When Sheryl placed food in front of her, Jo thanked her . . . then, because Grant grabbed Sheryl's attention for coffee, Jo went ahead and made good use of her proximity.

"How is Zanya, Sheryl? I haven't seen much of her."

Sheryl quickly poured the coffee and returned the pot to the warmer. "She's fine."

"And Blaze? Getting big, I bet."

No eye contact . . . her hands shook on the coffeepot.

Jo didn't like the body language.

"He's a big boy."

Jo eased off. She'd found out enough for one night. Besides, Thursday morning was only a few hours away.

Everyone in town knew Wyatt Gibson and his new wife were on their honeymoon.

And since teenagers were known to liberate a little alcohol from unsuspecting homes from time to time, Ziggy made sure to keep the small town tradition going.

Deputy Emery's squad car was parked in front of his house, which didn't sit very far from anything in River Bend . . . and Ziggy noticed the moment JoAnne sat her firm little ass in a broken-down bar stool at Sam's.

He socked away the fact his wife was talking to that bitch to use another time.

It was cold for late August, which gave Ziggy a reason to wear a dark coat to match the early dusk of night, and gloves. Well, the gloves were overkill, but if someone saw him, they wouldn't look at him as if he were wearing shorts in twelve-degree weather.

He didn't like the quiet of the town until he needed to hear every bark and whisper.

His senses heightened, and he worked his way to the house he'd seen but never been in. Nice little tucked away home. Perfect for his needs.

Ziggy had learned a few things in prison.

The art of disguise in case someone did see you. It wasn't hard to darken up his beard or wear a hat. A wig under the hat was a little hard to manage, but there were plenty of old women in River Bend who took advantage of the farmers' market, leaving their homes free for the picking. Alcohol wasn't a score there, but the occasional trinket could be, though Ziggy refrained from lifting petty things and having the town alerted to a thief.

Adrenaline heightened his senses and forced Ziggy to concentrate.

Breaching the door of Wyatt Gibson wasn't difficult. Because Ziggy had learned a few lessons, he made sure a mask was firmly in place when he was inside the walls of the house.

It didn't take long to find the liquor cabinet or a few water bottles. He reverted back to a teenager, making sure if it was noticed that someone had been in the house, they'd think it was a kid and not an adult.

Liquor went into the plastic water bottles, and enough water was put into the liquor bottles to mask the absence to the casual observer.

He filled his pockets, put the bottles back, and exited the house in less than ten minutes. Once he was tucked back into the trees, he walked the half a mile to the road to his trailer and ditched his disguise behind a fallen log. No use keeping that stuff in the house.

When he arrived home it was completely dark.

He turned on the TV and opened one of the water bottles.

And for the first time since he'd been out, he poured a shot of whiskey down his throat.

It burned.

And like every taste of freedom, it left him hungry for more.

Zoe worked a little harder, a little lighter on her feet at Nahana, knowing the days she'd be there were dwindling down to only a handful.

She'd had a conversation with Chef Monroe, the poster child for celebrity chef. When she'd told him she was giving up Nahana, he'd congratulated her. When she'd told him she was working throughout the summer and into early fall to keep Nahana lucrative while they found a replacement, Monroe had laughed at her.

"You're wasting your time."

"Oh?"

"You're too soft, Brown. They will use you until you walk. Be a bitch like all the rest of us and move on."

"That's not part of my DNA," she'd told him.

Monroe gave her ten more minutes of shit and promised to dine with her the next time she was in New York.

When she returned home from her shift, she kicked off her shoes and grabbed the phone.

She shared her day with Luke and listened to him talk about his. Yes, Miss Gina was doing well . . . no, there was nothing on the Brown home front. He said something about Zane being seen on the track with Jo but didn't have anything to add other than the *he was seen* gossip.

By the time she hung up the phone, Zoe decided it was just a little too quiet for her tastes.

The walls of her apartment were starting to squeeze in on her and feel like a foreign place where she didn't belong.

She looked up her lease paperwork and then turned her attention to a calendar. That would work out perfect.

The pounding on Luke's door before the sun rose had him grumbling, grabbing his bathrobe, and yelling en route to the front door, "What the hell is the—" His words faded.

Zoe stood in his doorway, suitcase in hand.

"W-what are you . . . ?"

Zoe dropped her case and smiled.

"I'm not moving in with you."

Luke's eyes dropped to her suitcase. Her large suitcase that had to have more than a few days' worth of clothes.

Her words started a slow dance in his brain.

"You're not?"

She bit her bottom lip. "I'm living at Miss Gina's. Mel's old room."

He felt his breath start to come, each inhale right on top of another, as if he were running.

"You are?"

"For six months, give or take."

"Give or take?"

"And I have to fly back to Texas a few times in the next couple of months. Finish my time at Nahana."

"That sounds reasonable." Sweet Jesus . . . she was back. His baby was back. He kept his smile firmly in his eyes. "But you're not moving in with me."

The seriousness of her face made him want to laugh.

He didn't dare.

"Of course not. People will talk." She turned on her heel and strutted back to his driveway.

In it sat a four-wheel drive, brand-new Land Rover with paper plates. "What's this?"

She opened the passenger side door. "Well, I'm not buying a house, and I need a car while I'm here."

He couldn't hold it in any longer.

Luke walked behind her, swiveled her shoulder until she faced him. "Welcome home, baby." And he kissed her.

Chapter Twenty-Nine

Word of Zoe moving back to River Bend spread like wildfire. She insisted it was temporary, a place to make a shift in her life . . . help Miss Gina to regroup at the inn after a year of turning away guests for fear something would happen to Hope. No one believed Zoe would be going anywhere.

"I think this calls for a party," Miss Gina said from the front porch.

"We just had a wedding." Mel was back from Fiji, tan, rested, and very sexed.

Hope was still in San Francisco, soaking up some serious grandparent time before school started in a week.

The phone to the inn rang, and Mel answered with the handset. "Miss Gina's Bed-and-Breakfast. Yes, this is the place." Mel held her hand over the mouthpiece and said in a hushed voice, "Another one."

Zoe shook her head with a smile.

"For the next two months Miss Brown will be in our kitchen the first and the third weekend of the month."

Miss Gina patted Zoe's hand as they all listened to a one-sided conversation between Mel and a future guest.

"Before the holiday? I'm going to have to consult with the staff and get back to you on that."

Zoe moved a thumb between herself and Miss Gina and mouthed the question, "Are we the staff?"

She nodded.

Mel had a pen and paper ready, along with the guest register. "And what name am I putting down for this reservation?"

"It sounds like you're going to have a busy season," Zoe said.

"Michael . . . and your last name?"

Mel dropped her pen and turned a little white. "Right . . . no, I understand." She dropped to her knees and fished under the wicker chair to find her pen. The register in her hand hit the deck, and she was all fumble and stumble as she attempted to get herself together. By the time she knelt against the chair with pen in hand, some of the color was back in her face. Or was that a blush? "No, no . . . Miss Brown is a close friend. I totally understand the need for that . . . ah-huh. Yes, we'll get back to you as soon as we can. Of course, thank you, Mr. Wolfe." Mel did a little beating of the air with her hands like a child who couldn't contain their excitement.

Mel disconnected the line and shot to her feet. She did an interesting version of a rain dance and squealed so loudly that Sir Knight lifted his head from his paws and tilted it in concern.

"Oh, my God . . . that was . . . that was . . ."

"Mr. Wolfe?" The name pinged around in Zoe's head like a silver ball in a pinball arcade.

Mel grabbed both Zoe's hands and squeezed. "Michael Wolfe!"

Zoe felt chills as recognition hit her hard. "The actor?"

Mel presented a toothy smile and screamed.

"Girls?" Miss Gina didn't share in their excitement.

"Michael Wolfe . . . action flicks. Totally hot." Mel fanned herself.

"He's just a person," Miss Gina said.

"An überhot celebrity," Zoe added.

"Jo is going to be stoked!"

"You know he's gay, right?"

Mel waved a hand in the air. "I don't care, he's still yummy to look at."

Zoe giggled. "Didn't you just get back from your honeymoon?"

Mel's jaw dropped and she reached for the phone. "I have to tell Wyatt." She ran into the inn and squealed.

"I think we need to go over your pricing and revamp the website."

"Do what you have to do. I'm just happy I'll be able to pay my property taxes this year."

"Are you struggling? I'm happy to—"

"I'm fine. Just a little tight, that's all."

Zoe sat beside Miss Gina and curled into her side. "We'll get you in the black before Santa gets here."

"As long as Santa is buff and riding a Harley, I'd be happy."

"What happened to Mr. Eugene?"

"He petered out." Miss Gina didn't sound too upset.

"He got involved with someone else?"

"No, I mean his peter petered out. What can I do with a man if *that* doesn't work?"

Zoe caught the giggles. "There's lots of things to do with a man other than play with his peter."

"Uh-huh . . . name one."

"Talk to them."

"I have you guys for that."

"Snuggle?"

Miss Gina wrapped an arm around Zoe. "Covered."

"They lift heavy things."

"And when Wyatt and Luke aren't around, I grab some of those young kids that drop by looking for odd jobs."

Miss Gina was still mentoring the youth of River Bend.

"Just keep them out of the lemonade."

"Are you kidding? That's what keeps the track team in this town full."

The giggles found Zoe a second time. "Petered out!"

Jo was on the second lap of her warm-up when Zane took up the spot beside her.

"It's not Thursday."

"I'm on to you, Jo."

"It's Jo now?"

"You'll get Sheriff on the days I have to be here."

Fair enough.

He had something to say, so Jo waited him out. It took half a mile. "I heard Zoe moved back to town."

"Looks like it."

"I feel like I can't get out of here, why would she come back?"

"That's a question you might need to ask her."

"I don't think she wants to see me." The remorse in his voice was a welcome relief.

"I don't think you give your sister enough credit."

They rounded onto Zane's first mile, and Jo caught something out of the corner of her eye.

The fog was thicker as summer rushed into fall, and either the fog was playing tricks on her eyes or someone was standing in the shadows of the trees surrounding the high school.

Attempting not to stare, Jo glanced at Zane, who ran with a little more ease than when he'd started. When she looked back up, the shadow was gone.

She had never run with a weapon, but maybe that wasn't the best decision.

"We've been doing this for three weeks," Zane reminded her.

"Feels good, doesn't it?"

He didn't confirm or deny. "You never ask about my dad."

"You being here isn't about your dad. It's about you."

"Why? Why not just write me up and make me do my time?"

Jo slowed her run to a stop, set her hands on her knees to catch her breath. "Why? I'll tell ya why. I think the inside just makes people meaner. Gives criminals more tools to screw up when they get out." She sucked in another deep breath and squared off to Zane. "And I think there is more Zoe in you than Ziggy. You just haven't figured out how to live without the cloud of your past."

Zane ran a hand through his hair. "I thought I was doing that."

"You were . . . got a job, and aren't you living in Waterville more than not?"

He shrugged.

"Zane?"

"I'm back and forth."

Not something Jo wanted to hear. "Why?"

"Keeping an eye on my sister."

Jo read more into those words than any he'd spoken in three weeks. "You do that."

Zane gave a quick nod.

"But Zane . . . if things get hairy, call me. I don't want you going in because someone drags you there."

He had a moment of confusion on his brow. "Why do you care so much?"

Jo took a step toward him and had to reach up to scruff his hair. "Because I was an only child, and you're the closest I came to having a little brother."

Zane stepped back and for the first time in a long time gave her a full smile.

Noise from the parking lot told them the teens had arrived.

"How many miles do you run with them?" Zane asked.

"A mile on the track, then we hit the trails for another five . . . why?"

He looked at his watch. "I don't have to go in until noon."

"You won't make six miles."

His smile fell. "Challenging me, Sheriff?"

Jo lifted both hands in the air. "Bring it!"

"What's this?" Zoe asked from near the open dresser drawer.

Luke poked his head out of her bathroom, brushing his teeth. "What does it look like?"

She lifted a pair of his underwear. "Man panties?"

He winked and ducked back into the bathroom. The sound of water followed a drawer closing with a slight creak. "I'm leaving a toothbrush here, too."

"Your house is three miles away."

"Well, I'm not moving in. People will talk."

Zoe pulled the length of her hair behind a shoulder and grinned. "We can't have that."

Luke pulled her into a playful hug and dragged her down to the bed, pinning her arms over her head. "You have a problem with my man panties?"

"No," she said with a giggle.

"Good!" He kissed her hard and quick before pushing off the bed, leaving her sprawled and a little short of breath. "Now go to work. I have cars to fix, woman."

She turned her head when he hesitated at the door.

His smile said everything. His wink told her he'd see her later.

When Luke walked out the door, Zoe curled up and hugged a lacy pillow. She couldn't remember being this happy.

Chapter Thirty

Ziggy held out his hand the minute Sheryl walked in the door. "You're late."

"It was busy. Took time for the place to clear out."

Once again, the smell of hamburger and french fry grease followed Sheryl around like a cloud. Felt like he was screwing a grease pit lately.

He snapped his fingers until she pulled a wad of bills from her purse and placed it in his hand. It amazed even him how quickly she fell back into her role.

He dug through the one-dollar bills to find the larger notes. "This is it?"

"It's the same as always."

He counted it again. "You said it was busy."

"Everyone came in late."

He took a swig out of his water bottle. Damn thing was almost empty.

"Late, huh?"

Sheryl's skinny ass moved into the kitchen. Ziggy looked her up and down, settled on her face. "Well, maybe if you wore a little makeup and tried to smile, you'd make more tips."

"Nobody in this town cares if I have makeup on."

He thought about how makeup and a dress could transform a woman. It could take a bitch cop and make her fuckable.

"You telling me I don't know what I'm talking about?" His hand tapped on his knee.

She stopped moving dishes around and looked up. "No. No, Ziggy. I just . . ." she stuttered. "I've been in Sam's for twenty years. None of 'em care if I have on blush is all."

He stood, real calm . . . and walked into the kitchen. His chest hurt with the pounding he felt in his veins. *Go for the hair. No bruises.* He twisted the pan Sheryl had in her hand away and set it in the sink.

"This needs to get clean."

"Uh-huh."

He took her elbow nice and easy.

"Ziggy, let me finish this first."

Poor woman thought he wanted her naked.

With careful ease, he inched his hand up her arm and to the back of her neck. When he grabbed a scruff of hair and pulled, she cried out.

"We need more money 'round here. And if I say you put on makeup, you put on makeup."

He pulled until she stumbled back and her knees started to give. His arms felt the power of her surrender. His cock decided maybe it wanted to screw after all.

Holding his scrawny wife in one hand, he pulled her out of the kitchen, through the living room, and into the only bathroom. He slammed his hand on the light, let adrenaline fuel his lesson. A cosmetic bag sat on the counter. He poured everything inside into the sink. With one hand, he managed to remove the top of a lipstick.

Sheryl held his hand to keep him from taking part of her scalp.

"Lipstick makes men think of blow jobs." He pushed the lipstick onto her lips, leaving a clump on one of her bottom teeth. He tossed the stuff back in the sink and grabbed a black tube.

"Ziggy, stop."

Using his teeth, he opened the mascara. Sheryl closed her eyes as he scraped it over her eyelids.

She cried and he tugged harder.

"Yeah . . . I like that." He rubbed against her hip, let her know what the makeup did for him.

The door to Zanya's room opened.

Ziggy pulled Sheryl all the way into the bathroom and slammed the door.

He dropped the makeup, put both hands in her hair and his lips close to her ear. "You say my name, real slow. *Ziggy baby.*"

He pulled her harder. "Ziggy. Baby."

He knew his daughter sat on the other side of the door, listening.

"Yeah, baby," he moaned, watching the door. "Moan!"

She didn't move fast enough. When he pulled, she moaned enough to sound like he was giving it to her.

"Not so loud," he said with a forced laugh. "Our baby will know how much you like it."

The sound of Zanya's door closing was like walking past a cop with a jacket full of dope. He turned his attention to Sheryl.

With a smile, he pushed her to her knees in front of him and opened the fly of his jeans.

The dinner party was at Wyatt and Mel's house.

"You know Mel can't cook," she told Luke as they walked the few blocks it took to get there. It wasn't raining, and since they planned on drinking, they decided to enjoy the warm September night.

"I know she's been poring over cookbooks ever since you announced you were writing one."

"Oh, has she cooked for you before?"

Luke cringed. "Lord, no . . . Wyatt has to be the guinea pig for that mess."

She lifted the bottle of wine she had in her hand and tapped it on the one in his. "We'll be fine."

Jo's squad car sat parked across the street, and Miss Gina was just pulling into the drive.

Zoe couldn't help but wonder if Miss Gina owned something other than a floor-length skirt.

Miss Gina eyed the wine in their hands. "Oh, thank God." She lifted her hand to show a jug of what Zoe had to guess was the famous hard lemonade.

"Open container, Miss Gina? That's naughty of you."

"Pft." She slammed the door to the throwback sixties VW van and headed for the door. "I have connections at the top."

Wyatt was a general contractor, and it showed in the work he'd put into his home. Mel greeted them at the door, all smiles, and Zoe had to admit, good smells came from the kitchen.

"I'm waiting to smell burnt," Miss Gina said right off.

Mel slapped the woman's shoulder and took the lemonade from her hand. "Do you want this or wine?"

"Or beer?" Wyatt asked from the living room.

"I'll take a beer." Luke lifted a hand.

Jo held Hope's hand as they drifted from a hallway.

"Auntie Zoe!" Hope pulled away and hugged her.

"What? No love for me?" Luke opened his arms.

"Oh, Uncle Luke." Hope shared the love.

Zoe followed Mel into the state-of-the-art kitchen and ran a hand over the edge of the oven. "Nice digs, Mel."

"Wyatt did all of it. It's beautiful, isn't it?"

Stone countertops, stainless steel appliances, downlighting from under the cabinets. "The wine fridge is perfect there." A well thought out wedding gift, she thought with a grin.

"Yeah, he'd planned the space for a beer tap. Can you imagine?"

Zoe almost choked.

Luke clearing his throat from the doorway had her standing taller.

"Let me open this." Mel took the wine from Zoe's hand.

Luke slid closer, took the bottle opener off the counter. He moved close, whispered, "Christmas present."

Zoe fluttered her lashes a few times and blew him off with a smile.

Luke kissed her without invitation and then left them alone in the kitchen.

"Do you have any idea how great that is to see?"

"I know how great it is to feel."

Mel offered a one-arm hug and continued opening the wine.

Marinated chicken, just slightly overdone, steamed vegetables, and brown rice that needed another twenty minutes to cook. Zoe had to hand it to her nonculinary friend. "I'm impressed," Zoe said after the first few bites.

Poor Mel looked nervous. "The rice isn't cooked enough."

"I like it, Mommy."

Luke ruffled the top of Hope's head.

"Timing is something you learn from mistakes. The more you cook, the more mistakes you make, the better you get."

"You should put that in your book," Jo said.

"Says the one who lives out of a microwave box."

Jo waved a forkful of chicken in the air. "The rice in the box is never undercooked."

Luke and Wyatt both agreed.

"Good Lord, what have you two lived on for the past ten years?" Zoe asked the men.

Wyatt filled his fork with half-done rice. "Pizza."

"Fried chicken," Luke added.

"Beer."

Luke kicked her under the table.

"I can grill a mean steak," Wyatt said.

"It's clear I moved back to River Bend in time save you all from high cholesterol and hypertension."

"What's hy-derp-teshion?" Hope asked.

"It's what you get when you eat tasty things," Miss Gina told her.

More than one set of eyes glared at the woman.

"What? It's true."

"What happened to peace, love, and all things earthy?" Zoe asked.

Miss Gina reached for her wine. "Oh, honey . . . we used that line before God created weed cards. Now that it's all legal-like, we stopped eating wheatgrass."

Jo blinked a few times. "You have a green card?"

"There is more in Eugene than my friend Peter."

Zoe almost spit out her wine.

"You have a friend named Peter?" Hope asked.

An hour later, once Zoe helped Mel load the dishwasher and put the men to work cleaning the rest of the dishes, Mel put Hope to bed. Zoe and Jo walked Miss Gina to her van.

"I can stay at the inn tonight if you want."

Miss Gina waved her off. "I have a nice couple from Eureka driving through."

"And you came here?" It wasn't often Miss Gina left the inn when there were guests.

"They have the emergency number. Besides, they were in bed before I left."

Jo kissed her cheek. "Call if you need anything."

They watched her pull out of the drive.

Zoe turned to walk back in and noticed Jo looking around.

"What is it?"

"Nothing."

~

"That's new." Zane pointed to the shoulder holster Jo had tried to hide under her jogging jacket.

She blew it off with a white lie. "I noticed bear tracks on the trail the other day."

If Zane didn't believe her, he didn't say anything.

They'd fallen into a routine of running two miles before the team showed up and then took off on the off track course for a few miles. It gave most of the kids the opportunity to go home and shower before returning for class.

"I'm worried about Zanya," Zane said once they stopped and waited for the teens to arrive.

"Why?"

"You know Mylo?"

"Blaze's dad, yeah. Seemed like an okay kid." But barely able to drink in a bar and certainly not ready to be a daddy.

"He got a job at the RV plant. Doing pretty good, actually."

"That's great."

"He told me he was going to ask Zanya to move in with him."

Get away from Ziggy. "So why are you worried?"

"She's afraid to leave."

"What? Why?"

"I think she's scared to leave my mom there alone."

Jo waited a beat, and then asked, "Because of Ziggy?"

One nod was his answer.

Damn it.

"I remember him yelling before he went in. Now he just sits there and watches you."

"Prison does strange things to people."

"Yeah." Zane tilted his water bottle back.

"Zane . . . has he hit her?"

"Zanya? No. Not that I know of."

"But you think he might?"

He was obviously torn. "People can change, can't they?"

Jo put a hand on her chest. "I drank more than all these kids in high school. My own dad put me in that cell I now hold the key to. You know what he said to me not long before he died?"

Zane shook his head.

"He told me the only way I was going to change was if I joined the military or lost something so precious it gutted me." Emotion threatened to overtake her with a simple memory.

"Damn, Jo . . . I'm sorry."

"Yeah, me too . . . because he was right, and I don't have the chance to tell him. Problem is, your dad hasn't lost something, and he didn't join the army."

"I wish he'd never gotten out."

"A lot of people agree with that."

"He's my dad. I shouldn't feel that way."

"Society can't dictate feelings, and you sure as hell don't need to put up with abuse to prove your love."

Zane kicked the stands. "I have one dad. One!"

Jo stood and placed a hand on Zane's shoulder. "I'm going to ask you something I asked your sister when she went through this . . . was Ziggy a sperm donor, or was he a father? Did he give his donation and leave? Or did he stick around to dedicate his life to make yours better to the best of his abilities? We all have choices in this life, Zane. Life's choices are what make us better or let us sit in the past and never grow."

"I hate this."

She did, too. "Try and get Zanya to leave. She doesn't need to suffer the sins of her parents."

Zane seemed good with that.

"And, Zane . . . call Zoe."

Chapter Thirty-One

Zoe's car sat in his drive, and the hope that she was cooking something amazing made his stomach grumble in happy anticipation.

That anticipatory happiness faded the second he breached the door and he found Zoe curled up on his sofa, a blanket in her lap, tears in her eyes.

He forgot about food and went straight to her.

Without words, she folded into his arms.

"Whose ass do I need to kick?"

She messed up the front of his shirt, and he waited. "I just got off the phone with Zane."

"Is that good or bad?"

"Both. He said he was sorry." She sat back, looked at him. "He cried, Luke. I don't remember my brother ever crying."

He ran a finger under the tears in her eyes. "Still wanna kick his ass."

She lowered her forehead to his chest. "How am I going to do this? Everything I love is here, and everything I hate is here! Zanya is trying to protect my mom, and Zane is trying to protect our sister, and all I can do is watch it all fall apart."

The pain in her words had him holding her tighter.

If there was one thing to drive Zoe away, it was her dysfunctional family.

He wouldn't survive losing her again.

"This place is crawling with new faces." Jo walked into R&B's wearing civilian clothes and no fewer than two weapons strapped to various parts of her body.

Josie cleaned the counter in front of her with a big grin. "Great for business. I'm told there was a developer looking at property on the other side of Waterville, by the RV plant. Considering a housing tract."

"Out here?"

"That's what I heard."

River Bend and Waterville were known for spec houses that didn't sit in cookie cutter yards. There were two old apartment buildings in Waterville that nearly everyone had either lived in or partied in when they were young. The growth came in bits and spurts . . . or not at all. "I guess the economy is turning around."

"What are you drinking?"

"Put something fizzy in a glass with lime. Make it look good."

Josie looked at Jo's outfit. "You're on duty?"

"Like I said, Josie. Lots of unfamiliar faces around here."

Normally, Jo's concern for the safety of her town would result in a backhanded remark from the lady who owned R&B's. *Nothing happens in River Bend. We're the safest town in the world. Nobody even locks their doors.* Something . . . anything to make Jo think she was acting paranoid.

Instead, Josie saluted two fingers in the air and said, "I got ya covered." Then she disappeared to take care of Jo's order.

She was simply the sheriff in town to most people. A few of her high school acquaintances would justify calling her Jo when she was dressed down and sitting at R&B's, which wasn't something she did often, and not at all since Ziggy was back.

The man had completely changed her routine. Even running with the cross-country team felt like she was exposing herself to some kind of danger. Danger that had nothing to do with wildlife.

"Here ya go."

Jo took her glass and moved from her perch of observation.

A couple of friendly waves escorted her as she walked to the lone pool table.

An entire group of men, probably in their midthirties, took turns rolling heavy balls into pockets with a stick. She didn't recognize any of them. Turning at least one head as she walked by, she stopped in front of the jukebox and pretended to scan her choices.

Eavesdropping on a conversation was always difficult in a bar, but she managed.

"It will be like prospecting in the Klondike. Livin' in our RVs for months." Jo didn't turn to see who spoke, she just swayed to the music and dug a quarter from her pocket.

"Don't mind that. Get away from my ol' lady," another voice said.

"She won't catch you boinkin' a new flavor either."

Laughter along with the sound of two balls colliding interrupted their conversation.

"I don't see much around here to play with."

"Oh, I don't know . . ."

Jo felt heat on her ass . . . the kind a woman feels when she knows it's being stared at.

She made a selection and moved away without turning around. The last thing she needed was someone in that crowd picking up on her. Anonymity was her friend right now.

She eased around the back and waved to Buddy in the kitchen. "Looks like you're gettin' your workout." The man was running like a real short-order cook.

"Yeah, how about you get that fancy chef friend of yours in here to help me?"

Jo laughed at the thought of Zoe in the back of R&B's. "Good luck with that. See anything off around here?"

Buddy shot her a glance.

"C'mon, I know Luke talked to ya."

He shoved something fried into the service window.

"I haven't seen that guy everyone is talkin' about," Buddy said. "There are a couple of quiet ones that come in. Seem to be lookin' more than drinkin'."

Jo turned back around to scan the place.

"They're not in here tonight."

"Any particular day they show up?"

"When it's busy. I'm guessin' to blend in."

"So the weekends?"

He rang the bell to get one of the waitresses' attention.

"Seems like every night is a weekend around here lately."

She tapped the counter. "Thanks, Buddy."

Jo felt eyes on her ass as she walked past the pool table and again when she set her drink on the counter with a five-dollar bill.

Outside, Jo walked the parking lot with her cell phone in her hand. To the casual observer she might look like she was checking her messages, but in reality, the video function did a great job of capturing license plate numbers that she could run when she went into the station.

Satisfied she had what she needed, she rounded the back of her Jeep, heard gravel kick behind her with footsteps, and turned around with her gun in her hand.

"Holy shit, woman!"

The guy behind her was one of the men at the pool table. He had both hands in the air, his eyes leveled on her service weapon.

She pointed the muzzle toward the sky and took her finger off the trigger.

"Sneaking up behind people will get you shot." She made no apology to the stranger, though she knew her reaction was overkill. Her heart rate was shooting over the top, her eyes hyperaware of the darkness beyond the parking lot.

Calm the hell down! she yelled at herself.

He took a step back, hands still high. "Way too much work." He stopped staring at the gun to look her up and down. "Too bad." Then he turned and walked away.

For a full minute, she leaned against her Jeep and pulled her shit together.

She returned her gun to her shoulder harness and opened the Jeep door.

Then she heard clapping.

"Well done."

The shadow of a man stood on the other side of the street, leaning against a tree.

Three steps out of the light given off by R&B's lot and Jo's focus matched the face with the voice.

"You're mighty close to breaking your parole, Ziggy."

"A hundred yards." He nodded toward the bar. "I'm guessing I'm at least two."

She stepped close enough to see his eyes, maybe catch alcohol on his breath. Anything to pull him in on a charge that would take him back to jail.

"You always threaten civilians with those guns of yours, JoAnne?"

"It's Sheriff to you, Mr. Brown."

He leered a slow slide down her body and back up. "You don't look like a cop tonight."

Jo shook off the feeling of walking into a spiderweb the size of a house, filled with a new hatch of eight-legged creepers.

"I'm always a cop, Mr. Brown. Now how about you tell me what you're doing out, in the dark, at ten o'clock at night?"

He shifted his frame off the tree and stretched his arms over his head. "Rained most the day. I needed to get my exercise in. I'm not much welcome in town. Can't help it if R&B's is on the road."

She didn't buy it. "You're out for a walk?"

"Free country. And I'm a free man."

"You're on a leash."

The smile on his face faded.

"You like to tie 'em up, do ya, Sheriff?"

The conversation made her want to heave. If it weren't for the fact that she had her gun within reach, she would have ended the conversation before it began.

Noise from inside the bar drifted out as a group exited the building.

"I'm watching you, Ziggy."

He lifted his defiant chin. "You do that."

She wanted to shoot him just on principle. Instead, she took the few steps to her Jeep, got in, and then blinded him with her headlights.

Ziggy put his hands in his pockets.

Jo put a hand on her gun.

Then he turned and made his way back toward home.

She passed him on the road ten minutes later.

It started to rain.

~

Ziggy had sat across the street from R&B's waiting for his contact. He needed a ticket out of this one-cop town. Needed a place where he could walk into a liquor store and buy a fucking beer. To do that, he needed money. The pennies Sheryl brought home were nothing, barely enough to eat off of.

When he noticed little JoAnne Ward's Jeep in the drive, he tucked back in the shadows and waited.

His contact pulled into the parking lot, flashed his lights . . . and when Ziggy didn't come out, he drove away.

He'd been pissed, but once he saw the sheriff walk from the bar, a man in tow, the voyeur in him came out.

Watching her pull a gun and hearing the waver in her voice when she told the guy off showered Ziggy with information.

The woman carried her gun, even in civilian clothes. Not sure why he hadn't seen that coming. The other thing he realized was that he had her running scared. Lord knew he loved the power of a woman shaking. The thought of doing more than scaring little Miss Ward had crossed his mind more than once. Taking what she was good for would result in him having to kill her. There would be no turning back from that.

He was told, on the inside, that once a man killed someone, beating the shit out of others didn't make sense.

Still, when she'd blown off Casanova, Ziggy just had to fuck with her.

He knew his rights and knew there wasn't much she could do but shake a fist at him. And if she did cuff him, all the better. He wouldn't resist . . . no way. He'd make her know just how willing he was to spread his legs to have her pat him down.

He watched her sitting in her Jeep before turning his way back to the trailer.

Only when it started to rain did Ziggy cuss out the night.

~

Mel stepped into the kitchen of the bed-and-breakfast, shaking the rain from her jacket. "Is it ever going to let up?"

Zoe juggled several pans full of crepes, eggs, and breakfast sausage.

"You've been back for over a year. You would think you'd be used to it by now."

Mel hung her jacket on the hook by the back door. "Living in California all that time thinned my blood."

"I didn't have that problem in Texas. Rains there all the time."

"That smells amazing." Mel removed an apron from the walk-in pantry and wrapped it around her waist.

The weekend routine was starting to find its pace. The inn was close to capacity on weekends, with bookings spilling into the week.

Miss Gina hired two of the high school girls to come in and help with the housekeeping while the guests were in the dining room, enjoying breakfast.

Knowing she was the draw at this point, Zoe made sure she welcomed the guests and wasn't opposed to showing up at the wine and cheese hour in the evenings.

It helped that Zoe had convinced Miss Gina to up her game with her selections. When Zoe had called a vineyard she especially liked in Washington State and asked if they would endorse—by means of cheaper pricing—the inn using their wine exclusively, they jumped at the opportunity. The chief sommelier himself had booked a trip to River Bend later in that week to finalize the deal.

Zoe felt good about Miss Gina changing her strategy and increasing her bottom line.

She'd set up an office in her room at the inn. Writing a cookbook was more difficult than she'd expected. Even with regular shipments of supplies, Zoe would sometimes run out of stuff she needed when sampling her own work.

The good news was the guests at the bed-and-breakfast had no problem devouring whatever she made.

"Here." Zoe handed Mel two finished plates. "The Wong family."

Mel put on her best waitress smile and left Zoe to finish cooking.

Chapter Thirty-Two

"Glynis, you there?"

Jo had ducked out of the rain to call into the station. It had been coming down in sheets for a steady six hours. And now that it was getting dark, the calls were coming in. *So much for small town living.*

"That's a big ten-four, Sheriff." Glynis had been studying call numbers and going completely out of her way to use them.

"I'm trying to get ahold of Luke, he isn't answering on the ham. I have a mess out here just past Grayson's farm. I need a tow." More like three, but she'd take one at a time.

The radio crackled when Glynis responded. "Last I heard he was pulling Mr. Mason's Dodge out of a ditch."

"Well, tell him my mess is cutting us off from Waterville. The road is completely blocked and Highway Patrol informed me there is a slide on the 101, and there aren't any reserves to send this way."

"You got it, Sheriff. I'll do my best."

With cell service being spotty at best on the back road, Jo knew getting ahold of anyone would likely take a rudimentary radio.

Jo sucked in a fortifying breath and stepped back out into the rain.

Emergency lights flashed on both sides of the six-car, one-RV pileup that had resulted from a blind curve and a boulder that slid onto the road, taking out the first car.

That many vehicles on the road at one time was a rarity but easily explained when she realized the group was the same that had spread around the pool table at R&B's. The men were caravanning back to Eugene . . . more accurately, they were wishing they'd left the night before instead of overdrinking and sleeping in the now-demolished motor home.

With water dripping off her covered sheriff's hat and yellow slicker, Jo walked back to the middle of the mess.

Deputy Fitzpatrick from Waterville was attempting to write down names and information on a small notepad.

"It's going to be some time before Miller's can get here."

Fitzpatrick turned as the only injured driver was leaving in a Waterville ambulance. "Thirty minutes on this side."

"I hate nights like this," Jo said.

"Yeah, nothing good ever happens when it's coming down this hard."

The buzz in his head matched the pounding on the thin roof of the trailer.

He had enough liquor to take him through the night, but scoring more when it rained this hard was impossible. Not unless you flat walked into a store and bought it. Which he couldn't do.

The local store turned Sheryl away, or so the bitch told him.

Lucky for him, he'd made a couple of friends who understood his plight. Didn't matter to Ziggy that the cost was triple what the stuff was worth. It was hard enough living in a shithole, he wasn't going to do it sober.

One headlight beamed through the window, signaling Sheryl's arrival.

She ran inside, shook rain from her hair.

With his eyes trained on the television, he yelled, "Shut the damn door."

She slammed it, forcing his attention her way.

"You gotta problem?" he barked.

"The wind caught the door."

He didn't believe her.

"Is Zanya here?"

Ziggy shifted his eyes to hers, then back to the TV. "In her room with her crying brat."

"Blaze is teething," she excused the kid's shitty behavior. Like she'd done for years when their own brats were little.

"Well, maybe if you hadn't raised a slut, we wouldn't be dealing with teething babies, would we?" Keeping the anger from his voice was harder when there wasn't anyone around listening.

"I was younger than Zanya when I had Zoe."

Damn bitch was doing it again. Telling him in her sly way that he was full of shit. He hated being talked down to. So many years of having to bend to the uniformed men on the inside, the warden that hated him.

"Like I said, a slut."

Sheryl winced but shut up.

He snapped his fingers and opened his hand.

She handed him a small wad of cash. "What the hell is this?"

"It was slow. Sam sent all of us home, said it wasn't a fit night to be on the road late."

There wasn't enough there to get the whiskey he needed. Even as he thought the words, he tilted back his Coke bottle that didn't hold any soda. He flipped the dollar bills in his hand like a switch. "You sure there isn't any more?"

She didn't look at him once again . . . and moved into the kitchen.

"That's all. Maybe if we could find you some work, we wouldn't have to worry about money so much."

His forearms tightened. "Don't you think I'm tryin'? No one wants to hire an ex-con."

"Didn't your parole officer say he knew some people in Eugene?"

"You tryin' to get rid of me?"

"No, baby . . ." she used her placating, *talk him down from the edge* voice. "We're just running out of money."

"You kept this place together without me for seventeen years, and you're tryin' to tell me you can't do it now with me here?"

She turned on the water and rolled up her sleeves. "Zoe helped before."

Just hearing her name shot his blood pressure high. "That snotty bitch daughter of yours. Too good to give it now, is she?"

"I can't make her."

Ziggy took another swig . . . his eyes landed on Sheryl's purse. "Funny how there is always money for that baby back there."

Sheryl tried to hide her eyes, but he caught her following his stare.

"You know something, baby?" His voice was nice and even. Nice and low as he stood. "I think you're lying to me."

He saw terror on her face when he lifted her purse.

"Ziggy . . ."

He tilted the bag, spilling everything on the dirty floor. Keys rattled alongside a wallet, and change took up the rest of the space. He shook harder as Sheryl reached for her bag.

He pushed her away and found what he was looking for. Two fives and a ten. "That's all! Maybe I should get a fucking job!" he mimicked her words.

"Ziggy, please, I can explain." She moved too close.

The back of his hand connected with her jaw and spun her into the coffee table.

Ziggy's gaze landed on his spilled drink.

He saw red. "I'll teach you to lie to me."

Sheryl threw up her hands to block the blow, and the front door swung open.

~

The power at Miss Gina's flickered all day and finally gave out after six o'clock. Mel, Miss Gina, and Hope entertained their guests with impromptu card games and Pictionary. By candlelight, Zoe managed to make a stove-top meal, so no one was hungry.

Eventually the guests made their way to their rooms, more than a little tipsy on the free-flowing wine.

Wyatt was out with Luke, helping with the accident on the road to Waterville, so the women decided to bunk down at Miss Gina's.

Hope had decided she wanted to sleep in Miss Gina's *mini house*, as she called it, and the two of them retired with homemade popcorn and hot cocoa.

By firelight, Mel sat in the parlor, reading, and Zoe used the quiet to write. With every recipe she decided needed to go in the cookbook, she wanted a short story telling how she came upon the idea and what she did to make it uniquely hers. A book filled with pictures and directions was not what she wanted to be known for.

She'd just unfolded from the chair to fill her mug with more chocolate when the phone to the inn rang.

Mel stirred.

"I'll get it."

They normally turned the phone for reservations on to voice mail in the evenings, but with most of their cell phones showing one bar, they left it on.

"Miss Gina's Bed-and—"

"Zoe? Zoe, come get me. Please come get me."

She turned stone-cold. "Zanya?"

"He's tearing the place up. My baby."

The sound of something crashing on Zanya's end felt like lightning to Zoe's system. "Oh, God."

Mel ran from the parlor.

"I'm on my way."

Zoe dropped the phone and ran past Mel to find her purse in the kitchen.

"What's happening?"

"That was Zanya. I need to get her from my mom's."

"You shouldn't go alone."

"No choice. Call Jo!"

Without any other words, Zoe ran from the inn, jumped in her car, and tore out of the drive.

~

"You wanna piece of this, boy?"

Zane stood in the doorway, rain blowing in behind him.

"Get off her."

Ziggy grabbed Sheryl's scrawny neck instead.

Her hands caught his, and she started to kick.

"You motherfucker!"

Zane charged him, knocking him off.

~

Through the rain, Luke felt his cell phone in his back pocket buzz. The number to Miss Gina's popped up, along with a picture of the flower child herself.

He smiled and answered, knowing it was Zoe checking on him. "Hey, baby."

"Luke? Thank God."

"Mel?" Not the person he expected to hear on the phone.

"Is Jo with you?"

Luke looked past the jumbled mess of cars, and the one he'd just loaded onto his truck, to find Jo talking with a deputy from Waterville. "Yeah, why?"

"It's Zoe. She ran out—" the call started to crap out.

"Mel?"

More static.

"Mel?"

"Can you hear me?"

"Don't move. What about Zoe?"

"Zanya called. Zoe ran out to get her."

His grip on the phone threatened to crush it. "At Ziggy's?"

"Yes. Hurry. It didn't sound good."

Luke turned and ran toward Jo, yelling her name.

Chapter Thirty-Three

The front door to the trailer was wide open. The motorcycle Zane rode was dumped in the yard, the lights blared along with a TV, and Blaze's cries rose above the screaming from inside.

Zoe hit the door at a run.

Zane and Ziggy rolled on the floor, fists flying.

Zanya stood in the hall, Blaze in her arms, yelling, "Stop!"

Zoe's eyes landed on her mom, who was picking herself up from the floor. Her face was bloody, one of her eyes already swelling shut.

Ziggy managed to get his feet under him, pulling Zane with him. "You wanna fight me?" His hand pulled back, sending a fist into Zane's face with a horrifying crunch.

When Zane fell, he tripped over a chair and into Zoe.

They both crashed to the floor.

That's when Ziggy noticed her. "Look who's here to join the party." He wiped the back of his hand across his lips—it came up bloody.

Blaze screamed louder.

"Get him out of here, Zanya!" Zoe yelled as she attempted to get to her feet.

Ziggy lifted a hand. "You stay right there."

Zanya cowered back, and Sheryl scrambled to her side.

Before Sheryl could get there, Ziggy shot a foot out, tripping her.

Zane shot up again and rushed.

Zoe rolled to her feet as Sheryl pulled Zanya back down the hall.

Ziggy's blows to Zane looked like a rabid dog on the attack, each blow harder, faster than the last.

Zane fought, catching Ziggy a few times, but as Zoe knew, her father was a vicious man who lived without rules.

The grunts and fists started to slow, until only Ziggy was fighting.

"Stop it! You're killing him."

Another hit and Zoe had to do something.

She rushed in, knowing the blow would come to her. But her little brother was hardly moving. Standing by and watching her father beat one of them, any of them, was something she vowed she'd never do again without a fight.

Ziggy laughed like a sick man on the edge of a complete breakdown and grabbed a fallen lamp.

Zoe charged before he could deliver a final blow to her brother.

She caught part of the lamp with her shoulder, but stopped it from hitting its mark.

First came a fist to her face, and when she fell, Ziggy's foot met her ribs.

Coughing hard, she rolled over beside Zane and covered her face when Ziggy lifted the lamp over his head.

Then the room exploded.

$\sim$

Jo saw blinders. Her speedometer shot past one hundred on the straights and sixty-five on the corners.

Luke white-knuckled it in the passenger seat, neither of them saying a thing.

The rain threatened their safety on more than one turn. The final stretch to the Brown home was open road.

Lights from the trailer spilled into the rain, cars were everywhere.

Their seat belts were off before they skidded to a stop.

"I go in first!" Her gun was already out, her feet running.

She heard Zoe scream, saw through the door when Zoe lifted her arms as Ziggy stood over her with something in his hands.

Before Jo could fire off a round, an explosion from inside the home stopped her feet at the door.

Luke ran into her back.

Ziggy dropped the lamp and looked down at his chest.

Blood pooled in the center.

Ziggy turned white, his face tilted up. "You bitch." He attempted a step, and another round caught him as he took his last breath and fell on top of Zoe and Zane.

Sheryl stood there, her eyes glossed over, her face void of expression. "Zoe?"

Jo kept an arm out, keeping Luke back.

"Sheryl?" Jo kept her gun in her hand until Sheryl lowered hers.

Jo moved quickly, capturing Sheryl before she collapsed and removing the revolver from her hand.

Behind her, Zoe screamed, "Get him off me."

Luke pushed Ziggy's body away and pulled Zoe into his arms. "I've got you, Zoe. It's okay. It's over."

She moved to Ziggy's sprawled body, checked his neck for a pulse. Not that she needed to, his dead stare told her it was over.

Jo met Luke's horrified gaze then reached for the radio pinned to her chest. "Glynis, you there?"

"That's a big ten-four, Sheriff."

Glynis's jovial voice stood in stark contrast to the scene in front of her. "We need an ambulance at the Brown residence."

"An ambulance?"

Jo turned her stare to the unmoving bastard in the room. "And the coroner."

Zoe didn't want the attention, or the cameras.

It appeared she wasn't going to get what she wanted, so she moved through the days that followed Ziggy's death, ignoring everyone that wasn't part of her core family.

Sheryl sat in a temporary cell in Eugene pending second-degree murder charges. While she may have been trying to protect her adult children, her life at the time of Ziggy's shooting wasn't a cut-and-dried case of self-defense. She'd purchased the gun before Ziggy was put away the first time. He didn't know she had it hidden in a heating vent in her bedroom.

Zoe was confident that in time, her mother would be free.

Or would she?

The image of Ziggy falling on Zoe in a bloody heap woke her up every night. If it wasn't for Luke being there, holding her, she would probably need inpatient therapy. Zoe could only imagine what her mother was going through.

Zane spent three days in ICU and the next few on an orthopedic unit, nursing a broken collarbone and wrist, and a concussion.

Miss Gina pulled in Zanya and Blaze, put them in the blue room on the third floor to keep the guests on the lower floors from complaining about a baby crying.

The day Zoe put her father in the ground, the sun was unusually warm.

More than one person told her she didn't need to go through the effort. What they didn't understand was that she wasn't burying him for his sake, but for hers . . . and her siblings'.

Luke drove her Land Rover with Zanya, Zane, and Blaze in the back.

A caravan of cars followed them to the cemetery. There wouldn't be a service, for no one had anything good to say about the soul that once filled the dead man's body.

The minister of the Little White Church told her he'd be at the site to say a few words to help them with this day.

Zoe agreed and said nothing more.

Zane carried Blaze in his baby carrier with Zanya by his side as they walked over graves to the site destined to hold Ziggy forever.

Dark sunglasses gave Zoe the ability to look around and not be forced to talk to people after making eye contact. They also aided in covering the green and yellow bruise on her face that makeup didn't hide.

Jo and Mel flanked her and Luke as they left the cars.

Wyatt took Miss Gina's arm and followed close behind.

Zoe saw the lone casket and tuned out those around her.

She stopped at the edge of the dozen chairs set up for people to sit in. Only she didn't want to stay that long.

When she looked up, car upon car pulled along the cemetery drive.

Mr. and Mrs. Miller, Principal Mason and his wife. Teachers, Deputy Emery, Sam, Brenda, Josie . . . the whole town poured in. One by one, they stood on the edges of the dug up earth in silence. A dark sedan opened, and out of it came Felix, September, and a few faces from her on-screen crew.

Zoe reached for Luke's hand, which was never far away, and squeezed.

He kissed the side of her head.

She kissed his hand and moved between her brother and sister. Together they linked arms but stayed standing.

Zane nodded to Minister Imman.

"Ladies and gentlemen, thank you for coming today to show your support to the children of Ziggy Brown. While every funeral has its own set of difficult circumstances, this one stands out. This man's troubled life fell on his children in ways none of us could ever imagine. While the support of your community is welcome now, may it be a reminder to us all to find that support earlier."

Zoe finally looked at Minister Imman.

"Many of you will say this man deserves to be in this grave. God forgive me, the thought has entered my own heart. But it could have just as easily been any one of the Brown family. While I have been called to help save the souls of River Bend, I found in this man's passing I must first do my part in saving the lives of those souls as well. I know that lesson was not given to me alone." Minister Imman scanned the crowd, and more than one head bowed.

Zanya squeezed Zoe's hand, tears in her eyes.

Zane stood stoic, his eyes never leaving the casket.

"Let us pray. Dear Father, please stand beside your children left in the wake of their father's passing. May you enter their hearts and help them find forgiveness so that they might move from this difficult time with joy in their hearts. And Father, please reach out to Sheryl Brown so she can feel your mercy. Amen."

Zoe refused to cry as she opened her eyes.

"Zane, Zoe . . . Zanya. I'm deeply sorry for your loss. Not of this man, may God forgive us all in that thought, but for the hopes and dreams of what will never be and what you now must put behind you. Peace be with you."

They stood there, silent. There would not be an outpouring of praise for Ziggy, or even one person wanting to say a single word.

Except Zane.

He broke away and approached the casket.

With his arm in a sling and stitches still holding his eyebrows together, he glared. "All I ever wanted was a dad. And this is what I got!" He lifted his arm in the sling. "You tried to break all of us. We survived *you*! May God have mercy on your soul, because if it were up to me, you'd burn in hell."

Zane turned toward her and Zanya and accepted their hugs.

"I love you, Zane."

"I'm sorry, Zoe. I should have listened to you."

"Don't. It's over." She watched as he picked up Blaze and moved through the crowd.

Zoe stood beside Zanya. "Do you want to say something?"

Zanya stepped forward. "When I was expecting Blaze, I was scared for my future. How was I going to support a child? How would I live? Then you came back and I feared for my life. I'm not scared of my future any longer."

Zanya followed Zane's path.

Luke took their place beside her. "What about you?"

She shook her head and let Luke lead her away.

Chapter Thirty-Four

"I'm scared, Jo."

It took a lot for a grown man to tell anyone he was scared.

"Why?"

"She hasn't cried. Not once since she came back from the hospital the day he died."

Jo watched as Zoe thanked the residents of River Bend for coming to the funeral and the gathering at Miss Gina's in show of their support.

"Do you ever think she's done crying? How many tears has she shed for that man?"

Luke looked distressed. "I don't want to lose her again. What if she can't live here now?"

Jo placed a hand on his arm and tried the warmest smile she could find. "Then you go with her wherever she needs to go."

"And if I remind her of all this?"

"Luke, look at me."

He did.

"That woman loves you. She isn't going anywhere."

A breath rushed from his lips. He kissed Jo's forehead and moved to Zoe's side.

"You're something else." Zane walked up, a soda in his hand.

"How you holding up?" Jo asked.

"I'm okay. Still hurt like hell, but I'm okay."

"Those were some powerful words you said today."

"Better than the ones I first thought of."

"Oh? And what were those?"

"That the bastard burn in hell."

Jo smiled. "I can't imagine he's anywhere else."

"I heard Zanya talking to Miss Gina . . . something about a job here."

"You know Miss Gina, she takes in strays all the time."

"That's good. I can leave without worrying."

Jo couldn't say she was surprised. "Where are you going?"

"I-I, ah, talked to a recruiter with the marines."

A strange wave of pride washed over her. "Oh?"

"Yeah, they went over my records. Looks like my past isn't going to keep me from enlisting. Just need to pass my GED, which I was already working on."

"You were?"

"Yeah, couldn't have those snot nose teenagers beating me on the track and in the school department."

Jo sent a silent thanks to her father for her influence on Zane.

She couldn't stop smiling. "Marines?"

"Yeah, badass, right?"

"I think it's a good thing."

He nodded, looked like he was holding back tears. "Feels right. Someone told me once that to change their life something bad had to happen or they needed to join the service. I figure I have two points in my favor going in. Well, three, if I'm as good a shot as my mom."

Jo couldn't stop the curt laugh from exploding from her lips.

Then she stepped into Zane's one arm and hugged him.

"You're gonna be just fine."

"I expect you at my graduation . . . or whatever pomp and circumstance I have to go through."

"I'll be there."

Most of the guests had left the inn before Zoe slipped out the back door to watch the sunset.

The door behind her opened, and she felt a throw drop onto her shoulders.

She leaned back against Luke's chest and enjoyed the warmth of his arms as they circled around her.

"How are you?"

"Hanging in there."

"Hard day," Luke said.

"I've had easier ones."

She felt Luke's lips on the top of her head. "I want to make it easier on you."

Zoe reached around, held his arms that crossed over her stomach. "You have, Luke. You and everyone here. I can't imagine going through any of this by myself."

Luke held her closer. "You're not alone."

"I know. I realized earlier how lonely I was when I lived in Texas. I had friends, colleagues . . . they would have shown up for a funeral, maybe even helped me plan one. But they wouldn't understand."

"Everyone here knows you, Zoe. There isn't any need for explanations in River Bend."

"That used to frustrate me."

"And now?"

She snuggled closer into his shoulder. "It's comforting. Which is surprising."

"Why?"

"I'm not sure. When the doctors were dragging me through X-ray after X-ray last week, I waited for the desire to run to hit me hard. How was I going to face this town? What would people say? I thought my need to get out of River Bend would dump on me like it had in high school."

Luke shivered, and she looked up to see him holding his breath with his eyes closed.

"It didn't, Luke."

He slowly opened his eyes and looked down.

She wanted to erase the fear in his gaze.

"I didn't feel the need to run away, I felt the need to hold you."

"Oh, Zoe." He kissed her temple and let his lips linger there. "I'm right here."

Zoe turned her attention back to the setting sun that started to boil in a small ball of fire over the trees. She needed to remove Luke's fears of her fleeing his side, regardless of what was to come, and she needed to start now.

"I've been thinking," she said with a sigh.

"Yeah?"

"Maybe we can have Wyatt remodel our kitchen."

Luke took a second for her change of subject to click. "Our kitchen?"

"Okay, *my* kitchen. You can call the garage yours. Maybe even get a beer tap for it."

His lips pressed close to her ear. She heard the smile in his voice. "Are you suggesting we merge our panty drawers into one place?"

She lowered her eyes and took a chance. "Yeah. I mean, once we're engaged, there's no need to pretend we're not living together."

Luke turned her around, his eyes bright and hopeful. "Engaged?"

She lifted her left hand in the air. "I'm a five and a half, and unlike Mel, I'm not opposed to tattooing that on your body in your sleep."

"You're serious." He was smiling like a kid on Christmas.

Zoe lifted her hands to his shoulders. "I left River Bend to find myself, to escape . . ." She didn't need to finish that sentence. "But I had to come back to you to realize what I had lost. I tried to stop loving you, thought I was successful for a little while there . . . but I was wrong. I've never stopped loving you, Luke. I'm really praying our timing is finally right."

"I'd follow you anywhere." His hands reached up and held her face. His eyes pierced hers with the sincerity of his words.

"How about down the street?"

"You mean it?"

"I'm staying in River Bend."

"Staying for good?"

"Yep, unless you and I wanna grow old in Fiji or something, I'm setting my roots down right here."

Luke bent his head and crushed his lips to hers.

He came up for air. "I love you."

His kisses came quickly between words.

"I'm never letting you go again."

Another kiss.

She pulled away, her arms around his neck. "Good, cuz I was kidding about the beer tap."

He tilted his head, pretended annoyance. "We'll negotiate."

It was her turn to kiss him. "What kind of negotiations?"

His kiss turned soft before he whispered, "The naked kind."

"I think I'm gonna like this." With swollen lips, she said it again. "Size five and a half."

"Marry me!"

"Is that a question?"

"I'll ask the question when I have a ring . . . just promise me you'll say yes."

The tiny, unshed moisture in the depths of his eyes mimicked the love in her heart.

"I promise, Luke. I love everything about us and never want to let that go."

He rested his forehead to hers. "Oh, baby . . . I love you hard."

~

"Agent Burton?"

"Jo, how are you?"

"Good. I'm good." She wasn't anywhere near good.

"Uh-huh . . . right. Why the out of character call?"

"How do you know it's out of character?"

"Because I suggested you call a year ago, stop by when you're in town, have a drink. Nothing. Now I hear from you. What's up, Sheriff?"

Jo peeked out the curtains of her front window. "Do you ever feel like you're being watched?"

Agent Burton laughed. "Depends on what I'm wearing and what bar I'm at . . . why?"

"I can't shake the feeling someone is watching me." A car drove by and Jo ducked behind the wall to keep that someone from seeing her.

"You sound scared, Sheriff."

She looked out the window again. "I am."

Acknowledgments

To the champions who survived a less than nurturing childhood and still went on to do great things, this is for you. My personal journeys through many aspects of this story were sometimes cathartic, and other times just plain painful to write. Survivors walk among us every day playing hero to their own stories. You don't always know it to look at them, but many fought through a childhood like Zoe with every possible hurdle placed in front of them to slow the pace on their road to great things. Like Zoe, some make risky and difficult decisions early on and persevere in the end. For those of you who didn't let your childhood define you, but instead gave it the chapter it deserved, and then turned the page to write your own book . . . kudos to you!

To Jane, my personal champion and cheerleader on every path I take. Thank you. To everyone at Dystel and Goderich Literary Management. Blessings!

To Kelli and the entire Montlake team. I swear I did pass my English Lit class . . . I swear! For all you do . . . thank you.

Back to Brandy:

We may not be bonded by blood, but that doesn't make you less of a sister. Our lives growing up were not ideal, and our friendship—yours, mine, and Kari's—was often the only anchor I had keeping me from drifting off to sea. While Zoe's story doesn't scream yours, the fact that you never left the general area of our hometown is why this book is dedicated to you. You bring up names of hometown friends, people who you see all the time, and I have to search the yearbook to remember. You were definitely Most Likely to Never Leave town. Your mammoth success in your chosen career came as no surprise to me since you were always determined to do so much more with your life despite the pitfalls that were placed in your path. Your kindness and loving heart . . . your smile and constant support, has never been forgotten.

I love and admire all you have done.

As always, I offer my unwavering support as you move forward in life.

Catherine

About the Author

Photo © 2015 Julianne Gentry

New York Times and *USA Today* bestselling author Catherine Bybee has written twenty-five books that have collectively sold more than two million copies and have been translated into twelve languages. Raised in Washington State, she moved to Southern California in hopes of becoming a movie star. After growing bored with waiting tables, she returned to school and became a registered nurse, spending most of her career in urban emergency rooms. She now writes full-time and has penned the popular Not Quite and Weekday Brides series, as well as the Most Likely To series.